take

nashoda rose

dedication

To the fans of the original Senses.
Thank you for waiting so patiently for this story.

Books by Nashoda Rose

Tear Asunder series
With You
Torn from You
Overwhelmed by You
Shattered by You (coming 2015)

Unyielding Series
Perfect Chaos
Perfect Ruin (Date TBA)
Perfect Rage (Date TBA)

Scars of the Wraiths
Take

http://www.nashodarose.com/

Glossary of Terms (alphabetical order)

Center World Other (CWO): For thousands of years, numerous organisms that survived the Ice Age remained hidden until a hundred years ago when they emerged to the Earth's surface in the form of insects. Intelligent. Can inhabit a recently deceased human body, possessing them body and soul. Transformation occurs within seven days, depending on the species. Immune to Wraiths' powers. Protected by heat and minerals from the Earth's core.

Deaconry, the: Assembly comprised of four Wraiths, two Scars, and one witch. Decide laws and punishments for all who live under the Goddess Azzurra.

Deep Sleep (DS): A state of sleep which one can be contained for short periods.

Grits (CWO): Derived from the common cockroach. Odorless. Difficult to track. Able to heal within seconds. Means of destruction: decapitation.
Assumes the bodies of attractive males with a strong presence. Will lure women to bed with the intent of siphoning the air from their lungs to live longer in their human states.

Goddess Azzurra: Goddess of the realm. Created the Scars and Wraiths. Also is the Goddess of Witches.

Ink: A tattoo on a Scar that can be called to life.

Lilac (CWO): Lepidoptera order of insects. Assume the bodies of females. Known to be strikingly beautiful to lure their targets. Their skin emits a powdered substance that smells of lilacs. Able to trap prey in webbing. Victims are stored in cocoons which are later used as sustenance.

Long Necks (CWO): Derived from the common beetle. Known as followers. Have unusually long necks. Characterized by bad acne, substantial bulk, and foul odors compared to rotten garbage.

Maite: Husband or wife of a Scar

Pests (CWO): Derived from the common mosquito. Spawn from swamp, or marsh-like areas near gravesites. Emit a buzzing only Sounders can detect. Possess excellent eyesight. Skin emits an itching agent.

Realm, the: An otherworldly dominion where the Wraiths reside and Deaconry convenes.

Rest: A coma-like state of mind a Scar is placed when punished. Length of rest determined by the Deaconry.

Scars: Immortal warriors with capabilities derived from the senses: Trackers, Sounders, Healers, Tasters, Visionaries, and the rare Reflectors.
Evolved in 1610 in Zugarramurdi, Spain during the Spanish Inquisition. In order to combat the devastation of the masses, five witches swore fealty to the Goddess Azzurra. In exchange, she granted them immortality, unique abilities of the senses, and an Ink that could be called forth for protection.

Scar Healers: Females with the capability to heal other Scars and humans. In rare instances, capable of healing animals and other entities. Able to envision the injury and heal the wound from the inside out. Experiences the pain of the injury.

Scar Reflectors: Possess a strong empathy toward emotions. Can alter emotions of others.' Characterized with stronger telepathic abilities.

Scar Sounders: Able to detect high frequencies from long distances.

Scar Tasters: Able to detect others' emotion by a distinct change in molecules in the air which affects taste.

Scar Trackers: Posses the ability to track shed skin cells.

Scar Visionaries: Able to see through certain objects. Some are able to read in hyper-speed or burn through objects.

Sublymns: Children living in the Realm who have died horrible deaths on Earth.

Talde: Group of Scars, similar to a covenant.

Taldeburu: Leader of a Talde of Scars.

Tracing: Ability to teleport to a past location.

Wraiths: Four witches, who had been burned at the stake, were offered a reprieve by the Goddess Azzurra. Each spirit was resurrected as a Wraith with the power of one of the four elements—Earth, Water, Fire, and Air.
Live in the Realm, but may walk the Earth for short periods of time.

him

1902 *France*

I COLLAPSED THE MOMENT THE *chains released my wrists from the overhanging branch and my knees hit hard on the dry, unforgiving soil. Hunched over, I took several deep, ragged breaths as the blood rushed back into my arms.*

The heavy chains around my shoulder and chest slowly unraveled and I knew it was too late for my Ink . . . I felt the emptiness. The engraved tattoo was still there, but what lived within was dead. Starved. Broken. Trapped for days beneath the chains, unable to release from my body with my call. It was the first part of a Scar that died when close to death.

My brother, Holden, lightly touched my arm and I jerked away. "Wasp, let me—"

I held up my hand, while keeping my head down, eyes closed. "Don't. Fuckin.' Touch. Me."

The image of her broken body tossed in the shallow grave like a rotten piece of meat kept repeating and cracked the fragile sane pieces I had left in me. I hadn't been strong enough to fight them.

Weak.

Pathetic.

When my limbs were functional again, I crawled toward the spot they'd buried her and stared at the disturbed soil. My palms flat on the ground, pressed into the earth. Emotions hit me like bolts of lightning. She couldn't be gone. I couldn't have done this.

I snapped as a wild frenzy took hold and I curled my hands into the soil and started digging.

I clawed.

Scraped.

Tore at it and tiny granules shoved up under my fingernails.

It was desperation as my sanity crumbled into fragments of the man I used to be.

Find her.

I had to find her.

Protect her. I hadn't protected her.

The ice-cold wind clutched at my naked skin, but I barely noticed. I was numb to the elements after hanging by my wrists for what felt like weeks. The days had been the worst as the sun beat down on me, a carcass dangling in the heat.

Then the nights came and the relief from the sun didn't last long. I shook so violently from the cold that the chains rattled constantly. But I'd suffer far worse if only I could get her back. Save her from them.

Faster. I had to dig faster.

They buried her here. I saw them. They had held my head up and forced me to watch as they tossed her limp lifeless body into the grave in front of me.

"Help me, damn it." I meant to yell the words, but my throat was so dry from lack of water it came out a scratched muffled sound.

A hand came down on my shoulder and squeezed. "Wasp . . . Jasper." The tone was barely audible, but being a Sounder, I could hear the snap of a twig or the flutter of a butterfly's wings a mile away.

Blocking out sounds was crucial to learn as a child or the chaos would drive a Scar Sounder insane. My hearing was ordinary except when I focused and used my unique ability.

But the vampires made me so weak I couldn't control the sounds. They hung me here, naked, fighting against the unbreakable chains, shouting until my throat was so inflamed it bled.

They knew I'd hear everything they did to her before they killed her.

2

They got off on hearing my screams. Her screams.

But when they brought her to me . . .

A sob caught in my throat and I dug harder. Faster. Soil flung into my face and I tasted the grit as some landed in my mouth.

I heard the voices of Holden and his best friend, Guise, along with a couple others, around me, but their words were muffled as my mind reeled into the darkness of what I was scared to find. It was descending, the reality trying to leak into my insanity of what I thought I could do—save her.

I did this.

She was mine to save and I'd been too late. I'd told them what they wanted too late and they killed her anyway. If I'd told them sooner maybe . . .

Unrelenting hands on my arms pulled me away. "No. Leave me the fuck alone."

I wildly fought against them, the roar in my chest pure agony. I kicked and punched, not knowing who I was hitting or fighting anymore, just that they were keeping me from getting to her. I heard a loud grunt and the grip on my right arm loosened. I yanked free then swung around and punched the other person holding me.

My fist connected with his jaw and for a second after the impact, I hesitated as my vision cleared. Blood ran from the corner of his lip and it matched the tears that streaked his cheeks.

My brother stared at me like I was a ghost, eyes wide and filled with grief. I caused that. I put that look in his eyes.

"Jasper. She's gone."

"No! A Healer can bring her back." I knew it was crazy, that somewhere in me my words didn't make sense, but it was as if I was gasping for air and the only way to breathe was to bring her back.

"It's too late. Jasper, look at me."

I shook my head back and forth, the soil that clung to my hair pitched in every direction. "No, a Healer . . . a powerful one . . . Lillian . . . Lillian can bring her back." I scrambled toward the grave, but my legs buckled and I landed on my side. "She was ten. She was only ten and I killed her." The words ripped from my throat in a haunted voice I didn't recognize.

I knew my brother and the Talde were watching, but they didn't try

3

to stop me this time as I dragged my broken body back to the grave and pulled at the soil again. I dug until the sun dropped and the moon rose. I couldn't stop. I had to keep trying. But I was so weak I could barely move handfuls of soil.

I finally collapsed onto my back and stared up at the starlit sky. The moment I stopped digging—there was a loss of who I'd been. And maybe that was why I tried for so long to get to her because I sensed as soon as I gave up and let the truth in . . . I'd never be the same man.

The final pieces of me burned into ash then scattered into the sky— disintegrating. Disappearing.

I stared up at the bright stars and they twinkled as if they were laughing at me.

I closed my eyes. Then coldness descended and sank into my heart.

one

Max

2015

"**M**OMMY, PLEASE." I FELL TO my knees and pressed my hand on the gaping wound on her neck. Blood surrounded me and when I looked down at my shirt I was soaked in red. I moved in slow motion as I trailed my finger down my shirt through the warm, sticky substance—syrup. And I had breasts. I was older. But I was supposed to be only ten years old.

I looked back at my mother and blood gushed through my fingers. Why didn't the bleeding stop? My hands burned with my healing ability but it was all wrong. I didn't heal her. I couldn't because he took me away from her.

Urgency ripped through me and I panicked. I had to heal my mom. I had to heal her. Now was my chance. My body burned as if I was in a furnace. God, why was it so hot?

"Mommy, please. I can heal you. Don't leave me."

My mom's neck stretched out as she inhaled a gurgled breath. Then she spoke, but it was different than before. Her voice was clear and strong and she was smiling at me.

I knew the words, every single one of them was etched in me. "Mom, don't talk."

But it was as if she didn't hear me and the broken record repeated the words I'd never forget. "It's too late for me, baby."

No. It wasn't too late. This time I could heal her and then I'd heal the Talde and we'd all be okay.

The record kept going. "Drake has an Ink that must never be healed. The Goddess Azzurra killed it." She coughed up blood and it sprayed my face over and over again. It wouldn't stop. God, stop. Please stop.

I sobbed hysterically as I sat in a pool of her blood as she calmly spoke. "He is too powerful with his Ink. Drake doesn't know about your other ability . . ." Her features melted together and then she burst into flames.

Oh, God, Mom. Mom. No. I tried to get away, but I couldn't move.

She reached for my hand and squeezed it. It was so hot. I had to get away from the fire. "Never tell anyone, Breanna. It's too dangerous. Never use that ability."

Suddenly, Drake was there, dragging me from her and out of the house. My mom. My Talde. They were all dead. He killed them.

I didn't want to go. I never had the chance to save them.

I kicked and struggled, but my body refused to obey my commands as it lay limp in his grasp. Why wasn't I moving? I tried screaming, but no words emerged.

His voice cut through the images and I was in complete darkness except for the echoing sound of his deep voice. "Shall we watch your mother burn?"

I jerked awake so abruptly, my head hit the wall. I was on the floor in the corner of the room, trembling and cold, yet sweat dripped down my brow. I hadn't had this nightmare in a while, most of the time I dreamt of the six years I spent living with Drake.

But this . . . I took a long, deep inhale . . . this was the worst one, the day I was taken. I hated this nightmare; my mom's voice . . . the burning. Ten years ago and it was like it was yesterday.

I crawled to my feet, using the wall to help gain my balance then went into the bathroom. I peeled off my damp pajamas, grabbed the plastic clip from the basket beside the sink and twirled my mouse-

6

brown hair up in a knot and fastened it. Reaching into the shower, I turned on the taps, noticing my trembling hand. It had been four years since I was rescued and still the nightmares lived in me.

It was Xamien and his Talde who found me in Drake's basement with a chain on my ankle to keep me from escaping. Although, to this day, Xamien had no idea it was Drake's home. Drake had been away and his vampire followers had been 'looking after' me.

Drake made it a habit to travel places he'd never been so that the next time, he was able to Trace, teleport, there. He told me that one day there wouldn't be a place in this world he hadn't been before. And his reasoning was so there was never a place in the world I could escape that he wouldn't find me. I'd become his private Healer and he was never letting me go.

But I'd been free for four years now, living in Xamien's pazo—his manor—in Spain. It was unlikely Drake had ever been here considering Xamien was a Taldeburu.

Unfortunately, with my freedom came the nightmares as I began to thaw and crawl out of the darkness.

I fought it.

I wanted to remain numb and alone.

Without questions. Without answers.

I could hide who I was from everyone and bury the past beneath the rubble. I even told Xamien my name was Max. I wasn't Breanna anymore and I never would be.

Within this protective shell of numbness, I was strong and I'd fought hard to be this way, closed to the fear that woke me in the night. That was the only time it found me. The only time I had no control. I became a windmill in a storm, spinning out of control, my fear gusting through me unable to be stopped. But the detachment was fading. The light that had been snatched from me when I was only ten years old was struggling to find a way to repair.

I didn't want to repair. I couldn't. Not if Drake was still alive.

I touched the white gauze bandage on my neck and trailed my finger over it, the stickiness of one corner of the upturned tape catching my skin. I pushed it back down, ignoring the tenderness as I pressed harder than necessary.

The hybrid vampire-witch Xamien had living in the attic had sunk her teeth into me yesterday and then picked me up, tossing me across the room as if I'd been a weightless plastic figurine. My body had slammed into the wall then crashed to the floor. I'd hit hard, leaving my side knitted with yellows and greens.

The new wound on my neck was just another scar to add to my collection. Reminders of why it was safer locked away. Every burn. Every mark Drake scored into me. It was *him* tormenting me. Never letting me go.

That was what he'd done to me. That was what woke me in the middle of the night screaming. He was the only thing I feared. Pain, death, torture . . . none of it frightened me anymore. But him and the power he had over me . . . he owned me and *that* fear I couldn't bury because if he was alive, one day the monster would find me again.

My only hope was that no one discovered I was the little girl, the powerful Healer, who was killed in the fire along with her Talde ten years ago. It was my only chance to stay hidden from Drake.

I stood under the hot spray until the trembling stopped then turned off the taps and climbed out of the tub. As I reached for a towel on the hook, I heard footsteps on the hardwood floor outside the door. It was after midnight, and Xamien rarely had guests and if he did, he told me they were coming.

The steps stopped outside the bathroom door. I expected a knock and Xamien to ask if I was okay. Often he'd come check up on me if I woke in the night screaming; instead, the doorknob turned and the door swung open.

My breath hitched and I yanked the white towel up in front of me while I staggered back a few steps. A shiver brushed through me as the cool air from the open door hit my wet skin and the humid air dissipated.

I clutched the towel to my damp skin as I met the hard, grey eyes of a man I'd never seen before. The first thought that came into my head was panther—a deadly panther. Sleek and lean—his muscles defining every inch of him even through his clothing.

It was as if he was ready and eager to pounce on whatever prey he had in his sights. And at the moment, that was me. What softened his look were the lazy walnut curls that fell in disarray over his head and the slight twitch in the corner of his mouth as if he was . . . amused.

"Who are you?" Maybe I should've asked what the hell he was doing walking into my bathroom in the middle of the night, but I was more concerned as to who he was and what he was capable of. He had to be a Scar because Xamien rarely allowed anyone in his manor except Scars; however, recently, he allowed a vampire-witch to be incarcerated in the attic.

"Are you a Scar?" My shields around my thoughts to hide my abilities were pretty resilient, but it still made me uneasy meeting new Scars. This guy, with his cocky stance and arrogant expression, looked like he had an overabundance of confidence. I only hoped he didn't have an ability to match.

"Sure am. But if you'd rather I be something else, I'm willing to *play* for a night."

Oh, my God. What a dick. "You're standing in my bathroom in case you haven't noticed."

"Oh, I noticed." His eyes boldly roamed down the length of my body, hesitated on my foot where my disfigured Ink tattoo lay, and then dragged back up to meet my eyes again. His expression remained composed and unconcerned as he casually leaned his shoulder up against the doorframe and crossed his arms.

"Can you please leave?" I attempted to keep my voice courteous like I always did, but there was grit to it this time and it echoed in the bathroom.

"A polite little thing, aren't you," he replied with a harsh baritone, which held a hint of Scot accompanied with the softening lilt of Irish.

My blood pumped faster through my veins as the sexy sound vibrated through me. The nightmare had obviously damaged my brain. "If you don't leave, I'm calling Xamien."

The corners of his lips twitched. "I don't think you will."

I glared. "Why not?"

"Because you like me."

I snorted. "I don't even know you. And I certainly don't like strange men who come into my bathroom in the middle of the night." The clip in my hair slipped out and fell to the floor, making a clink as it bounced off the ceramic tiles. My hair tumbled down my back and over my shoulders. His eyes watched the strands until they settled in place then his gaze slid over my skin to linger on my collarbone before

9

dragging up the curve of my neck.

Goose bumps scattered across my moist skin as his eyes changed from a light charcoal grey to glistening black, like wet pavement in the night. It was utterly captivating . . . and I didn't like it one bit.

Scars had much stronger emotions than humans, sometimes, so powerful, it was debilitating, but I'd never had my body react to a man this way. Not that I had much experience.

The muscles in his arms flexed and my eyes darted to the ink etched into his skin in an intricate pattern from his elbow upward to disappear beneath his plain black t-shirt. I peered closer trying to distinguish if it was his Ink, but it was nearly impossible to tell them from a regular tattoo. My only advantage was I had a connection with Inks. I studied his tattoo, searching for the familiar living being beneath—

"You see, you like me."

My eyes shot back to his and an idle emotion rose inside me—anger. It clawed at my shield as he stood in the doorway as if it was his right to be there. "Are you done having your fun? I'd like to go back to bed."

The corners of his lips curved upward and I caught a glimpse of his perfect white teeth. "Don't think I'll be *done* for a while." The word *done* came out as a drawl that lingered in the air between us.

For years, I'd kept my emotions contained, yet within one minute, this guy was charging it like a wild boar. I had the urge to walk up to him, smack him in the face then slam the door on him. It was an urge that surprised me. I hadn't thought of reacting to anyone in a long time. I was calm, patient and disconnected, but all of those were teetering on a tightrope. What I didn't like was the strange whirl in my stomach as if I was nervous.

"How old are you?" he asked.

"None of your business." Scars were immortal and aged until thirty-two, so it was hard for me to guess how long he'd been around. I was only twenty, and for a Scar that was really young.

"Oh, baby, right now, you are my business."

A splattering of sensations peppered through me and begged to come out and play. I couldn't let them. I wouldn't let him unhinge me with a few looks and a couple words. I was stronger than that. But there was something about him that put me on edge.

God, why was he just staring at me as if he could see right through my towel? Why wasn't I calling Xamien? He was close enough to speak telepathically, but I hadn't used that form of communication since I was ten.

Fine. If he wasn't going to leave, then I was. I leaned over to reach for another towel to cover my shoulders, but I kept my eyes on him. I wasn't stupid and suspected if I took my eyes off him, he'd take advantage. I didn't know how yet, but I wasn't taking any chances with this asshole. But my mistake was I should've been paying attention to what I was doing.

It happened fast. I leaned too far. The heel of my foot slipped in the puddle of water beneath my feet and I lost my balance. I scrambled to grab hold of something . . . that something was the towel rack. But even my one-hundred and fifteen pounds was too much for it and the metal rod snapped out of the holder and clanged to the floor.

A weird strangled cry emerged from my throat as I landed sitting on the toilet with the bundle of towels now on the floor at my feet—including the one I'd been using.

My cheeks burned as I grabbed one and pulled it up in front of me then jumped back to my feet. Our gazes clashed and I noticed the quick change in his expression from lowered brows over his annoyed charcoal eyes to amusement again.

He grinned and half-snorted. "Impressive."

Momentarily speechless, I had no idea how to respond. The polite response would be a shy, embarrassed smile; my gut response was 'get the fuck out!' Instead, I kept my thoughts to myself. It was safer that way. I had to stay safe.

No confrontation. Simple. Yet there was nothing simple about this man. I could see it hidden in the depths of his eyes—dark, hard. And he'd changed expressions so quickly as if not wanting me to witness the dark parts of him.

He crossed his ankles, appearing casual and comfortable, and I ground my teeth together. "So, do you normally shower in the middle of the night?"

"So, are you normally rude?"

He laughed and a soft curl fell in front of his eyes. He casually pushed it back behind his ear. "You don't know who I am, do you?"

No. And I didn't care.

"Jasper Kyelin."

Kyelin. Then it clicked. The rogue Scar. The mercenary or assassin—both. He'd stayed here briefly a few times, but I'd never met him. When I'd been attacked a couple days ago by the witch-vampire, he'd been there, but I was in so much pain I hadn't looked at him.

"And your name, sunshine?"

Sunshine? *God, I hate endearments.* They were degrading. I wanted to tell him to take his sunshine and shove it up his ass where the sun didn't shine, but I wouldn't play his game and from his cocky amused attitude, this was a game and I was the play piece. "My name is Max, not 'Sunshine,' although I suspect you already know that," I replied.

He shrugged.

Yeah, he had. God, his asshole meter was rising by the second. "You're Xamien's little pet."

The meter shot off the scale and exploded. I met his eyes and held them, glaring. *Bastard.* I had no intention on having any further conversation with him and he was quickly proving my theory that people rarely listened, and if they did, they didn't give a shit. It was all pretenses to get something from you for their own benefit. The question was . . . what did Jasper want from me?

He shoved away from the doorframe and casually strolled across the tiled floor toward me. Confident. Self-assured. Not a trace of unease.

"What are you doing?" My voice quivered and he grinned. *Jesus, get your shit together, Max.*

He crouched in front of me and my eyes followed his agile movement as he picked up my hairclip. He slowly stood again and took another step forward. He was so close to me his breath brushed across my face when he exhaled.

My chest tightened as his scent drifted into me. It was fresh soil mixed with a hint of dry cedar—sensual. I tried to ignore it, but when I breathed in, it settled in my lungs and caused a wave of heat to spread across my skin. I quickly lowered my gaze, intending to ignore him; instead, my eyes trailed down his long, muscular thighs.

I swallowed and curled my fingers into the edges of the towel pulling it tighter to my body. I kept my eyes glued to the floor, attempting to ignore the new sensations raging through me.

"Standing right here, best look at me, babe." His finger came under my chin and I clamped my jaw as he tilted my head up so our eyes met. "And I'm not one for repeating myself." He held my clip out in his opposite hand.

I didn't move until his brows lowered. I snatched my clip from his palm and curled it in my hand.

He watched me with such intensity I was unsure of what he was doing. And *that* I didn't like. He was a Scar and I didn't know what type and some Reflectors were really good at breaking through shields. There was slight heaviness in my head and it was him attempting to read my thoughts, but I knew from the pressure he wasn't strong enough. Fortunately, it was one advantage I'd gained from my captivity, a concrete wall around my thoughts. It took several years before I managed it, and even Xamien, who was almost as powerful as the North American Taldeburu, Waleron, was incapable of reading my mind.

"A Scar with unreadable thoughts." His brows rose and the corners of his lips curved up. "But . . ." His thumb caressed my chin. "There's something more to you than that."

I stiffened, eyes widening then I yanked my head to the side, dislodging his hand. How did he read that? Oh, God, he couldn't know just from touching me could he?

"Sunshine, I don't give a shit what you're hiding." He boldly looked me up and down then drawled, "Except perhaps what's under that towel."

I bit my lower lip—hard. So hard I tasted blood. I released the pressure then flicked out my tongue to caress the damaged surface.

"Liking the tongue action, but best keep it locked away or you'll be losing that towel. Morals rarely cross my mind." I yanked my tongue back inside my mouth. He grinned, but it didn't match the piercing look in his eyes.

"Just get out of here."

He tsked. "Not the way to treat a guy who was concerned for your . . . safety."

"Safety?" Was he crazy? I wasn't in any danger.

"I'm a Sounder, babe. Heard your thrashing from my bedroom." He hesitated as if he was deciding what to say. "I realize some erotic dreams can be rather . . . vivid, but you might want to keep them under wraps while I'm here. Or . . ." he grinned. "I'll be tempted to make them real."

I tried to blanket the desire that suffocated me, but he was messing up all my control and I was spiraling into unknown territory.

"Unless of course you and Xamien are fucking one another?"

My mouth dropped open. *Bastard.* First of all, it was none of his business and second of all . . . it was none of his fucking business. I clamped down on my retort which was going to be my fist belting him across the face, but instead used the response Drake had enforced in me. No confrontation meant I stayed protected.

"No, sir," I ground out and looked down at my feet.

Suddenly, I found myself shoved back against the wall, his hands gripping my hips with a fierce bite. I gasped, my eyes flashing to his. Gone was any sort of teasing humor as his eyes narrowed in on me, brows low, mouth tight.

"Sir? Not your fuckin' sir. Anything but a sir—best you remember that."

Just as sudden as it came, the violence in his expression disappeared and the corners of his mouth curved upward and sparkling warmth invaded his eyes. His hands left my hips only to slowly move up my sides until his thumbs were resting just below my breasts. "Fuckin' beautiful."

He pushed away from me, and for a brief second, I wished he hadn't.

Then I wished I'd nailed him in the groin.

He turned and walked out, leaving the bathroom door ajar.

I collapsed onto the toilet seat and put my head in my hands.

What the hell just happened? I'd lost my calm. My control. He'd broken through my shield and had my emotions sparking off like fireworks. He was dangerous to me and what I was hiding.

I crawled back in bed, but failed to sleep. Instead, images of Jasper inundated my mind causing me to toss and turn.

The next morning, according to Xamien, Jasper was gone before the sun rose. I should've been relieved; instead, I found myself thinking of him and it wasn't just that day. It became days afterward.

Then a week later, I woke in the night and smelled his scent in my room. I leapt out of bed, turned on the light expecting to see him, but Jasper wasn't there. Day after day for weeks, I sensed him near me, but Jasper hadn't returned.

I became obsessed with him. Thinking about him all the time and then constantly berating myself for it.

And the worst was, my nightmares reminding me to stay hidden and safe became riddled with erotic dreams of Jasper.

But the feeling of him being near me was never consistent. It was as if he was there and then . . . he was gone. I couldn't understand it and after several months, I gave up trying. What I did know was when I didn't sense him around, I felt . . . alone.

two

Max

Six months later

I ROLLED OVER MOANING AS the deep roar of a bike's muffler sounded outside my bedroom window. I put the pillow over my head as it skidded in the gravel and then the engine revved before it shut down.

I flicked an eye open and glanced at the red digital number on the clock sitting on my nightstand—one fifteen. What was Xamien—?

The front door slammed shut and I bolted upright.

Xamien was in Toronto with Waleron.

Xamien didn't have a motorcycle.

Darts of fear speckled my skin as I heard the footsteps downstairs. My heart slammed against my chest and I threw back the covers, jumped out of bed then knelt on the floor and felt around until I found the slightly raised tile. I dug my fingernails underneath and pried it loose then slid it aside.

I reached in the hole, pulled out my handgun and quickly checked it was still loaded, although I always left it that way. I never assumed I was safe even after years of being free of the monster. Nor did I pretend to believe the feeling would ever go away.

A gun wouldn't stop him though. Nothing would if he found me.

I clutched the gun, finger curved around the trigger as the booted feet took the stairs two at a time. Two at a time . . . Drake would never take the stairs like that. He'd do it calmly, quiet and with grace. Complete control. Dignified.

I quickly glanced at my hands . . . they were normal, no heat. After years of healing Drake's lungs week after week, my hands used to automatically heat up whenever he was near. It became my warning sign he'd arrived . . . home. Despite what happened there, it still had become my home for six years. I had nothing else. I had no one. He'd made sure of that.

My heart beat steadied and the trembling in my body stopped as I realized it couldn't be Drake. I may no longer be afraid to die, but I was smart enough to be scared of Drake and going back to him. Of what he'd do to me if he ever found out what I'd been hiding from him all those years I'd lived with him.

My one strength was that I'd learned to be numb. To shut off the inner coil of emotions. It was my way to not feel the pain. To stop my abilities. To stop everything.

Until him. Jasper.

I tried to ignore the spark igniting inside me at the thought of him, but for months, I imagined the touch of his fingers on my hips when he pressed me up against the wall. I smelled his scent on the breeze that drifted through the window at night as I lay in bed. And those times, I swear he was watching me . . . that he was in my room when I was sleeping. It unleashed a craving for him that refused to be dulled.

And I hated him for it. I hated how he awakened something inside me. He was like a maggot burrowing deep in my skin that I couldn't get rid of.

While he'd so easily controlled his emotions, mine had been all over the place like butterflies in a wind storm.

Steps strode confidently down the hallway and I quickly tiptoed behind my bedroom door and pressed my back against the wall.

I held the gun with both hands in front of me, my finger firm on the trigger as I waited for my door to open. I glanced at my window and thought of running, but I didn't want to run. I'd spent four years learning how to handle weapons and I was good at it.

A few times, I'd caught Xamien watching me from the kitchen window as I relentlessly practiced wielding my circular blades. I saw the sadness in his eyes and the disappointment. He never pushed me, but I knew he wanted me to trust him. To tell him who I was and what happened to me. All he knew was that I was a Scar and my name was Max, although the latter was obviously a lie.

My breath hitched as Jasper's familiar scent trickled under the heavy wooden door. My heartbeat rocketed and my nerve endings stood at attention.

I heard the creak of the handle turning and then the door burst open so hard, my foot that was meant to stop it—didn't, and I was crushed between the door and the wall.

He strode in, turned and kicked the door shut with the heel of his boot.

That cocky smirk he'd worn so easily at our last meeting was gone. Now he looked . . . vicious. Merciless. And suddenly the relief that it was him was washed away and uncertainty took over. His narrowed grey eyes blazed with a steady gravity as he looked at me. The sharp outline of his jaw pulsed and the corded muscles in his neck tightened.

"Get changed," Jasper ordered. There was no apology for hitting me with the door. No explanation. No acknowledgment of the gun in my hands pointed at his chest.

And I wasn't going anywhere with him. I had no clue why he was here in the middle of the night, but I certainly didn't trust a rogue assassin Scar, no matter how much I'd thought about him in the last six months.

"We need to get the fuck out of here." I watched as he strode over to the window, parted the curtains then looked out. He was wearing black cargo pants that hung easily off his hips and a snug black t-shirt with a holster slung over his shoulder. My eyes slid down his tatted arm to his hand that was curled around the hilt of a knife.

He swung back around and came toward me. "Fuck, sunshine. You have an issue with instructions?" He grabbed my forearm.

I immediately reacted to his rough touch and tried to wrench my arm away, but he refused to budge. "Let me go. I'm not going anywhere with you."

"This better be fuckin' worth it," he mumbled.

I had no idea what he was talking about, but to suddenly take off with him in the middle of the night . . . stupid considering rumor was this guy took jobs that were far past the edge of being moral.

Jasper raised something in me, a rebellion to my coldness and I had the urge to try and break that control he held onto. "I'm not going anywhere with you, *sir*. Now, let me go."

His bruising grip tightened and his eyes drove into me. "Call me that one more time and once we get the fuck clear of here, I'll throw you over my knee and spank your ass."

My breath hitched and I pulled back again, but failed to dislodge his grip, so instead, I raised my gun and pointed it at him.

"Fuck, you're pissing me off. Save the bullets for the assholes who are on their way here." He yanked on my arm—hard. I stumbled into him and his hand went for my gun.

I squeezed the trigger.

Bang.

The sound echoed through the room in a loud vibration along with his accompanying roar. "Fuck."

He let me go, staggering back a few steps, his hand on the side of his upper thigh where blood trickled between his fingers. The crushing path of the bullet left a gaping hole in his pants that was fast becoming soaked in blood.

He growled and then his head jerked up and our eyes locked. The penetrating look was unsettling and my nerves fired off and it wasn't from the possibility that this man would kill me; it was for what he might do beforehand.

I remembered him looking at me in the bathroom, wearing a towel and nothing else. How his eyes roamed over my body as if he was going to throw me on the counter and have his way with me.

I backed up a step, gun still pointed at him. But this time, I was having trouble keeping it steady. I'd never shot anyone before and I hadn't meant to shoot Jasper, well, not really.

Jasper lifted his hand to look at his wound then snorted. "You remember what I said six months ago?"

Of course I did—I remembered every word. I just didn't know which part he was referring to.

"No morals, sunshine." He walked to the bed, picked up the sheet, and then with his knife, he ripped off a strip. He looked up at me. "Nothing affects me. Not your contempt or anyone else's. I don't care whether you hate me or can't wait to get your mouth around my cock. 'Cause when it's all over—I. Don't. Give. A. Fuck. What I do care about is getting paid." He took the piece of linen and wrapped it around his thigh several times and blood instantly seeped through. "And now my fee for saving your ass just tripled."

Fee? Saving me? What was he talking about?

He grunted as he pulled tightly on the self-made bandage. Then in one fluid move, he leapt forward and kicked the gun out of my hand. It slid across the stone tiles and disappeared beneath my bed.

I dove for it.

Jasper dove for me.

We both landed in a heap on the floor. Me on my stomach, Jasper on top, his hands latched onto my wrists above my head.

My cheek pressed into the cold floor and I panted hard and it wasn't from exertion. The feel of him on top of me, his scent awakening a rabble of butterflies, a rabble I never knew lived in me until I'd met him, a rabble I'd been fighting for months. Well, now they were having an illegal fluttering party and I needed to lock them up and throw away the key.

The sudden hard swelling between his legs on my ass sent my pulse racing and that low octane tweak into a full-blown panty-dampening ache. I tried to wiggle to get out from under him, but stopped when he groaned.

"Babe, loving this position, as I'm sure you're aware. But we really don't have time for this."

"Get off me." I thought my voice would be steady; instead, it quaked and damn if he noticed.

"Cute," he whispered next to my ear. "Wishing we had more time. I'd fuck you just like this. Maybe bring your ass up a bit. Better for both of us."

Shivers trickled across my skin like tiny pebbles being washed over by a fast moving stream. His breath had a hint of raspberry as it wafted over my face and I inhaled, closing my eyes. Then I tensed as the iron scent hit me. The instinct to heal was strong in me and the

20

burning in my hands began as the urge to heal his thigh raced through my veins.

"Get. Off. Me."

"Oh, I'll get off," he murmured. His cock twitched and I shoved back my leg trying to hit his thigh. "Yeah, sunshine, I feel it too. We'll get there."

Oh. My. God. Did he really think I'd have sex with him? Probably. No, not probably—likely.

I hated unpredictable and Jasper's middle name was quickly becoming unpredictable. I was good at reading people, knowing what they'd do before they did it. Jasper was a broken puzzle piece, one second sexy and flirty, the next dark and scary and I was certainly no sunshine, more like a dense fog. I was plain and impassionate . . . well, at least I was until those butterflies showed up and then the fire within me sparked into an inferno.

Suddenly, his weight lifted and I was hauled to my feet in front of him. "I dare you to make another move, angel." He cocked a half-grin and it was that grin I hadn't been able to get out of my head for months. "Never hit a woman. Never will. But I sure as hell will put her in her place some other way. And spanking . . . that's fair game."

I took his warning seriously. Jasper didn't appear the type to make idle threats. I may think I could take him, but I was practical and realistic. He was an assassin and could snap my neck before I took my next breath.

His gaze jerked to the window and his eyes narrowed, head tilted as if he was listening. "We need to leave—now," Jasper ordered. "They're nearly here."

"Who?" I asked, but Jasper was opening drawers and throwing clothes at me. "What's going on?" A vise clamped around my chest as I thought of the one person who would come after me.

"Humans. Not very strong, but I'd prefer not to get shot again." Jasper strode toward me. "Change or you're going like that."

I darted for my nightstand where my cell phone charged, but he got to me first, latching onto my wrist. "Let me call Xamien."

Most Scars were telepathic, but it was limited within a mile or so except for a rare few who could reach further. I had to call Xamien. I didn't trust Jasper and I sure as hell wasn't walking out the door with him until I found out what was going on.

Jasper reached over and grabbed my cell then threw it on the floor and smashed it with his foot.

I stared at the crushed pieces and then back at Jasper. "What—"

"No phone calls."

I was fast getting that I wasn't going to win here. "I can't just leave with you. I don't know you, and I certainly don't trust you." I held the clothes to my chest with one arm, my mind whirling with distrust and unbridled emotions that were playing with me like I was a ragdoll.

He shrugged. "Never asked you to trust me and it's better you don't. But you sure as hell know me. I'm the guy you've been thinking about fucking for the last six months." *Oh, my God.* "And you're coming with me because you want to see me get paid a large sum of money for saving your ass."

It was like Jasper was chipping away at my numbness with a mallet and I couldn't stop myself from punching back. "I'm not leaving until you tell me what is going on."

Jasper scowled and his entire body stiffened. Any hint of humor vanished as he took a step toward me. I backed up until my spine hit the barrier of the wall. Shit. I'd really pissed him off and I had no weapon, although I was uncertain whether I'd have the guts to shoot him again. He was a rogue Scar assassin, who looked as if he was going to kill me.

He stopped inches from me then raised his knife to my neck. I didn't breathe as he pressed the tip to the hollow of my throat and I felt a tiny pin prick. I held completely still, afraid to look away from him or move. His eyes held a dangerous glint in them as he stared at me.

Without a word, he grabbed the neckline of my pajama top. Then with his knife, he ripped it straight down the middle. I gaped. The clothes I'd been holding now held up in front of my naked breasts. He didn't stop there as he put his hands on my hips and yanked down my white silk pajama pants.

"Oh, my God." I stood in my pink panties in front of him, but he wasn't even paying attention to me; instead, he strode to the window again.

"Put the fuckin' clothes on or you go naked." His tone was rough with a deep Scottish brogue as the tension pulsated from him.

I knew when to stop fighting and at the moment, Jasper was furious and I was certain any second, he'd either shoot me himself and take a loss on whatever money he was being paid, or throw me over his shoulder with nothing but my panties on.

I quickly pulled on the khaki shorts and pale pink t-shirt with the sparkly white horse on the front. A present from Xamien on my first Christmas here. It came with my favorite weapon—my circular blades.

By the time I was dressed, he was in front of me again, grabbing my arm and before I even had the shirt pulled down, he tugged me toward the door.

Then I heard it; cars driving up the gravel driveway and skidding to a stop and then doors opening and slamming shut.

"Looks like I'll have to work for my money now. Hope you know how to kick some ass because I plan on living to get paid for this job." I never had the opportunity to use my weapons, but I practiced with them and thought I could hold my own. "Our best scenario . . . we get out of here alive. The worst . . . I have to use you to bargain for my life."

I gawked at him. "You wouldn't." But from the snippets of info I'd gathered on Jasper, I was betting he would.

His brows rose. "You want to test it, sunshine?" I heard the front door splinter as it was forced open. He waited for my answer and I finally shook my head. He smirked and then opened the door and pulled me into the hall.

My breath hitched as glass shattered and I slammed my back against the wall. Jasper didn't stop though and pulled me behind him until we were close to the bannister overlooking the front hall. I banged into his side when he stopped abruptly. He glanced at me and scowled, but didn't say anything. He tilted his head and his eyes narrowed as if listening for where the men were located downstairs.

Then he turned to me and said without a hint of teasing. "In case I die, you should know I've wanted to fuck you since that day in the bathroom."

Wow, he really had no filter, and why would he want to fuck me? I was a pin cushion of scars and burns.

"Yeah, I saw the scars. Don't give a fuck either. Means you have a story is all. One I plan on reading while sinking between your thighs." Jasper didn't tiptoe around me like I was some glass figurine with scrapes all over it. He was direct, honest and . . . completely offensive.

I caught his gaze looking me up and down as if he was contemplating whether to toss me against the wall and fuck me before we died or take his chances and hope we made it out alive then fuck me. And for some crazy screwed-up reason, the thought had my heart racing and my sex clenching. But when Jasper looked at me with heat blazing in his eyes I felt—wanted. Desired.

But I was damaged goods and I didn't have sex—period. Sex was carnal and filled with emotion. There was too much of a chance my shields would falter and he'd see more of who I was. And the consequences of that ever getting out . . . it was safer for everyone this way.

He lowered his voice and nodded to the stairwell. "I'm guessing ten trained men with high-powered guns. That's the bad news. The good . . ." he grinned. "I fight harder turned on."

I never wanted to slap someone before; I just didn't care enough to have anyone piss me off—until Jasper. Now I wanted to slap him and then . . . kiss him. Jesus. What the hell was wrong with me?

The men's footsteps crunching on broken pieces of glass, china, and whatever else they'd destroyed, blanketed any crazy desire I was fighting. Xamien was going to be pissed and Xamien pissed meant there would be hell to pay. He was cool, calm and had the patience of a saint, but when Xamien lost it he was a tsunami.

"Stay the fuck behind me. I get shot, knifed, whatever, you can heal my ass."

My stomach plummeted. "What?" How did he know I was a Healer? No one knew.

He opened the door. "Babe, the moment I touched you, I knew."

My head spun and knees weakened. "Did you tell anyone?"

He hesitated, eyes watching me as if he was assessing something. "Nope. Let's go." He chin-lifted to the left, which led to the rear of the house, then let go of my hand. His back to the wall, he moved along it, knife in his hand, gun in his pants at the small of his back. His steps quickly ate up the ground, but he was quiet and calm.

Jasper stopped, turned toward me, dragged his eyes down my front and then yanked off his black t-shirt and tossed it to me.

I stared at it for a second, then at his naked chest that was a hard slab of muscle with tats drawn across his left shoulder to link with the ones on his arm.

"Put it on. You stick out like a fuckin' cotton candy with those stupid horse sparkles."

I quickly put it on over my top and it hung down to my mid-thigh. The scent of him drew into my lungs and I inhaled deeply with my chin down until I heard his distinct chuckle. Then I wanted to shoot myself in the foot.

Jasper's hand came around the back of my neck and he jerked me toward him. He cupped my chin with his blade still in his hand so the handle was cold against my jaw. Then he leaned in and before I could take my next breath, his mouth was on mine.

I was so astonished I just stood there and let him kiss me. We had men coming after us. He was shot in the leg and he was kissing me and it was . . . Jesus, it was penetrating and unforgiving and hard.

It was beautiful.

I hadn't had much beauty in my life, but this . . . the urgency in him. The need. It encompassed me and I sagged against him, while his unyielding mouth moved against mine with possession.

He let me go and without a word headed for the stairs.

I stood frozen, lips swollen and knees weak.

He glanced back at me. "Wait until I have my cock in you."

I huffed as each butterfly was murdered and plummeted to a painful death in the pit of my stomach.

three

Jasper

FUCKIN' KISSED HER. I hadn't planned on it . . . well, not yet at least, but seeing her inhale my scent on my shirt . . . that snapped my control. It was fuckin' hot as hell.

I heard two sets of footsteps start up the stairs and quickly shoved Max back against the wall. I put my finger to my lips then gestured for her to stay, and crept down a few steps to peer over the railing.

I glanced back at Max to make certain she was following my instructions, because I was fast realizing that underneath the submissive shell she hid behind, lay defiance. I hadn't expected it until she shot me. Now that was one fuck of a surprise. I didn't think she'd have the guts, but having watched her for the last six months between jobs, I knew she was capable of handling a weapon. I just didn't expect her to use one on me.

She'd trembled when I kissed her and those lips, that mouth had been warm and pliable beneath mine. Jesus, it was better than I'd imagined and I imagine a fuck of a lot. The thing was this was now a job. She was a job. I didn't want it to be. Fuck, it was the worst fucked-up job ever, but there was no way in hell any other fucker was getting near her.

It had to be me.

Jesus Christ, I wanted to fuck the girl I was hired to kill.

Yeah, well, I may not get the chance to do either if we didn't get out of here. I threw my legs over the railing and leapt, landing hard on top of one guy and taking him down. The shooting pain in my thigh from the bullet wound made my vision go black for a second and I shook my head trying to clear it.

I heard movement in front of me and kicked out with my good leg and bashed the other guy in the chest, sending him rolling down the stairs like a beach ball that popped and deflated at the bottom as he lay on his stomach stunned for a second.

I flipped over, punched the guy in the throat and he dropped the gun to clutch at his neck with both hands, gasping for air. Still straddling him, I half-turned and threw my knife at the guy at the bottom of the stairs who was now on his feet, gun pointed at me. My knife embedded in his chest, but not fast enough as I heard the distinct click.

I rolled to the side as the bullet whizzed past my left ear. I yanked his buddy up in front of me as the gun continued to go off. The harsh impact of the bullets hitting the body caused it to jerk several times. Stupid bastard. I tossed the body forward when he was out of clips and it tumbled down the stairs and hit the asshole and the two of them landed in a heap.

When I reached them, the living guy was attempting to get free of his dead buddy as I stood over top. "Need some help?" I hauled the dead guy off him. Then before he had a chance to go for his knife in his boot, I landed a hard blow with my fist to his chest wound where my knife had been. "Who hired you?"

The guy coughed up blood and it splattered my chest in a fine mist. When he caught his breath, he lifted his head and met my eyes. "Fuck you." Then he had the balls to spit in my face.

Too bad I had bigger ones.

I sliced my knife across his throat and watched as his narrowed eyes widened and he gurgled as blood sprayed from his neck. I had no time for bullshit and the asshole wasn't going to tell me anything. Of course, that might have changed if I took him with us then tortured him for a while. But despite what I did for a living, torture wasn't my thing and those who'd heard of me knew that.

No fucking around. Tell me what I want or die. Saved me a hell of a lot of wasted time ripping fingernails off and pulling teeth.

I heard her come up behind me, and then smelled the delicious scent of her coconut shampoo. Jesus, I didn't like the fact I was thinking about kissing her again with two dead bodies at my feet and several more men who no doubt heard the gunshots and were going to be on us any moment.

I should be thinking about getting the fuck out of here. I may like to fuck women, but my job came first. Always. And this job was pretty damn important because Max had something I wanted. That was if I could keep her alive and out of the hands of the guy who was after her. If he got too close, I'd have no choice . . . I'd have to kill her.

That was why they picked me. I was the only Scar who'd kill her if need be. I wasn't proud of it. Fuck, I never thought about the jobs I did and who I had to kill. They were a means to an end except my end never came. I couldn't get out from under the storm that brewed inside me. Trapped in a vicious circle of my family's haunting grief and my guilt eating away at my insides.

"Jasper?"

I stiffened then glanced at the girl I'd been stalking for months. At first, I played it off as lust, and being the sick bastard I was, I wanted to break the girl I met in the bathroom. But when I left to go on a job, she fucked with my mind and she was all I could think about. I couldn't wait to get back and watch her sip her coffee out on the patio or see the sweat drip down her flushed cheeks as she practiced with those kickass circular blades. The worst was slipping in her bedroom at night and having to leave when she began to thrash around and moan.

Her hand touched my arm and I jerked my gaze to her. She was looking down at the bodies. Steady and calm as if she'd seen death regularly. I had the urge to throw her against the wall and kiss her again. I couldn't help it. It turned me on. She turned me on and it was even worse now I'd tasted the rebellion inside her that was desperate to come out and play.

Jesus, I had to get my shit together. She needed to learn the rules and I had to start thinking of her as a job.

I linked my fingers with hers and then we ran into the kitchen and out the back door. As soon as we were a few feet from the house,

I heard the shout above us from the second floor window. "Fuck." I picked up the pace, my thigh burning as we weaved through the garden. "My bike's hidden up ahead near the shed."

Her hand suddenly slipped from mine and I thought she fell; instead, when I stopped and looked back, she was frantically digging in the fuckin' dirt with her hands.

I froze.

For one second. One fuckin' second it hit me and I froze, staring at her.

Digging.

Frantic.

On her knees.

The façade slipped and I stumbled back a step. My hand holding my knife trembled and my heart thumped erratically. The memory was raw and harsh like sandpaper rubbing at my mind grinding the image into me over and over again. It was me. It was me searching for Beth.

Weak. I'd been so weak. Not strong enough to save her. Then my parents' wails . . . bile rose in my throat as I remembered my mom's fists pummeling my chest, screaming and crying hysterically. It had been Holden who pulled her off me.

Max looked up and our eyes met, but I didn't really see her. It was Beth being tossed in the grave, the dirt carelessly thrown over her while they laughed.

I couldn't stop them.

I couldn't save her.

I couldn't—

The faint click of the gun cocked fifty feet away snapped me out of it. Jesus Christ, I curled my hand around my knife as the anger blanketed the memory.

"You trying to get me killed, girl? Fuck." I came up behind her and hauled her up underneath her armpits.

Dirt crumbled from her hands. "My blades. I need my blades."

Shit. I'd seen her put them here often enough and I saw the look in her eyes every time she took them out. It was power. Need. Desperation all rolled into one. She needed them, just like I needed to kill. Fuck, I'd even jerked off to the image of her in the courtyard wielding her blades.

29

A twig snapped. Then the distinct sound of a heartbeat—one guy.

I crouched then nudged Max in the arm and chin-lifted to the rose bushes on the right. She pulled a box out of the hole then lifted the lid and grabbed her knives. They reminded me of table saw blades, except these had grips on them.

My first impression of Max that day in the bathroom—a sweet, quiet rabbit scared of her own shadow. That lasted about two seconds when I saw the flash of emotion in her eyes, but it came and went like lightning, and then she was cold and detached.

And I didn't like it. I liked seeing the defiance she tried to keep locked down; that flash of rebellion blazing in the core of her body. But those scars—and Jesus there were a lot of them—made me want to break her wide open and then heal every single one of them with my kisses.

Fuck. I might have to kill this chick. I have to get a fuckin' grip.

Max leapt to her feet, a blade in each hand, and damn if my cock didn't harden.

I frowned. "Try and remember you're a Healer and don't do anything stupid." I grabbed her arm and we started running again, although it was more a jog with my leg slowing me down.

Two guys emerged out of the side door and raced after us, bullets flew past, but I noticed they were aimed low, at our legs so as not to kill Max. I yanked her forward trying to get her in front of me so she was protected when I heard her swift inhale. She staggered, her weight pulling me to a stop as she fell to her knees.

Her hand went to her side and came away covered in blood.

"Fuck." I picked her up in one swoop and dove behind the shed for cover. I put her down then crouched and lifted her t-shirt to look at how bad it was. She couldn't die. I needed her alive. I tried to convince myself it was because of the payment if I kept her alive, which was much more lucrative than my payment if I was forced to kill her. But I knew it was something else. Something dangerous to feel. Something I didn't let in because of shit just like this.

The wound was bleeding, but the bullet had nicked her and gone right through. I yanked the shirt down, grabbed her hand and pressed it to her side—hard. I knew it must have fuckin' hurt, but she didn't react to it. Actually, she looked calm for a chick who'd just been shot.

"Stay here." I got to my feet and then took off after the assholes. I enjoyed the odd cat and mouse game, but we'd fucked around too long and I was betting these guys were calling in reinforcements. Humans were an easy kill, vampires a fuck of a lot harder, but from what Adrian had told me, this was one of our own, a Scar who was after Max and he had the ability to Trace. If he traced here before we got the fuck out, I'd be out of a deal and more than likely my life.

I calmed my breathing as I heard them approach. I slipped my gun into my belt and took out my knives. I calmly waited, using my ability to focus on their movements. I took them both out within seconds of one another. Clean. Calm. And only a mild protest from one guy as he went down.

I was good at what I did. That was why I did it. I didn't give a fuck as to why I was hired for a job. I did what I was paid to do and walked away. It was simple. My life was simple. I kept it that way.

Until Max. Then simple became complicated because I'd been unable to forget the image of her as she stood half-naked against the wall. Her silky white skin moist and heated from the shower; droplets trickling down the curve of her neck; nothing between us except a white towel. I saw the scars weaving across her skin and rage had burned inside me at whoever had done that to her. I wanted to rip them apart for even touching her.

I couldn't forget Max no matter what I did. I'd tried to stay clear of Xamien's, but I kept coming back, craving even just a glimpse of her. I fuckin' stalked her. For weeks I watched her until I was needed for a job, but then . . . then I was back. I always fuckin' came back.

The way she quietly moved through the gardens, her subtle movements like a rose petal floating on a gentle breeze. Quiet, subtle, beautiful. But Max had thorns. She just kept them hidden; at least she thought she did.

And then there were the nights I heard her screams from the nightmares. I had the overwhelming urge to say fuck it and run to her, hold her. But I couldn't. I couldn't care. I had to stop caring. Those were the nights I left and found something to kill.

Xamien found out I was there, lingering like a black shadow on the outskirts of his property. He only contacted me once telepathically, asking me what the hell I was doing. I left that day and didn't come back for a month. And when I did it was after Adrian's call about the job. The one I refused at first and hung up on him.

Then the ice cold feeling intensified as I thought about what he was asking and I knew it had to be me. My usual job was killing and I did it well. Protecting a girl I obsessed about . . . one I'd have to kill if there was a chance the Scar could take her . . . but I'd rather it be me. There was no way in hell I was letting anyone else near her.

If shit went bad, then she'd die and so would my unhealthy obsession with it. Kind of a win-win.

But the longer I watched her the more I wanted to see what was beneath the hard outer shell she hid behind. I wanted to set her free, crack the seal and hear it hiss and bubble and scream.

Everything about this was fucked. I knew it, but there was a chance I could get what I needed and walk away from this—from her.

I ran back to the shed where I left Max one minute ago, expecting to find her moaning in pain, but I should've known better—she was fuckin' gone.

"Jesus." I ran for my bike, well, limped because my fuckin' leg hurt like a son-of-a-bitch. I stopped when I saw her and nearly blew my load. She was sitting astride my bike looking for the keys. I did wonder if I'd left them in the ignition if she would've taken off without me.

She looked up and I pulled them out of my pocket and dangled them. I imagined her smiling at me—she wasn't and I realized this chick never smiled. I'd watched her sporadically for months and never heard her laugh or seen her smile. And that bothered the fuck out of me.

I noticed her blades were tucked in my leather satchel on the side of the bike and couldn't help but be a little impressed. And damn her sitting astride my bike—a fuckin' angel.

Thing was I bet she didn't have much of an angel in her anymore. According to Adrian, who was responsible for finding me most of my jobs and just as corrupt as me, maybe worse, had said Xamien found her chained in a bedroom on the floor when she was sixteen. It took a year before she spoke and told Xamien her name was Max. Whoever had taken this chick as a child had sucked out any happiness and encased her in stone. Well, I was capable of chiseling through stone. You just needed to know how to handle the fuckin' chisel.

"I'm thinking I should've ripped that towel off six months ago."

No, I knew I should've. I moved in and noticed her stiffen. "Too bad you put a bullet in my leg that is starting to fuckin' hurt like hell; otherwise, I'd go kill the rest of those fuckers then sink my cock inside you, right here on top of my bike."

I expected some kind of reaction; that was what I pushed for in her. But Max merely looked at me with those blank eyes, her hand pressed to her side. Looked like I'd have to work a little to sink between her legs. Because that was what this was. A lusty obsession with a girl I shouldn't take, but I was good at doing the wrong thing. Had done the wrong thing my entire life, now I just accepted it and didn't make excuses for who I was.

"Slide back, sunshine." I focused my hearing ability and heard men running through the kitchen toward the back door.

She didn't hesitate. I liked that. It was me who had trouble when I got on then had to tug her forward on the leather seat so her pelvis was snug against my ass. I grit my teeth as my cock strained against my pants. "Arms."

When she didn't put her arms around my waist, I was going to make her when two guys came barreling around the side of the shed. I kicked the bike into gear and skidded down the driveway.

They didn't shoot and I knew why—I wasn't the only one who wanted Max to live.

four

Max

WE RODE FOR OVER AN hour with my body pressed up against his. I managed to hold on to the metal bar on the back for about five seconds before giving in and putting my arms around him. Jasper rode his bike like it was glued to the road and when he took the first bend and our knees nearly kissed the pavement, I grabbed for him. I was pretty certain he'd done it on purpose when I heard his chuckle. Asshole.

My palms flat against his stomach, I felt the deep contours of muscles, ridged and hard. I swallowed and tried to think of something else, anything else, but nothing came to mind except the feel of him beneath my hands. His ass and my pelvis snug, the vibration of the bike under us.

I clenched my elbow hard against my side where the bullet had penetrated and grunted in pain. *Much better.* Pain I knew. It was familiar and I knew how to handle it. What I was feeling for Jasper was new and exhilarating and had no place in my life. I had to control my emotions, and Jasper made them snap and crackle.

Jasper slowed after twenty minutes and we cruised along the winding roads of Andalusia, Spain. I relaxed a little, my arms resting lightly around him as the wind brushed through my hair, the woodsy scent of the piqual olive trees and the warmth of his body close to mine.

He was so casual, easily maneuvering the bike with an air of confidence as if nothing could throw him off-balance. And I knew that was what attracted me to him—that inability to be agitated. The control. It was also what made me uneasy because my usual knack to keep others at a distance wasn't working with him. Jasper didn't treat me like I'd shatter; instead, he pushed me to the edge.

The warmth of his hand on my naked thigh made every muscle tighten and my breath hitch. A quiver travelled through me then goose bumps spread. The heat from his hand seeped into my cool skin instantly soothing.

In a slow casual glide, he slid his hand down to my knee, cupped it, his fingers squeezing then moving back up again. My heart went from one beat per second to ten while my murdered butterflies resurrected.

I was determined to ignore him and it wasn't as if I could get away either, or push him off me. I suspected he knew it, too. He had to know exactly what he was doing and I was pissed off that I was pissed off. That he could easily throw me off with a simple touch of his hand.

I clamped my teeth together and squeezed my eyes shut, hoping to ignore his soft caress. Instead, the image of him on top of me as he thrust flashed and I quickly opened my eyes again.

I couldn't take it anymore when his finger stroked the sensitive spot beneath the crook of my knee and a tidal wave of desire hit me.

My hand shot to his wrist and I latched on then pulled his hand off my leg. He didn't object, merely placed his hand back on the handlebar. I took a deep breath and my erect nipples pressed into his back. The bike jolted forward and the corners of my mouth twitched.

We rode for hours giving me plenty of time to contemplate what I was going to do. All I knew about Jasper was that he was an assassin and a friend of Xamien's. Although, I was leery of calling them friends, as according to rumors, Jasper didn't have friends.

I'd managed to stay clear of any business regarding the Scars until six months ago when I'd met Jasper. He'd been at Xamien's to help with a situation involving the Scar Delara.

It was the first time I'd met the Taldeburu, Waleron, who lived in Toronto. He sat on the council with the Wraiths and he was known to be cold, unemotional and would do anything to protect the Scars. He also had an Ink that had tried to take control of him.

That was when Waleron found out I had the ability to communicate with a Scar's Ink. What no one knew, and what was imperative to stay that way, was that I had the unheard of ability to bring a dead Ink back to life.

I'd kept it from Drake for six years. He never knew I could've healed his Ink and then his failing lungs would've repaired with his Ink's rebirth. But I knew the consequences if I'd done it.

Drake had killed my entire Talde just for my ability to heal his lungs. If he knew I could heal his Ink, an Ink the Goddess had killed because of how dangerous it became, Drake would stop at nothing to find me again and that sat in the pit of my stomach every day since. My only hope was that he was dead. That his lungs had finally given in to the blackness that suffocated them.

But Drake was one of the original Scars, older than Waleron, who was known as the most powerful Scar alive. He was determined and sought to one day either rule or destroy the Scars.

Jasper suddenly veered off the paved road into a parking lot and pulled up to the front door of a bungalow-style building then stopped, letting the engine idle for a second before he shut it down. I glanced over at the tilted half-lit flickering sign on a metal post that occasional flashed hot tub in Spanish and English. Below that, it read vacancy.

I settled my hands on his hips while I got off the bike and winced at the sharp pain in my side. I stood facing him, arms crossed over my chest. "What is going on? Who's after me?"

There was something behind his dark eyes, a merciless hardness that even when he flashed that cocky grin, it was settled there like a speck of wet sand in the desert. "Don't know who, but Xamien will be calling tomorrow and you can ask him, although I doubt he knows either. Right now, I'm tired as hell and need a bullet out of my thigh."

"Why should I stay with you?" Although, at the moment I had no place to go, no money and I certainly couldn't go back to Xamien's.

He shrugged. "Because you want to live a few more days." He reached in his pocket and pulled out a pile of bills. "Go, get us a room. They're more likely to ignore the blood on you rather than me. We don't need added attention."

"Two rooms you mean."

Jasper frowned then got off the bike, grabbed my wrist, shoved the money into my palm and closed my fingers around it. "No, babe, one. You get two, you're wasting my money 'cause you're in my room tonight."

I wanted to throw the money back in his face; instead, I crumpled it in my fist and glared back at him.

"You waiting for a kiss or a smack on the ass? Both are up for grabs, sunshine."

I didn't think I was capable of a girl growl, but I made some kind of noise that came from the back of my throat and Jasper heard it because he laughed then leaned back, resting on his bike, ankles crossed.

Then I spun around and walked into the office where I procured two rooms. When I came back, I tossed him a key with the little yellow tag that displayed the room number then reached into his bag, grabbed my blades and proceeded to my room which was right next door to his. I was hoping that would make him more willing to bend on the issue because I wasn't sharing a room with him. Shit, he was a Sounder and could hear my heartbeat from next door if he wanted to.

I just put the key in the lock when I was suddenly airlifted and thrown over a shoulder—Jasper's shoulder. And damn if it didn't bring tears to my eyes as I landed hard and it felt as if someone punched me in my wounded side.

"Told you how it was going to be. Should've listened." He carried me next door, stuck the key in the lock and then opened it. He slammed it shut with the heel of his foot, walked into the room and tossed me on the bed.

The mattress squeaked as I bounced on it a couple times when I landed. I quickly turned over and crawled to the opposite side of the bed, and scrambled to my feet.

"Not chasing you, Max." It was the first time he'd used my name and I hesitated. "Sit your ass down." His words were like rocks banging together and his stance was wide, ready to make a grab for me if I even tried for the door. "I'm going to clean that wound on your side then you're going to heal my leg that you so kindly put a bullet in. After that, we're both getting some shut eye." He crossed his arms over his naked chest. "In this room. Together."

I looked down at the orange and brown bedspread, hiding my anger behind my curtain of hair. He was really an asshole and normally I could escape from people, but I was being forced to deal with Jasper and any anger I'd kept locked away was bending the mental shield around me, ready to release all the rage I'd kept locked up tight since Drake.

He walked toward me, stopping inches away. Then to my surprise, he reached over and squeezed my waist. It was a gentle and reassuring gesture and so unlike Jasper. Our eyes stayed locked on one another for a few moments, before he turned and disappeared into the bathroom.

I considered running next door. I still had the key curled in my hand, but like I'd learned a long time ago, sometimes it was easier not to fight. I had scars to prove it.

When he came out again, he had a wet cloth in his hand. He strode over to a leather satchel by the door, unzipped it and sifted through until he pulled out a plastic bottle. He strode toward me, chest still naked, the vivid lines of his muscles speckled in dried blood. God, he didn't have a single scar on his lightly tanned skin—perfect. The complete opposite of me.

I stiffened, sitting up straighter as I placed my hands on my scarred thighs. Then I lifted my chin and stared straight ahead.

It didn't matter.

Nothing mattered.

I don't care.

He crouched in front of me and I heard the rustle of his pants and his mild grunt. Shit, now I felt guilty shooting him and I never experienced that emotion. I had no reason to—until now.

Jesus, he was screwing me up.

The crackle of a seal breaking sounded and I looked at the bottle in his hand—whiskey. This was going to hurt like hell and maybe that was exactly what I needed to get my shit together.

He shrugged. "It'll have to do until we get to my . . . friend's place tomorrow." I didn't like the sound of that. And he hesitated at the word friend and I was guessing it was because Jasper didn't have friends; he had business acquaintances.

"A Scar?" I hoped not. I'd been able to keep my abilities hidden for years, but I was careful with who I encountered. Meeting Waleron a number of months ago had been a mistake and then Jasper had sensed I was a Healer. All it took was for one Scar to get into my head and find out I could give life to Inks and then word would spread and I'd be a liability.

"No. She's human." He reached for the hem of my shirt—his shirt—and I scooted back. His hand gripped my hip and held me steady. "Yeah, I want to fuck you, but right now, it isn't about that. So you need to suck it up and let me do this."

"I can do it myself," I shot back and grabbed for the bottle.

"No you can't." He snorted. "Ironic the Goddess gave the ability for Healers to heal everyone except for themselves. A real fuck up if you ask me."

The pads of his fingers heated my skin through the material and there was nothing sexual about it, yet it was everything sexual. My pulse pounded in my throat and tingles like shooting stars burst through me everywhere. It was unrestrained and I hated it. I shoved his hand off me then abruptly pulled up the shirt.

It was supposed to be one fluid motion. It turned into several when I had to lift my butt to get the shirt out from under me; then it stuck to the wound because of the dried blood and when it finally peeled away, it went too high revealing my abdomen and ribcage.

My eyes locked on his, but he didn't say anything, merely kept his steady gaze on me. It was almost better when he did say something because then at least I knew what he was thinking.

He lifted the whiskey bottle and the pungent smell drifted into the air and burned the small hairs in my nostrils. "You want to lie down for this?"

I shook my head.

He nodded then titled his hand and I watched the amber liquid spill from the bottle. The second it hit my flesh, the fiery pain sliced through my side. I squeezed my eyes shut, tensing, but remained still.

After a few seconds, I opened my eyes as the pain dissipated . . . until he started wiping the dried blood away from the torn flesh. He was gentle, the corner of the warm wet cloth rubbing lightly over my skin.

He set the bottle on the floor and then put his hand back on my hip, his fingers steady and splayed over my skin. I was surprised he never once looked anywhere but at my side and what he was doing, his brows drawn together in a deep furrow of concentration.

I was contemplating thanking him when he said, "Might have avoided this if you hadn't shot me and we got out of there sooner. Try and remember you're a Healer and act like one."

Asshole full on.

Jasper leaned back on his heels, pulled out a knife from his boot then reached for me. I didn't move. I was accustomed to knives on my flesh and if he had to cut away or debride flesh, then it had to be done. My fingers curled into the bedspread and I couldn't stop the sharp inhale as he came closer with the knife.

Instead, he pierced it through the cloth and ripped it in half then poured whiskey on it. Without warning, he dug the piece of soaked cloth into my wound.

"Jesus." My vision blurred and I would've been halfway across the bed if he hadn't anticipated that reaction and clamped down hard on my thigh.

"You don't like it, don't get shot next time."

I bit my lower lip hard to keep myself from saying something back. *Don't let him make you react.*

By the time Jasper finished cleaning the wound, it was pretty numb. He poured more whiskey on it then got up and went to his bag.

I think the only way I got through it was repeating over and over in my head what an insensitive bastard he was. But he was right. I should've been more careful and I wasn't sure what pissed me off more, that I hadn't been or Jasper's comment. I decided to focus on Jasper's comment because he was being a dick and I was betting most chicks fell at his feet and spread their legs as soon as he smiled at them.

"Go shower and then I'll bandage it."

I was going to tell him I'd heal his leg first so I could get it over with and then decided he could suffer a little longer. I scooted off the bed, went into the bathroom and shut the door. I searched for the lock— no lock.

I paused for a second remembering when Jasper walked in on me before. The way his eyes roamed over me as if I was . . . like he wasn't repulsed by my scars.

I sharply spun away from the door, avoiding the mirror as I took off my clothes, and then turned on the taps. The bottom of the tub looked like it had a ring of dirty soap scum around it, but I hadn't much of a choice. I stepped under the spray, tensing a few seconds as the water hit my wound and then grabbed the motel's cheap packaged soap off the ledge. I ripped off the paper and quickly scrubbed myself. My hair needed washing to get rid of all the dust from the road, but the motel had no shampoo or conditioner and I was forced to use the soap.

I finished up and had one leg out of the tub when the door opened. I grabbed the edges of the shower curtain and pulled it around me.

"Clothes," he said and placed a pile down on the counter. He smirked at me. "Might get in the habit of locking the door."

"There is no bloody lock," I shouted. I froze, realizing I'd shouted. God, I hadn't shouted since . . . since Drake cut it out of me. I wasn't allowed to shout or scream or fight.

He lifted his hand and wiggled the gold sliding latch at the top of the door. Shit. Who puts a lock there? "If you want me to see you naked, all you have to do is ask, sunshine. I'm a pretty straight forward guy. Don't need the games."

Games? He thought I was playing games? I wish like hell I could easily lower my head and say 'yes, sir'—but I couldn't. Jasper riled me way past that ability to keep my mouth shut. "Get out!"

He chuckled and nodded to the shower curtain. "Orange doesn't really suit you. I'd stick with reds. You look fuckin' beautiful in red." What? He'd never seen me in red. "I'm thinking spiky black heels too. Maybe we could pick some up and—"

I picked up the bar of soap, but before I could throw it at him, he was gone. I was so angry with myself for rising to his words. He was enjoying himself watching me flounder and I had to get my shit back in control then call Xamien and find out what was going on. Then I had to get as far away from Jasper as I could.

I left the water on straight hot as I dried off, and by then, the entire bathroom was in a dense fog of heat. I pulled on the over-sized V-neck shirt he left me—his. I lifted the boxer shorts into the air—his. I felt the small pull upward at the corner of my mouth as I stared at them. He expected me to wear his boxers? I glanced at my shorts covered in my blood and then back at the boxers.

The thought of wearing his boxer shorts . . . How they had been next to his thighs, had his cock brush against the material . . .

Stop.

I yanked them on, rolled them at the top so they would stay on my hips and then went and turned off the hot water which wasn't hot anymore. I came out of the bathroom and stopped. Jasper was leaning back against the headboard, arms crossed behind his head while he watched some Spanish news channel on the television. He looked like a king, confident, casual and completely ignored me.

I made it to the side of the bed and sat before he said anything.

"Long shower."

I shrugged. No doubt he knew exactly what I'd done.

"Don't worry. I thrive off cold showers. And if I'm real cold, I'll have you to warm me up." Before I could come back at him with anything, he said, "You going to put those healing hands on me now? Been sitting here thinking about them touching me for the last hour you've been using up my hot water."

"It wasn't an hour." My lips pursed together. I was not going to play into his hands. We needed some ground rules before I touched him. "No kissing me again—ever."

He lowered his arms from behind his head. "Hey, I only take what wants to be given, sunshine. And I'm only referring to women. Anything else . . . I pretty much just take."

Yeah, I was betting he took anything he wanted and didn't think twice about it. "Well, I didn't ask to be kissed."

His brows rose. "Might want to rethink that answer because you're lying to yourself and to me."

I ignored him. "And you're sleeping on the floor."

He didn't say anything, merely looked at me and damn it, I couldn't tell what he was going to do. "You going to heal me or admire me?"

Clamp it down, Max. I took a deep breath, climbed up on the bed and crawled over to his wounded thigh. My eyes hit the slight swell in his pants between his legs.

He shrugged. "Out of my control, angel. Hot chick crawling on her hands and knees toward my lower region . . . it's any man's fuckin' fantasy. Even better is one that you're wearing my briefs."

I gasped, sitting up straight, mouth falling open. Then I grumbled, "Boxers."

He laughed, a sound which made my insides heat up and send that rabble of butterflies in my belly into a frenzy. Graveled and deep, like it came from deep within him, but never did the lighthearted sound match that speck of hardness in his eyes.

What sucked was I liked the sound of his laugh—a lot. Good thing he rarely laughed. His chuckle and grin I could handle, the laugh, not so much.

So I did what would end his laugh and pressed my hands hard on his wound. He stopped abruptly and scowled, muscles flexed. I glimpsed at his tats on his arms that were bulging with tension.

From what I'd heard about other Healers, they couldn't touch any-one with a wound without their hands reacting. But I was different, I had to concentrate and focus on the healing and only then would it begin to take place. Sometimes, it felt as if I could do the opposite, take it away. That I had to tell my ability which way to go, heal or destroy.

Shivers racked through me as my hands burned, and I closed my eyes. The images came with the ability as did feeling the same pain as the person you were healing. I grit my teeth as the impact of the bul-let slammed into my own leg. I let the pain in, sweep across me then pushed the feeling away. I knew how to block out pain, but I also knew how to embrace it.

My healing took hold as the burning increased in my hands and the images moved faster through my mind like a movie on fast forward. I thought of all the times I'd healed Drake, week after week for six years, healing his lungs so he could breathe. I knew it was because his Ink was dead. My mother had told me that before she died. The Goddess had killed his Ink to weaken Drake, and without my healing, he may not have died, but he'd be fragile.

He used to get so angry when the wheezing started only a week after I'd healed him, then the pain in his chest. The punishments were to make me try harder, to force me to heal his lungs completely, but I couldn't. I couldn't without healing his Ink at the same time and I'd never do that. He'd killed everyone I ever loved. And no matter what he did to me, I'd never fail my mother or the Talde. I'd never heal his Ink.

"Max?"

I jerked back. The heat in my hands and the images fading instant-ly. He reached for me and I shuffled back, quickly pulling my gaze from his. I picked up the bullet I'd extracted during the healing and Jasper plucked it from my grasp and shoved it in his pants' side pocket.

"Why would you want that?"

Jasper swung his legs over the side of the bed. "Not often you get to keep the bullet you were shot with by a woman you're going to fuck."

I huffed. Then found myself staring, eyes wide and heart slamming against my ribs as Jasper undid the buttons on his pants and I caught a glimpse of the scattering of hairs that led downward like a pointing arrow. His pants dropped to the floor and he kicked them off his bare feet.

"Jasper, what . . ."

"I'm having a shower and I expect you to be here when I get out. You're not . . . we have a problem and you won't like how I solve it."

I couldn't stop staring. The contours of his thighs were like mountains with crevices in a valley, long, hard and firm. I had the urge to run my fingertips over them and . . ."Oh, God."

Jasper stopped just outside the bathroom door and half-turned. "What's wrong?" He was alert in an instant, eyes focused, body tense. I knew he had to be using his Sounding ability to search the area around the motel for any danger.

The funny thing was *he* was the danger.

"Nothing," I squeaked and lowered my head. I peeked up at him just as his fingers went to the edge of his boxer briefs.

I swallowed. Froze. Then stared from under my long lashes as he bent over and yanked them off in one swoop.

Shit.

I caught a glimpse of his tight ass before he disappeared from view. Not because he closed the door, no, he left it wide open, but because he stepped behind the gaudy shower curtain.

I fell back onto the bed, covering my face with my hands. I was turned on. Hot, wet and throbbing. I was turned on by a guy's legs and ass. But Jasper didn't have just any ass; it was rock hard and round and curved perfectly into his sculpted thighs. This was mortifying. I was wearing his boxers, wet and feeling emotions I never knew I had. And the worst part was he knew it.

I'd never been concerned what others thought about my scars, but suddenly I was. Now it mattered. Now I wanted to keep myself covered from him and I hated feeling insecure about myself, but Jasper looking at my marred skin . . . it raised my awareness of what I looked like.

I heard the crinkle of paper and suspected he'd found the cheap soaps I'd thrown in the trash along with the one I used.

"Fuck, that's cold," Jasper shouted.

I bit my lower lip and smiled. I didn't realize how good it felt to smile, how much I missed it until I did it. It was like I was lighter, warmer and the dredge of blackness faded for a single second.

Then I locked it away again. Because with one emotion came others. Others that would break me wide open.

I got up, yanked the comforter off the bed then threw a pillow on the floor beside it. I tugged back the white sheets, crawled underneath and curled on my side, my hands beneath the pillow. The sound of the shower mixed with the steady drone of a newscaster's voice on the television lulled me to sleep within seconds.

five

Jasper

I TOWELED OFF MY HAIR while standing naked beside the bed watching Max, curled up fast asleep. A strand of hair fell across her nose and when she exhaled, the fine hairs lifted then fell back. I reached forward to push them aside then stopped myself.

What the fuck was I doing? Jesus. I had no business touching her like that. No business liking this chick and yet . . . I did. At first, I thought it was lust and it was; I wanted to fuck her, still did, but after watching her . . . seeing how she held back the smile as she ran her fingertips through the wildflowers every morning. How she blew on her coffee every single time before that first sip. The way her brows drew together when she was practicing with her blades. It was the only time I saw that hidden determination in her. She hid it from Xamien with the way she bowed her head and quietly spoke to him, but there was always tension in her shoulders. And once when he walked away from her, I saw the flicker of sadness in her eyes as she stared after him. And that I didn't like. I knew there was nothing going on between them, but I still didn't like the fact she felt something for the powerful and noble-as-hell Taldeburu.

What I loved was fucking with her, seeing her hackles rise and the heat in her cheeks. It was the only way I could get a reaction from her and I craved it. Needed it. And fuck if I didn't want to kiss every inch of her until she purred in my arms.

But I don't soothe.

I fuck.

Fucking wasn't emotional. It was a basic need. But for some screwed-up reason, the idea of fucking her was all-consuming.

I stepped back from the bed and my foot landed on the comforter. My eyes hit the pillow next to it. Like hell I was sleeping on the fuckin' floor. This chick really had a few lessons to learn in how this all was going down.

But Max had boundary issues. I didn't do well with that. I liked to peel the layers back, make them bleed then if I needed to I could use what I had to against them to get what I wanted.

I was good at breaking boundaries, rules and whatever else. Living my way of life there was no time for personal bullshit. Mine was locked down so tight, not even a Scar Reflector could reach my secrets.

The way Max subtly flinched when I touched her—boundary issue.

Wanting her own room—boundary issue.

Comforter and pillow on the floor—boundary issue.

Fuck that.

I broke that boundary with the kiss. She'd been stiff under my lips at first and I guessed she'd had fuck-all experience or if she did, it was with some piss poor kisser who couldn't take what he wanted. I made no mistake about showing a woman what it was like to be taken. Shit, they wanted that and if they didn't, then they weren't a chick I cared to sink my cock into.

I'd purposely undressed before going into the bathroom. If she'd seen my smirk or my hard-on from thinking about her watching me—because I sure as hell knew she was from the sound of her racing heartbeat—she'd have run for the door. I almost wished she had because then I'd have had to catch her. My cock stirred at the thought of holding her struggling body up against me.

I had no doubt she'd fight me the first time. It would be a battle of wills, but she'd be wet as hell and throbbing for me. I'd feel the leashed desire pulsing through her veins, needing to be set free. And I was going to be the one to unsnap it while I drove inside her.

I ran my hand through my damp hair, and then kicked the pillow. Fuck. I needed to get laid. I hadn't been with a chick for months.

Months. Yeah, fuckin' six months.

I was always clear to any chick I sunk my cock into—take and leave. My motto. I'd give her the best sex she'd ever had then leave. I didn't see it as selfish, the opposite in fact. I gave her the best pleasure she'd ever had then left before she ever got to know me—I was doing her a favor by leaving. Sometimes, I came back for seconds, months later, but staying too long in one woman's bed led to attachments. Attachments led to caring and caring had no business in my life. It would get me killed and anyone else close to me.

I'd chosen this life and nothing could get in the way. Not even my little obsession. I'd have to end it soon and the only way was to sink between her thighs. Once I had her, all this bullshit I was feeling would go away. It was the chase. It was not being able to have something and wanting it more.

I snagged the pillow off the floor and tossed it on the bed, and then went and pulled the curtains closed. I strode back to the bed and glanced at Max again—A fuckin' angel with an attitude.

An angel stuck in Hell. Sunshine blocked by dense clouds. Yeah, those marks on her body had one hell of a story. Normally, I'd shrug it off, not my business, but I wanted to make it my business. I wanted to kill the bastard who did that to her. No, I wanted to do more than kill him. I wanted to crucify him, make him suffer, make him beg for mercy, for his life while I laughed. Only then would I kill him.

Torture. *Fuck.* I didn't do torture, but suddenly I wanted to see another person suffer before they died.

I slipped under the sheets and lay on my back, elbows bent and hands beneath my head. I tried to block out the sounds of her heartbeat, her breathing, but I'd listened to them from a distance for months and now they were so close, it was as if they were inside me.

And if I had to kill her, I couldn't deny the fact that the pieces of her that had settled deep inside me would detonate.

six

Max

I ROLLED OVER, HUGGING THE pillow in a rare moment of bliss after having slept through the night without any nightmares. I sighed, feeling refreshed as I stretched my legs out and hit warm, hard—

My eyes flew open and I came face to face with a naked smooth torso with black ink lines running the length of his side. The sheet covered his legs then stopped in a crumpled chaos at his hips. My gaze trailed down the path of hairs to . . . I bolted up right, yanking the sheet with me.

"Morning, sunshine." He was sitting up in bed leaning against the headboard, eyes glued to his phone as his fingers tapped on the screen.

"You're in bed." Jasper had ignored the hint of blanket and pillow on the floor and slept in bed with me. I should've known he would. His leg rubbed against mine and abruptly, I pulled mine away.

"You're certainly observant first thing in the morning."

"And your asshole button doesn't have an off switch."

He chuckled. "About time you woke-up. Been awake for hours listening to you snore like an elephant with its trunk kinked."

I gasped. "Elephant . . . kinked . . . you're such an asshole."

"Hmm, you also lack variety in your vocabulary." His mouth

twitched and I wanted to smack him. I didn't because I had no intention of putting my hands anywhere near him. He was naked or partially naked. I was in his t-shirt and boxers and I couldn't decipher if the fast pumping rush through my veins was from anger or from the thought of him being naked in bed with me.

I'd coasted through the last four years without having to say much and suddenly in the last twenty-four hours, I was talking back, arguing and even smiling. "What are you doing?"

"Playing angry birds. Addicting. Red bird is the shit—"

I exploded. Not like me. So not like me, but I was furious. I hadn't felt emotions like this since . . . my first few months in captivity. "What the hell are you doing in bed with me?"

He continued to play on his phone without even reacting to my outburst. His brows lowered in concentration and his lips pressed together as he slid his finger across the screen.

"Are you listening to me?" Jasper's nonchalance was making me react irrationally and I had a feeling that was exactly what he wanted. And this was why I preferred to be silent rather than talk because people rarely listened to anything but themselves. "God, so typical."

"Oh, I'm anything but typical. And I heard you, just chose to ignore you. My right. It's your right to get out of my bed."

"Your bed?"

Jasper's brows rose and there was no sign of his playful grin. "Yeah, sunshine, my bed. I clearly remember shoving a handful of bills in your hand to pay for this room. And I paid for the room next door, which by the way still pisses me off. I don't like to waste money."

"Well, it wouldn't have been wasted if you let me sleep there."

"It wouldn't have been wasted if you'd listened to me in the first place."

He lowered his hand from his phone then slowly stroked his abdomen, fingers moving over the blocks of muscles. I watched, breathless, unable to look away from his smooth, hard body. Then his hand slid lower, down the trail of hairs . . . the sheet lifted and his hand disappeared. I swallowed. The sheet tented . . . I wasn't sure if it was his hand or . . . I jerked my eyes away, but my gaze didn't go far; instead, I was staring at his chest, admiring the hard mounds and valleys.

"Done with your perusal?"

My already heated cheeks burned. "Surprising you even know a word like that."

"Oh, baby, you'd be surprised about a lot of things I know. Care to find out?"

I scrambled out of bed taking the sheet with me. Big mistake. Well, it wouldn't have been if I hadn't looked, but I did and he only had boxer briefs on and his cock was obviously rock hard—and huge. My eyes flew to his and there was no smile, no cocky smirk . . . he was smoldering with desire.

"Oh, God." I spun, ran into the bathroom and slammed the door. I heard Jasper's deep chuckle following me.

Damn it. I felt like a nuclear weapon traveling on a road ridden with potholes. Unsteady and ready to explode at any minute. Everything he did was testing my control. Shit, he wasn't testing it; he was splitting it apart.

I put my hands on the lip of the sink, closed my eyes and tried to will the eruption of emotions away, but the image of Jasper, lying in bed half naked, casual, confident, making no apology for his erection, wouldn't vanish.

He desired me. He was turned on and we hadn't even touched. It made me feel . . . wanted. Desired. God, why did I want him to want me? He was arrogant. Selfish. An assassin who was hired to protect me from someone . . . a someone who had no reason to want a girl who lived for four years tucked away in Spain.

"Max. Let's move." Jasper knocked on the door. It was a no nonsense voice, stern as if telling his soldiers to move out.

I had to stop this . . . this . . . well, whatever it was. People used people to get what they wanted in life. I'd learned that really young and Jasper was certainly at the top of the list of using others, except he didn't try to hide it. I knew he was being paid to protect me. I also knew he was playing with me and enjoying it.

I turned on the taps and washed my face with cold water, the burning in my cheeks slowly dissipating. It took a good five minutes before I pulled my shit together.

When I opened the door, Jasper was dressed and on his phone, standing with his back to me. Whoever was on the other end must have been doing all the talking because Jasper said a few short curt words then hung up. Without looking at me, he opened the door and left.

When I heard the bike start up, I noticed his bag and my blades were gone. I went outside and came up beside him. "I need clothes. I can't wear this." I gestured to the boxers and t-shirt.

"You look fine to me." Jasper was sitting astride his bike, his hands resting on his thighs looking completely in control. Shit, he was in control.

I cocked my hip and put my hand on it and then I saw the slight twitch at the corners of his mouth. He was playing with me again.

"I want clothes and a phone call before I go anywhere with you."

Jasper shut down the engine, pulled his cell out of his front shirt pocket and handed it to me. It was so casual, as if he'd expected me to ask. "Have at it, sunshine. And tell him his house is a write off."

"How'd you—"

Jasper quirked a brow. "You have no friends. No boyfriends. You never travel, and spend your days looking after Xamien's garden and practicing with those blades of yours. The garden thing is boring as hell, but guess it's a Healer thing . . . making things grow and shit."

"You know a lot about me having just met me."

He clenched his jaw. "My job to know." He chin-lifted to the phone. "Call him if it makes you feel better. Number three."

I pressed number three and Xamien picked up on the second ring. "Jasper."

"No, sir, it's Max."

"Max. How are you? Are you guys somewhere safe?"

I glanced at Jasper and he leaned his elbow up against the handle bar. I noticed his eyes remained focused and intense, even when he was being annoying and flirting with me.

"Your house . . . it's ruined, sir. Jasper says the men who did it are after me and he's been hired to protect me. Is that true?" Then I added, because Jasper was pissing me off by looking so cocky and full of himself, "Should I kill him?"

Jasper burst out laughing and the sound made me smile, but I turned slightly so he couldn't see it.

Xamien chuckled and I heard him murmur something to someone in the background. "Do what he says and he'll keep you safe. I trust him."

"Xamien, what's going on? Why would anyone want me?" I held my breath as there was silence at the other end of the line.

A cold wave of dread came over me and my breath locked tight in my chest. "Max . . . I know you're a Healer." I closed my eyes, hand tightening on the phone. "Healers are always in danger and I think that's why you've kept it hidden."

I looked at Jasper. He smirked. "Did Jasper tell you?"

"No," Xamien replied. I don't know why I cared, but I was relieved Jasper hadn't lied to me. That he'd kept my secret. "I've known for years, but I'd never force you to use your ability if you chose not to, Max. I've never told anyone either. I'll meet with you and Jasper tomorrow. By then, I may know more. For now, do as Jasper says. He's the best at . . . what he does. Keep close to him." He paused, then, "And Max . . . be careful. Let me talk to him."

I said goodbye then held the phone out to Jasper.

"Stay with the bike, babe." He lifted his leg over the seat then walked away, phone to his ear. I couldn't hear what was said, but his grin had vanished and his spine stiffened, fingers gripping the phone a little tighter.

He strode back to me and put his phone back in his pocket. "Satisfied?"

"Not really." But I could wait until I saw Xamien tomorrow.

"Don't worry, Xamien's warning to keep my hands off won't deter me."

I ignored his attempt to get me riled. "Do you have clothes for me or are you going to continue to be a dick?"

He grinned. "Nice to see we've moved up from asshole."

I frowned. "Who says dick is any better than asshole?"

He raised his brows and looked down at the bulge between his legs. I rolled my eyes and he laughed, a sound which made my insides light up like I swallowed a flare. He nodded to the leather saddlebag. "Jeans and a shirt in the bag. And a sweet-ass pair of red panties." My mouth dropped open. "You have one hell of a panty drawer."

What? "What?" I dove for the bag and sifted through his clothes and there at the bottom, I caught the flash of red. I yanked my panties out then my jeans and t-shirt. By the time I stood up straight, my clothes in my hand, I was seething. "You had clothes for me?"

"Guess you're not going to thank me for taking the time to grab a couple things for you."

"When?"

"When what?"

I stomped my foot and that pissed me off because I didn't stomp or get angry or become flustered and I was all of the above. "You know damn well what I'm asking."

Jasper snagged me around the waist and brought me into him. I landed hard against his thigh, my hands going to his chest with my clothes the only thing separating us. "Babe, you and me . . . it wasn't a spur of the moment thing. Grabbed a few of your things when you were out in the garden a few days ago just in case shit went bad. Then shit went bad and I had to get you out of there." He tugged me closer and his knee went between my legs. My breath locked in my throat. "Now, angel, you want to get changed or stand here talking about how I got your clothes because I need coffee."

The fastest way to get him to release me was to agree with whatever he said. "Yes."

His fingers curled into my waist. "Yes what, sunshine?"

I bit my lip to keep from smiling as I said, "Yes, sir."

His brows lowered and his lips pursed together, just like I knew would happen. Then he shook his head and chuckled; the vibration sent my insides haywire. "Fuck, you're cute when you try to piss me off." He slapped my ass and I jerked away, staggering back a couple steps then darting for the motel room. I expected his laughter to follow, but it didn't.

When I came back outside dressed in my clothes, I didn't even look at him as I threw my leg over the back of the bike. This time, I wasn't going to hold onto him no matter how fast he went or how sharp he took the corners. I'd rather become road kill. I grabbed the sissy bar behind me and Jasper didn't say anything as he took off.

Thirty minutes later, we pulled into a cute roadside restaurant, venta, with large bay windows and orange stucco walls. It was called Medina's and it was packed.

We found a booth and I noticed Jasper scan the place as if he was expecting one of the customers to pull out a gun and start shooting. Jasper ordered two black coffees, churros, sweet rolls and rye toast with butter. I was more of a coffee and toast breakfast person, but suddenly, I was starving with the smell of sweet pastries wafting around me.

The waitress brought over the carafe and poured us each coffee. I noticed she poured Jasper's slower while her eyes kept flickering up from beneath her mascara-caked lashes to look at him. The girl was cute, with a short brunette bob and bright blue eyes. She also looked young, not that it would matter to Jasper.

I grasped my coffee and curled my hands around the mug. "Who is paying you to protect me?"

Jasper ignored the girl who was desperately trying to get his attention by leaning over the table and placing napkins near the opposite end of the table. I rolled my eyes and blurted. "Thanks. We're good now." The waitress straightened abruptly, looked at me briefly and walked away.

"Adrian."

"Is he a Scar?"

"Yep." He lifted his coffee and I watched his lips curl around the edge of the mug then his Adam's apple move up and down as he swallowed.

"Why does he care if I live?"

He hesitated then said, "He doesn't exactly."

"What does that mean? Why would he hire you to protect me then? And I don't understand why Xamien wouldn't."

Jasper set his coffee down, stretched his legs out to the side and crossed his ankles. "A lot of questions for a chick who doesn't like to talk."

I hated talking. Worse was talking and asking questions to a guy who was being cagey. It was like prying open the mouth of an alligator. Then sticking your head inside and waiting for it to snap closed on the answer you didn't want to hear. "Why are you being evasive?"

"Not my job to give you answers, babe."

Fine, he didn't want to give answers then I was leaving. Well, not really as I had nowhere to go and no vehicle, but I wanted answers and Jasper had them—or at least a few. I was halfway to my feet, when Jasper's hand shot out and grabbed my arm.

"Sit. Now."

I didn't.

His grip tightened. "Not playing here. We cause a scene—and babe, I will cause a fuckin' scene if that's what it takes to stop you from walking out—then whoever is after you will have a lead on which way we're traveling." He nodded to the patrons. "You think these people won't talk about the guy and the girl who caused a disturbance at Medina's?"

The clatter of plates plopped down on the table. "Need anything else, sexy?" The waitress asked, ignoring me standing there.

Jasper was still staring at me waiting for my response and didn't acknowledge the waitress. "You going to sit?"

"You going to give me something?"

His jaw clenched and then he let me go, leaned back and half-grinned. "Sure. I'll give you something."

I glared. "Jasper."

"Fine. Sit down."

The waitress looked between us. "Is there a problem?"

I sat and quirked a half-smile and so did he. He reached for a napkin. "We're good, thanks," he said to the waitress without looking at her and she walked away. "Eat up, sunshine, and I'll tell you what I know."

I gestured to the all the food he ordered. "I'll become a hippo if I eat all that." I wasn't afraid to eat, but the amount of sugar on the plates in front of me was like slapping a tub of lard onto my butt.

"Angels can't be hippos. Won't happen."

I couldn't keep back the twitch at the corners of my mouth. "Why not?"

"'Cause a hippo is a mean fucker. Angels aren't. And I've decided you're an angel. With issues of course. You know the ones, stuck on earth in limbo because they shot some guy in the thigh."

This time I couldn't control the smile as I shook my head. "That's ridiculous."

He chuckled and a rare bubble of laughter rose in my chest. He chin-lifted to the plate. "Eat. Don't know when we'll be stopping again." He took a bite of a sweet roll and powdery sugar sprinkled onto his plate.

I wrapped my hands around my coffee mug and lifted it before blowing a stream of air on it then took a sip. When I went to put it back down, Jasper's eyes were on me. He quickly looked away and it was the first time I thought he looked uncomfortable. It was surprising and even more surprising that I liked his eyes on me. I liked him watching me as if . . . as if I was more than a job. More than a woman he wanted to fuck.

After a few minutes, he started talking, keeping his voice low, although there was no one at the booth next to us now. "Adrian runs a . . . quiet organization."

"Secret?"

He nodded. "It's for jobs that are . . . different."

"So, he breaks the Scars' laws?"

Jasper bit into a piece of toast then tossed it down on the plate and leaned back against the green plastic backrest. "More like looks after situations he doesn't feel should be brought to the Deaconry. That should be dealt with internally."

I'd been taught by my Talde about our history and knew how we lived by an oath to the Goddess who created us to uphold the laws. By the sounds of it, this Adrian guy and his organization was finding a way around them. "But how did he know someone was after me? And if you and Xamien didn't tell anyone I'm a Healer, then how does anyone else know?"

"Don't know that. Adrian has connections, lots of them, and he knows shit is going down before anyone else. My guess . . . that is how he heard that someone was looking for you."

"And you don't know who or why?"

"No, I don't know who. All I was told was he was a Scar and can Trace."

A wave of fear went over me as I thought of Drake. No. It couldn't be. How could he find me? Why now? It couldn't be him. His lungs required healing and he wouldn't have survived all these years, and if he did, he'd be weak and wouldn't be able to Trace. He needed healing in order to use that ability.

He met my eyes, unwavering, dark and swirling. He took a sip of his coffee as the waitress came over, cleared away our plates and placed a bill on the table. The girl hesitated at the table, and Jasper for the first time looked at her and then grinned. The girl blushed and I scrunched up my nose with disgust. Jasper saw it and it was that deep graveled laugh that had my stomach flip-flopping.

I waited until she moved way before I asked, "Does Xamien know about Adrian?"

"Nope."

"Waleron?" His mother was one of the original Scars from Zugar-ramurdi and from the one time I met him . . . Waleron was powerful.

"Waleron knows pretty much everything."

"So, Adrian must have a lot of money." Because I was betting Jasper didn't come cheap.

"Adrian keeps his business, his business, and I've never really given a shit why or how."

"And you take jobs from this guy?" I couldn't understand why Jasper would do this. Why he'd take jobs from a man he didn't really know anything about.

"Yeah, babe. I do. That's who I am." His voice hardened and he abruptly took out his wallet and threw down some money. He was silent and his brows lowered with a slight twitch in his jaw. "And my life and what I do is none of your business."

I shoved my mug aside and asked the question I was afraid to hear the answer to, but had to know how far Jasper would go. "Would you take money from whoever offered you the most?"

He stiffened and his eyes narrowed and darkened. "Probably."

"So if this guy who is after me offered you a lot of money to give me to him, would you?"

"Jesus, Max." He got up so brusquely, my mug toppled over as the table moved and the remnants of coffee spilled onto the table. Then he spat, "Yeah, I would. Is that what you want to hear? That what you've heard about me? Don't worry, sunshine, he could never match what Adrian is giving me."

I should've expected that answer. I did expect that answer, but for some reason, I'd expected more from Jasper. I thought when he'd touched my arm, softened his voice, and the grey in his eyes warmed, that there was good in Jasper.

Apparently, I was wrong.

"Let's go." He snagged my hand and before I could take my napkin off my lap, he had me up and walking out of the restaurant.

seven

Max

WE RODE UNTIL DUSK, ONLY stopping twice for washroom breaks and a snack. I never said anything and neither did he. I kept my hands off him while we rode and he kept his speed reasonable.

He turned down a long, narrow driveway and then cut the engine in front of a cute Spanish-style house with a wraparound porch. I slid off and briefly looked around, noticing the beautiful red carnations and bluebells at the side of the house.

My pulse slowly rose as I admired them. Wildflowers had a fragile beauty about them with incredible resilience to withstand the test of nature. Their stems swaying and bending to the harsh winds and rain, yet if they were strong enough, they'd stand tall again when the sun's rays shone down on them.

And yet . . .

When people easily snipped their stems, each day the flower's life slowly faded.

That was what had been done to me when Drake took me. Cut from my stem—my home. Taken from my element, and each day I dried up until I had nothing left.

A stem of who I'd once been. Who I was supposed to grow into.

Xamien may have saved the shell of me, but I'd never be the same. And now Jasper . . . he was the violent storm, trying to unearth me and I was holding on with both hands and fighting back. I couldn't let go. I had to stay hidden for my own survival as well as for the safety of others. Already I'd lost my mother and Talde because of who I was.

My breath hitched as his hands settled on my hips, his chest up against my back.

My pulse spiked.

I clamped my teeth. Pursed my lips. I went to elbow him in the gut when his hands tightened and his low voice drizzled into my ear like a distant muffled roar of thunder. "Be nice, sunshine."

Oh, he had no idea how nice I'd been to him.

I heard the bang of a screen door and looked up at the house. A woman, who looked to be about thirty, stopped on the top step of the porch, and then shielded her eyes with her hand. A brilliant smile surfaced and a dignified squeal, if you could call any squeal dignified, but this woman managed it somehow.

"*Mon cheri.*" And she was French—great. "You should've told me you were coming." She walked . . . no strolled toward us, hips swaying rhythmically side-to-side like a pendulum—a voluptuous pendulum.

Jasper shifted closer and his cock pressed against my lower back— his hard cock. And instead of thinking what the fuck was he doing with a hard cock, I was thinking if his hard cock was because of me or her?

He whispered, "Play along, please. She's human and knows nothing about the Scars."

I hated playing along. That was why I kept to myself. "Why are we here?" We'd passed a nice bed and breakfast fifteen minutes ago.

"Because her coffee rocks."

I was pretty sure Jasper thought her coffee rocked because the French woman had rocked something else beforehand. And I was pretty sure if the woman served him mud after sex, he would've thought it tasted good.

He stepped away from me and for a brief second, I wanted him back. I wanted it to be me who rocked. I crossed my arms, my back stiff as I stood watching the scene unfold.

The woman with the chic shoulder-length blonde hair with a few streaks of subtle red interwoven, bit her lower lip then slowly let it slide from between her teeth. She certainly wasn't paying attention to me. I could flap my arms and dance around like a chicken and the woman wouldn't have noticed. Her eyes were on Jasper as he walked toward her.

She fell against him, long spider-like arms wrapping around his neck, painted pink nails disappearing into his hair. She dragged his head down . . . dragged was the wrong word as Jasper didn't look like he was being dragged anywhere he didn't want to go. And then she kissed him.

Jasper had both his hands on her waist and an odd pain clutched at my chest as I looked away.

But it was like trying to not look at a car wreck and I glanced up again just as they broke apart. The woman whispered to him and I heard him chuckle quietly. I think the woman might have completely ignored me if Jasper hadn't turned to me and then said something to her which made her look over at me and laugh. It was a high-pitched shrill that sounded like an off-tuned cello.

I was good at acting impassive. That was how I'd survived living with Drake for so long. So, when Jasper and lip biter turned to me, I held my chin high and met them head on.

"Max. Julianna has offered us dinner and a place to crash for the night. She also has some disinfectant to put on that *scratch* of yours."

Fucking lovely.

Julianna ran a finger down his cheek to his chin then lower to trail a path down his chest. He grabbed her hand and pulled it away, and then said something to her. She glanced over at me and glared. Jasper leaned toward her again and said something else and she smiled, her white teeth sparkling against her blood red lips.

She slid her hand down his tatted arm until her fingers linked with his and then turned, heading back inside with Jasper in tow. I crouched beside the bike and started unhooking the bag.

"I'll get it later. Get in here, Max. We need to re-bandage that wound," Jasper called over his shoulder. Then the screen door clanged shut behind them.

I ignored him and grabbed the bag, stood and threw it over my shoulder. I'd never cared about my looks before, but now I was running my fingers through my tangled hair that had become a bird's nest after riding for hours on the back of his bike. Juliana had her hair done, make-up perfectly drawn and she was wearing a cute pair of beige shorts and a button-down white blouse that was tied at the waist to show off her tanned stomach.

The screen door creaked open again. "Angel," Jasper yelled. He scowled when he glanced at the bag and waited while I walked across the yard. I avoided looking at him as I slid by him. He took the bag off my shoulder then stopped me by snagging my hand. He pulled me into him, so my back was snug against his chest. "Julianna and I . . ." He stopped and a tremor erupted in his chest as he growled.

I had no qualms about finishing what he was about to say. "Have fucked? No need to explain. I really don't care." The words were ground out even though I tried my best to hide my anger. Jesus, why was I angry? I should be happy he was getting laid. Then he'd leave me the hell alone.

He leaned in and lowered his voice, his lips next to my ear. "You sure about that?" His arm around my waist squeezed and I dug my fingernails into the back of his hand as hard as I could.

He abruptly let me go and I turned around and waited until his eyes were on mine before I mimicked Julianna's lip action, the slow glide of my tongue wetting my lower lip. "Yes, *sir.* I'm sure."

His jaw clenched and the confident smirk erased as his lips pressed together. "Careful," he murmured.

I knew I was playing with a dangerous man, but I was tired of being careful and Jasper unleashed my recklessness. I inhaled his scent and it felt as if a latch lifted and I could finally take a deep breath. I smiled and he scowled.

I heard footsteps and looked past him into Julianna's quaint house. She stood on the oak staircase watching us and with her thin red lips pursed and her nails digging into the handrail, she looked like one pissed-off cat with its hackles up.

I didn't know why I did it, maybe because Jasper was opening up a part of me I didn't understand. But something rose inside me and it was spiteful. I considered myself clever, calm, sane . . . until this moment.

I stepped closer to Jasper and put my hand on the waistband of his jeans right at the button then fiddled with it, making sure my fingers brushed against his abdomen. His body tensed and I could feel his eyes driving into me, but I kept my head lowered.

Then when I thought he might crack and grab my wrist and yank me away, I slipped my hand lower over the straining bulge. Shivers immediately flowed through my body, but it wasn't cold shivers; it was sparks of fire. The touch of him beneath my hand was magnetic and it took me a second to get control of my expression before I peered up over my shoulder at Julianna.

She had no idea what I was doing with my hand as I stroked up and down then gently squeezed. And that did it. Jasper roughly latched onto my wrist and yanked my hand away.

And this was the stupidity part. I shouldn't have looked up at him—I did. And what I saw was a blazing, heated look in his eyes that was anger and desire all rolled into one.

I wanted him to throw me against the wall and fuck me right there. I didn't even care that Julianna would see it happen. Shit, I wanted her to.

Get control of yourself, Max. I was slipping, but for once, I wanted Jasper to be the one out of control.

I forced a smile then leaned in close, went on my tiptoes and whispered in his ear, "Who am I to you?" I knew my question could be taken in two different ways and I was no seductress; actually, I'd never seduced a man in my life.

Jasper wasn't smiling. He looked pissed off. "Don't fuck with me, Max. You're nothing to me except a job."

It was cruel, harsh, but what had I expected? "Not what I was asking." His hands settled on my waist and I tried like hell to keep my breath steady. "I meant who am *I* to *you*. As in what does the sex goddess over there know?"

Jasper's brows lifted and his hands rose a little higher so that his thumbs rested just under my breasts. He leaned in and whispered, "My sister."

I huffed. "She'll never believe that."

"I don't give a fuck what she believes. She'll accept whatever I tell her." Then his hands dropped from me and he turned and walked to Julianna and looped his arm around her waist. "Anything to *eat,* Jules?"

Her laugh sent a shrill down my spine and the cold ice wall

slammed shut over my emotions. They walked toward the kitchen arm in arm; Julianna leaned over as if to nibble on his ear and I saw him pull away from her, but then she said something and he chuckled.

I hated him.

eight

Max

CRIED AND SHOOK SO badly I could barely stand. He stood behind me, making sure I didn't bolt, although I'd learned a long time ago that running and disobeying only caused more pain, more scars.

I looked over my shoulder at him. "Please. I'll do better."

He glared at me; arms crossed, a barricade against any escape. I lowered my head and then stepped into the shower, the freezing cold water instantly soaking into me.

Pain.

How could water cause so much pain? But within minutes, every inch of me was so cold it felt as if I was burning. I wrapped my arms around myself to try and control the shivering, but nothing would stop it . . . except him.

He controlled my pain and my comfort.

Finally, he nodded and I scrambled from the tub. He waited with the towel and then wrapped me in its warmth, his hands gently rubbing my arms and back.

Suddenly, it all changed and I had chains on my wrists and ankles and he was coming at me with the scorching metal rod. No. God no. My Ink. He was going to kill my Ink.

I sobbed on the floor, my foot with my Ink tucked under me. "No. No."

Now we were at my Talde's house and I was ten years old again; the day he took me. I was looking in on the scene as Drake and I stood together, his hand casually over my shoulder as we watched my house burn. I wasn't crying. I was calm and accepting.

Then he said, "Let's watch Jasper burn."

I woke screaming.

I bolted upright in bed, my skin damp, hair stuck to my cheeks like cling wrap. The sheet was wrapped around my body like a cocoon. I panicked and scrambled out of the tangled mess, falling out of bed and landing on my knees. I knew it was just a dream but still I rubbed my wrists and ankles, making certain the shackles weren't there.

The blanket of fear smothered me. I was that girl again, squeezing my eyes shut with a desperate plea that the imaginary world I was living was just that; imagined—it wasn't.

Desperate.

Alone.

Scared.

I staggered over to the corner of the darkened room, the moonlight lending its hand to show me the way and sank to the floor. Bringing my knees to my chest, I wrapped my arms around them and weaved my fingers together. I was sweating but freezing cold, unable to stop the violent trembles.

The door burst open and I jerked my head up.

Jasper stood in nothing but his jeans which had obviously been hastily thrown on because they were undone and revealed the trail of sparse hair. His dagger was in his right hand, stance wide and ready as he scanned the room. Every muscle was flexed, eyes black and narrowed with brows drawn over them. There wasn't an inch of him that didn't look tense and ready to slice apart any that got in his path.

This was the Scar assassin. The man who had every right to be cocky as hell. A beast. Threatening and virile. A predator.

And yet, it was comforting. I took a shaky breath as he saw me sitting on the floor in the corner of the room. He lowered his arm and his shoulders sagged.

"Jesus, Max." He kicked the door closed with the heel of his bare foot and strode toward me. He came closer and crouched in front of me. I heard the creak of his denim jeans as they stretched. He reached out and picked up a strand of damp hair and rubbed it between his fingers. Letting it go, he traced a finger down the moisture on my cheek. "You're sweating. And crying."

"It's hot."

"Bull. You have a fever? How's the wound?" He put the back of his hand to my forehead and I shoved it away.

"It was just a dream."

His scowl deepened and the lines around his eyes accentuated. Jasper looked primitive; every bone displaying its purpose. There was no uncertainty with the structure of his face, or his expressions. And in some sort of fucked-up way, I liked his scowl the best. It breathed emotion. "One hell of a dream to be screaming like a horde of vampires are in your room."

I shrugged.

"Don't fuckin' shrug at me."

The remnants of my dream washed away as my anger rose. "Get out, Jasper. I'm fine. Go back to your woman."

His frown wavered for an instant and then returned full force. "It's called a nightmare." Whatever. "What was it about, Max?"

Crouched, arms resting on his thighs and eyes penetrating. And it wasn't with heated smoldering desire; this was heated anger. He was pissed off. I wasn't sure why this annoyed him so much. Because I'd woken him up? Or maybe he'd been in the middle of fucking Julianna.

"Nothing."

"What the fuck was the nightmare about, sunshine? You haven't had one like that in months."

I stiffened, eyes darting to him. "What?" How would he know? I knew I had one tonight because of what was happening, but he was right. "How do you know that?"

"My job to know."

I didn't believe him. Had he been there? All those times I sensed him near me. Smelling his scent in my room. Feeling as if he was watching me. Had it been true? "Where were you for the last six months?"

He tensed, but after a moment, he sighed and then his face softened. "Been around. Now, what was the dream about?" He moved over to the wall beside me, sat on the floor and leaned against it. Then he stretched out his legs and crossed his ankles as if he was making himself comfortable for a long haul.

Been around? I stared for a second at his bare feet, how his nails were kept short and tidy. For some reason that didn't surprise me . . . that he looked after himself. "Watching me?"

He ignored my question. "What was the dream about, Max?"

I think that was the second time he'd called me by my name, and despite hating myself for liking it—I did. The way it rolled off his tongue in a deep roguish sound sent tingles across my skin. "My past. Nothing unusual," I said.

He raised his arm and then in a gentle movement, hesitant, he tucked the hair behind my ear. The second the pads of his fingers touched my face, goose bumps rose and my breath hitched. His expression softened and then he wiped the tears away with his thumb one by one. "They about whoever put those scars on you?"

My breath hitched and I looked away.

"Whoever he is . . . I'll never let him near you." I didn't believe him and why should I. I was a job to him and when it ended, he would leave and those words meant nothing.

"Do you lie to all your *jobs?*"

It was like a light switch went off in him and suddenly he was stiff and tense. The softened expression was gone and in its place was a harsh, cold anger.

"You scream like that in the wrong place, wrong time and it's a fuckin' beacon. I plan to live long enough to get my *job* done."

I had no misconceptions of who this man was. However, Xamien probably did. He was an assassin and killed for money. But this job was the opposite. He was getting paid to protect me. I wondered why he'd even do it? Why would an assassin take this job? It didn't make sense.

"Do you really not know who is after me?"

"No. I wasn't given that info." His harsh grip on my chin slipped away and he was silent a minute. I started to get up to go back to bed when he seized my arm. "Are you going to have any more nightmares tonight?"

I shook my head. I never had more than one a night. At least that was how it had been for the last few years.

He nodded, got up, walked into the adjoining bathroom and turned on the shower. My heart stopped and a sliver of unease shifted through me. Why would Jasper do that? How did he know I had a hot shower after a nightmare? Even when we'd first met, he hadn't known why I'd been showering at midnight.

He came back out and walked straight to me and reached out his hand. I stared at it for a second and it was a second too long because he leaned over and grabbed my arm, hauling me to my feet.

He led me into the bathroom then turned to leave.

"How did you know?" My words stopped him.

He paused and I saw the tension in his shoulders, but I wanted to see his face, because unless Xamien told him, which I was a hundred percent sure Xamien wouldn't talk about my nightmares with anyone, then Jasper had found out some other way.

"You're cold and sweaty. Simple deduction."

Before I could say anything more, the bedroom door opened and I caught a glimpse of Julianna standing there wearing a red negligee that accentuated all her curves and left nothing to the imagination. I never had the need to feel jealous, but I did now. I wanted to run over to the door and slam it in her face. Better yet, grab Jasper and kiss him right in front of her.

I did neither.

"Everything okay, *mon cheri?*"

My chest tightened and I ground my teeth together. The tension in the room was so intense it was as if the pin on a grenade had been pulled.

"Yeah. It's good." Jasper strode to the door, and started to shut it, but not before I caught a glimpse of Julianna placing her hand on his arm.

I didn't sleep the rest of the night.

Jasper strode into my room before the sun had even risen. He was properly dressed this time, hair wet and tussled, and smelling like papaya and lavender. It didn't suit him. Jasper had a natural earthy scent—erotic.

He stopped just inside the door and briefly looked at me curled up in the rocking chair by the window. I caught the twitch of his brows lowering and the unsettled storm in his eyes. Something was off and I wondered if Julianna hadn't satisfied him.

I'd been sitting here ever since the shower, trying to figure out my options. Jasper might not think I had options, but I did. I could've left last night and I was betting he would've been too busy fucking his French princess to realize I'd gone.

But Xamien told me to stay close to Jasper, that he'd explain everything to me, and I trusted Xamien's judgment. I could decide what to do when I saw Xamien.

"Get dressed. We need to be on the road in five." He walked out, leaving the door open.

A minute later, I heard the roar of the bike's engine and then three revs. *Shit.* I threw on my jeans and ran to the adjoining bathroom, quickly peed and stuck a wad of toothpaste in my mouth. I slipped on my shoes, ran out the bedroom door and smacked right into sex goddess.

I should've politely thanked her for her hospitality and walked away. The old Max would've done that. But the rumble inside me from seeing Jasper walk out of my bedroom last night still simmered. My anger was directed at Jasper, but Julianna was playing me and I didn't like it.

"Don't think you're special because my *brother* was with you last night." I kept my voice calm and controlled.

Julianne slowly smiled, her lips pulling back to reveal her pearl white teeth. "We both know he's not your brother." She raised her chin and my hand curled into a fist as I imagined punching her in the nose and seeing her land on her ass, fawnlike legs in the air. "He was in my bed, not yours. And has been a number of times. *That* makes me special."

I raised my brows. "Oh, didn't you know? *Specials* are whatever needs to be used up before they go bad." Her back stiffened.

"Max!" Jasper shouted.

I looked past Julianne's shoulder and saw him standing at the other end of the hall looking all-encompassing with his stance wide, shoulders broad nearly filling the width of the hallway. I knew he'd heard me; the question was whether he heard the entire conversation. Of course he did; he was a Sounder.

"Get your ass on the bike. Now!"

Julianna snickered.

I glared at him and muttered. "Yes, *sir*."

He heard me. "For fuck's sake." He turned on his heel and two seconds later, the front screen door slammed.

I glanced at Julianna then raised my chin and met her glare. "Thank you for your hospitality." Then I brushed by her, followed Jasper outside, walked to his bike and climbed on. He started it up again and I put my hands on the back bar. He reached behind, grabbed both wrists and pulled them forward so my arms were around him.

Then we left Julianna's.

It was an hour before we stopped again and it was only because I had to pee so badly. I tapped him on the shoulder when the next roadside café came into view and he pulled over and stopped. I was already off the bike and running toward the bathroom before he shut down the engine.

He caught me at the door of the diner, latching onto my wrist.

"Jesus. You have a guy after you who can Trace. Might want to remember that before you go running off? 'Cause, sunshine, no matter how good I am, I can't fuckin' Trace, so if he gets to you first, you're history."

I hesitated for a second as his words caused a tremor to shift through me. Even the word Trace reminded me of Drake.

Jasper crossed his arms, his foot holding the door open. A man and woman walked toward us, took one look at Jasper, and opted for the other door.

"I'm not scared. I want to know who is after me. It's important I know."

His jaw clenched. "Told you. I don't know. He never told me. But I do know that you are scared. You're terrified as hell of whoever put those scars on you; otherwise, you wouldn't be having nightmares about him. Fear is eating away at you from the inside out. I can see that as clear as the fuckin' sun."

"Don't think you know me, Jasper." Because all he saw was a damaged girl with a fucked-up past and the wad of cash he'd get when the job was done. "You will never know me."

We stood staring at one another before finally the tension in his arm holding the door relaxed. "Didn't you have to pee?"

I did have to pee—bad. I attempted to walk away, but Jasper snagged my hand and led me up to the front counter. He chin-lifted to the waitress. "Washroom?"

She replied in Spanish and pointed toward the right of the counter. Jasper didn't say thank you, merely pulled me behind him, slammed the flat of his palm into the door and walked inside. A girl reapplying lipstick balked at him, eyes widening. She dropped the lipstick into the sink and it clanged, swaying back and forth inside the porcelain bowl. I was getting that Jasper had that effect on girls. Whether she was shocked at a man in the ladies room or because he was currently radiating anger was debatable.

"Out," Jasper ordered.

I was going with the anger.

The girl fumbled with her make-up bag then quickly ran by us. I was about to say something to Jasper about his rudeness but shrugged it off. Like I always said, people rarely listened to what they didn't want to hear. Jasper certainly didn't want to hear what I had to say, so it was a waste of breath.

He leaned up against the vanity, hands curled around the lip of the laminate counter. His brows rose as he stared at me by the door. Was he really going to stand there while I peed? This was about dignity and peeing in front of Jasper even with a closed stall door was . . . well, I wasn't going to do it.

The tap dripped.

The shitty cigarette-stained counter creaked under his grip.

Dishes clanged in the nearby kitchen.

"Sunshine, Jesus. Have a piss."

Shit. Double shit when he crossed his arms. There was no point asking him to wait outside; his answer would be no.

I went into the stall, slammed the door, slid the latch aside and then undid my jeans, sat and peed. When I came out, he pushed off the counter and walked to the door. I washed my hands then went to push the dryer button when he caught my wet hand with his and pulled me out of the bathroom.

"Hey, I need to dry my hands."

He kept walking. "Blower that loud when I'm trying to listen for anyone coming . . . common sense."

"You need lessons in basic human civility," I muttered.

"Not human, angel." He touched a waitress's arm on her way past. "Two café solo's and two rye toast with butter. To go."

It was annoying that despite his rudeness, the woman looked at him with a dazed look and a brilliant smile. What was it about hot men getting away with being rude? If I had done that, she'd have called me a bitch and I wouldn't have been served.

"Sure thing, sweetie," she said with a heavy accent and a wink.

"Thanks, love." Jasper cocked a grin.

I rolled my eyes. "How did you know that I took my coffee black?"

Jasper guided me over to a stool and I sat. "I notice things."

"At the first diner, you told the waitress two black coffees. How did you know?" The shower. The coffee. My nightmares. He knew I ate rye toast with butter in the morning instead of the traditional sugary churros. "Jasper?"

He shrugged. "I told you I was watching Xamien's place for a few days."

"You got all that in a few days?" A trickle of unease tap danced across my skin.

"It's my job, Max."

Suddenly, everything changed in him and the tension shifted to the easygoing playboy. He had this aura about him, a magnet that awakened the molecules in my blood stream from the slow lazy river to an ocean of tidal waves.

His hand casually swept my hair away from my neck and my breath hitched. I glanced up at him while his finger traced over the nodules at the top of my spine. The butterflies fluttered, panties dampened and my heart tripled its pace.

"We need to play a role here, babe." I thought he might let me go when his finger stopped caressing me. Instead, he leaned closer and kissed me. It was a soft kiss on the lips, but the moment our lips connected, the sparks ignited.

He deepened the kiss, his hand tightening on the back of my neck. My mouth yielded to his harsh assault of carnal fluidity. Saturated warmth of raw need broke the boundaries of what we were.

I didn't think either of us expected it. Nothing could have prepared me to be taken by him with a power that didn't just grab me—it changed me.

I couldn't breathe as I swayed into him, my hands coming up to rest on his chest, fingers curling into his shirt. It was knee weakening, panty dampening and heart pounding. I should've pushed him away. I didn't.

Jasper Kyelin was an overbearing, morally deficient asshole. But for that one moment when his lips took mine, he made me his. And for the first time, I felt wanted and beautiful.

Then he groaned.

And the sound broke through my moment of vulnerability. I pulled back so hard, I nearly toppled over the back of the bar stool. I would have if Jasper hadn't still had a hold of my neck.

Our eyes locked. My lips parted as if to say something, still breathless from his kiss. I hadn't expected it to be so potent, like a drug hitching a ride through my veins. I wasn't stupid. I knew he wanted to fuck me and I suspected he knew I wanted him.

But I needed to stomp it down before he stomped all over me. I wasn't being sloppy seconds to Julianna.

His fingers wove through my hair and he pulled me closer. I resisted and he scowled. "Your mouth is one hell of a place to be, sunshine. Didn't expect that." His grip tightened. "If there is a next time, and I suspect there will be, your mouth touches no other. Not while its playing with mine."

Whoa, what? "A next time? Are you kidding me? There shouldn't have been a first time. You had your lips locked on some other chick how many hours ago? No, there won't be a next time."

"Didn't kiss her, Max. She kissed me and I stopped it."

"Oh, is that one of your rules. No kissing, only fucking?" Why did it bother me if he fucked another woman? I shouldn't care. I didn't care. But I did.

"Didn't fuck her either. Haven't in years." He quickly let me go as if I'd burned him. "We have company."

I tensed and went to look around when his voice penetrated my mind. *Men by the door. Two of them. We're going to walk right by them. They make a move, you head for the bike and I'll meet you there."*

It was the first time he'd spoken to me telepathically. It was a very intimate way of communicating, as if the person was inside of you, part of you. Jasper's voice was different, raspier and his accent was more distinguishable. But the subtleness of it made it mysterious and dark, yet with a gentleness as though he caressed me with his words. I also sensed the black hole that encased his heart.

Jasper Kyelin was more than a Scar assassin with an arrogance that warred against the Goddess who made us. Against the laws of the Scars. He had parts of him that lay hidden beneath his assholishness.

"Max," Jasper hissed. He was trying to get my attention, hand on my arm and eyes drilling into me. "A hell of a time to be daydreaming about my kiss."

There was a slight pressure in my head as he attempted to get past the walls around my thoughts. He'd have a while to go because living with Drake had taught me to learn how to block others out. It had taken years, but having Drake read my thoughts had set me up for more punishments because he knew exactly what I was thinking.

Jasper being a Sounder, had probably heard the two men talking and knew instantly that they were searching for me. The tension hummed in his body, the coiled up muscles ready to react. A guy like Jasper stayed alive by being vigilant and cautious.

His fingers casually played with my hair, tantalizing and sensual. Yet his attention was elsewhere. If I'd been an observer, I'd have seen a man intent on his girl, the smoldering eyes, and the closeness of bodies.

Mechanical. It felt and looked sensual, but if you looked beyond what was there, read the signs, it was mechanical. A well-oiled machine. Rhythmic. Focused. Unyielding to the threat.

This was why Jasper was paid to protect me.

"Here you go, sweetie." The waitress plunked down the order on the counter and Jasper reached into his pocket and pulled out a few bills and tossed them on the counter. He picked up the cardboard tray with the coffees and the brown paper bag which he placed in the tray between them.

"Thanks," he mumbled, snagged my hand, pulled me off the stool and started walking straight toward the men.

There was no hesitation in anything he did. I wondered why we didn't go out a back door maybe through the kitchen. The men stared at us as we approached. I knew from the lack of black licorice scent that they weren't vampires nor Long Neck Centered World Others, CWOs, who looked like they had just crawled out of a dumpster. Smelled like it too.

"What are they?"

Jasper ignored me.

He walked straight toward the men and my grip on his hand tightened. What the hell was he doing? I stared at my feet and leaned in closer to him. I hated not having my blades with me. I had no defense as a Healer.

"Excuse me," he said to the one man who partially blocked the door with his bulk.

I held my breath. Waiting for the strike. The gunshot. Being grabbed and taken away.

Feet shifted and then we were walking past them and out the door. Jasper tossed the coffees and toast into the bin, and within seconds, we were on the bike and back on the road.

I had no idea where we were headed, but wherever it was, it was fast. Jasper never let up for a good hour. When he finally pulled onto the shoulder, it was on a quieter road where few cars passed by. He shut off the bike and I slid off. And waited. Because Jasper remained where he was, hands resting on his thighs and not saying anything.

Then he did. "You trying to get us killed?" I was standing slightly behind him so he had to turn to look at me. And fuck, it was a look. One that raised the hairs on the back of my neck and had me grinding my teeth back and forth. "Never . . ." he snagged my wrist, fingers bruising, "speak telepathically around anyone when you don't know what the fuck they are."

"You did." Maybe I should've kept my mouth shut and just said, 'yes, sir' like I had done with Drake. But Jasper had split me open and I could no longer stay quiet. My fight to get back the control I used to have and the ease of living in the dark . . . it was slipping away.

Jasper had ripped down my black shield and splattered me with a spectral of colors. And despite hating him for it, with each breath I was feeling more alive than I ever had.

"From fifty feet away and I know my limits. Do you understand

76

me?" He let me go and shook his head back and forth. "And if you say fuckin' 'yes, sir,' I'll do what I should've days ago and spank your ass right here on the side of the road."

The pull upward at the corner of my mouth surprised me. He really was an asshole, but for the first time since he'd barged into my bedroom, Jasper looked and sounded worried. Yeah, it was subtle like the slight shift in the direction of the breeze, but I'd felt it when he held my wrist. The peppering of his nerves awakening under his heated skin.

Had he been worried about those men? About himself? About me? Or was it simply my imagination?

"Get on the bike."

"Can you at least tell me where we're going?" I knew we were meeting Xamien, but I wasn't sure where or when.

"To France."

"France?"

"There's a place that's safe for you to lay low. Xamien will meet us near there. Now, will you get on the bike?" he ground out.

Shit, he was still pissed. I threw my leg over the bike and settled in behind him. There was a time for pushing him and this wasn't it. It wasn't fear of him that kept me silent. It was the simple deduction that it wouldn't have done any good. He'd been right. I shouldn't have spoken telepathically so close to those men because if they had been rogue Scars, they'd have known instantly we were too.

"I'm sorry."

His back stiffened and then he punched the handle bar and turned to look at me. "You didn't know any better. It's fine." I knew it wasn't, but he was trying to make me feel better and that was a first. He started the bike back up and I put my arms around him.

We rode for another hour before he pulled off onto a dirt road. We bounced along the unkempt winding path barricaded by trees on either side of us. A few minutes later, we broke into a clearing and I peered over Jasper's shoulder.

Now, this I hadn't expected. There was a small plane and a grass runway. A plane with wings wearing the age of time. Black spots littered across the base of the upper wing and what appeared like rust speckled the propeller on the front.

Jasper pulled up beside it and we dismounted his bike.

"A plane?"

The right corner of Jasper's mouth curled upward and his eyes brightened. "Meet Fiona."

"Fiona?"

The anger had washed away and it was the playful Jasper again. "My plane."

"Yeah, I got that. But Fiona needs a facelift. Maybe even a new Fiona."

Jasper chuckled. "She's never let me down. I trust her."

I don't. "Are there parachutes in the plane? Helmets? Fire protection suits?"

He burst out laughing and the sound sank into me, sparking heat from the tips of my fingers straight down to my toes. It was obvious from the lightness in him that Fiona was his pride and joy. I was surprised Jasper had a pride and joy as I had the impression there was nothing he cared about.

I did wonder who she was named after. I'd never really been curious about anyone. Didn't care to. But I wanted to know how Jasper came to be the way he was. Why he lived without ties to anyone. Why he killed for money. He couldn't have always been like this.

I watched him stride over to the plane, his arm reaching up then his fingers running along the edge of the wing. It was a caress, soft and gentle like he was stroking the curve of a woman's side. I stared, my pulse spiking, imagining it was me he was caressing.

His hand smacked the metal and I jolted.

A machine. Nothing that could love him back. Something he could easily destroy if he needed to. No attachment.

And it could be argued that I had no attachments either, but I had my reasons. The question was . . . what were Jasper's?

I heard the roar of another bike and glanced at Jasper who was now in front of the plane checking the rusted propeller. I quickly flipped open the saddlebag and took out my blades, one in each hand. I backed toward Fiona, keeping my eyes on the direction of the sound of the bike. Had those men followed us? No, there would be two bikes or a car.

I kept backing up until I bumped into something hard—Jasper. His hands slid down my arms to cover my hands on the blades at my sides.

"Planning on cutting up my plane, sunshine?"

I nodded to the tree-covered area where we had come from. "Someone's coming."

I shuddered when his breath drifted across the lobe of my ear. "Damien. And I'd advise not fucking with him. He's still pissed off at the female race."

Damien and Xamien were brothers and nothing alike. Damien's nickname was 'women hater,' he was impatient and volatile and had one hell of an attitude. He lived as a Solitary in Florida and used to be called into assist a Talde when needed. That changed. Now, he hunted a girl—Abby.

Damien hopped off his bike, not a cruising bike like Jasper's, but a red racing bike, and strode toward us.

Jasper leaned into me. "Feel free to use 'yes, sir.'"

I jabbed my elbow back into his abdomen and hit solid mass. He'd been ready for it.

Damien stopped in front of us, legs braced, arms crossed and not a sliver of the man I'd encountered a number of months ago. His eyes were like looking into muddy water, unable to see what was beneath the surface. Damien looked as I had at one time . . . void of emotion. Living and breathing, but only in the mechanical sense.

There was no hand shake, slap on the back, how are you, formalities between the men. Right to the point.

Jasper threw him his keys. "If we're lucky, they'll follow you," Jasper said. "I suggest going South. You have a chick to ride on the back?"

Damien nodded. "Yeah. Down the road. Anything else?"

Jasper shrugged. "Run by Adrian's and see how he's doing?"

"Fuck you," Damien muttered then shook his head. I was wondering what the big deal was when he said, "I'm not falling for that again. Fuckin' bullet hurt like hell."

Jasper chuckled then gestured with a head tilt toward me. "She shot me in the thigh."

Damien's brows lifted. "Did you not get her off after you fucked her?"

I snorted. "Jesus, I'm standing right here."

Jasper, whose hands still rested on top of mine that held my blades, tightened. "Don't worry sunshine. I'd never do that to you. My women come first—literally."

This time, I slammed my heel onto the bridge of his foot.

He grunted then let me go, but I heard the subtle chuckle follow me. "Luckily, she's a Healer. Unluckily, she has an attitude." I pulled away from him and turned my back, pretending to admire the rust bucket Fiona while I listened to their conversation. "Any leads on Abby?"

"No," Damien said.

"You look into what I asked?"

"Yeah. Sounds like it might be him and if it is . . . more than you can deal with." Were they talking about Abby or me? "Might want to . . . end this. Odds aren't in your favor on this one."

Silence.

I looked over my shoulder at them. Jasper had his head down, arms crossed and back stiff. Damien stood braced, arms at his sides and was looking at me with his shadowy eyes.

"No," Jasper said.

Damien's gaze jerked back to Jasper. "You invested?"

"You know me better than that. Just don't like losing."

Damien looked at me again and his penetrating gaze hesitated on my arms—my scars. I shifted uneasily and rubbed my arms, not liking how intensely he was staring at me.

"Don't let her fool you. They're all cruel bitches," Damien said and then turned on his heel and strode to Jasper's bike. He unhooked the saddlebag and tossed it toward us.

What the hell did he mean by that?

"Come on, sunshine. Let's get Fiona in the air." Jasper tapped the wing with his fist twice then grabbed his bag.

The roar of the bike started and I watched as Damien disappeared behind the cover of the trees. "What was that about?"

"Nothing. Let's go."

I wasn't so sure about whether Fiona would *go* anywhere. Did he know what he was doing? It wasn't like I was scared of flying or dying, but my choice of deaths wouldn't be a fiery spinning nose dive into the ground.

"Angel. Ass. Here. Now."

Jasper was already at the top of the stairs.

I climbed up, following him into the cockpit and squished between the seats. I sat in the seat beside him and fastened my seatbelt. He flicked switches then placed a headset on and began speaking to someone.

The engine spurted and the propellers groaned a few times before they suddenly spun. Jasper grinned. "That's it, baby." Slowly the plane jerked forward and I watched the propellers out the side window spinning. I was surprised I didn't see the rust flicking off into the air.

Jasper put his hand on my thigh and I looked at him. He wore a cocky grin and his eyes twinkled as if he knew something I didn't. "Not going to ask for my qualifications?"

I shrugged. I suspected Jasper wouldn't do something as stupid as fly a Cessna without being damn good at it. Actually, Jasper seemed the type to be damn good at everything he put his mind to—including, he claimed, sex.

Jasper chuckled shaking his head. "Think I'm going to like hearing you scream and writhe beneath me." I stiffened, wondering if he'd read my thoughts. But that was impossible. I'd feel it and my shields around my mind were intact. "Tilting your world on its axis with my cock inside you . . . seeing your eyes fill with desire. Angel, that fake blasé attitude won't be touching you when I'm inside."

I crossed my arms, more to keep my heart from leaping through my ribcage than anything else. Just the thought of Jasper inside me was catapulting me through a maze of emotions.

The plane started down the grass field and my emotions were taking flight at the same time as I watched Jasper easily maneuver the plane into the air at a steep angle.

He looked completely at ease, his face relaxed, muscles flexed, but not with tension. No, Jasper exuded so much confidence in his stature I didn't think he was capable of vulnerability.

Waleron had that same confidence, sure of himself, fearless and stoic, yet he carried it differently. The Taldeburu had a stern intensity about him. I'd experienced it intimately when I'd placed my hands on him to try and calm his Ink. The unyielding power that lay beneath his skin was a powerful turmoil, swirling like an out-of-control hurricane ready to sweep up anyone in its path.

But Jasper, he was different. I had trouble reading him. He had no morals. What did that mean? How far would he go to get what he wanted? Did he kill innocent people? Would he betray a Scar? On the outside, Jasper was arrogant and self-assured with an unbending no-bullshit attitude. But I was yearning to know what was beneath.

What made him an assassin? What made him this way? Because we were all a product of our past; it was just how we lived with what we experienced that shaped us into who we became.

I glanced over at him as he spoke to someone over his headset—and it wasn't in English. He scowled then said a few sharp words before his hands tightened around the controls. He suddenly moved his mouthpiece away and looked at me.

The heat in my cheeks came to life at being caught staring at him.

He threw off his headset. "See something you like?"

I'd spent years keeping quiet, and I'd learned to appreciate it. The less said the better, but with Jasper, I was having trouble keeping my mouth shut. He pushed my buttons and I wanted to push his back.

"Nothing I haven't seen before." I shrugged and peered out the side window. "I live with Xamien remember." Xamien was one of the most attractive men I'd ever seen—worldly with a casual air about him. I also thought of him more as a father figure than a man I'd ever be interested in. "Nothing unusual in my world."

"Your world?" Jasper scoffed. "Your world consists of Xamien and his butler guy, Glunk, about one-hundred acres and a manor. You, Miss Sunshine, haven't even experienced a teacup of the world."

I tensed, hands gripping into the leather armrests. A teacup? Did he just compare my life to a teacup? "At least in my 'teacup' I have morals and can sleep at night."

"Oh, I sleep just fine." His voice was low and soft as he said, "Can you, Max?"

My breath hitched and my gaze jerked to his.

"Why do you have to be such an asshole?"

"Because you're cute when you get riled." His mouth twitched at the corners.

Bastard. He liked this. He liked getting a rise out of me. He was enjoying seeing me stutter and thrown off balance. Well, I may not have his experience, but I did know what a man liked and what would throw him off.

I slowly ran my tongue over my upper lip.

Twitch gone.

I caressed the silver chain at the base of my throat.

His brows lowered as he watched me.

Then I bit my bottom lip and slowly dragged my teeth over it.

His lips pursed together and shifted in his seat.

Game over.

Now, I was taking control.

nine

Jasper

MAX WAS ASLEEP, FEET TUCKED under her, hair lying in soft tendrils against her cheek begging me to run my fingers through it. I loved a woman's hair; it said a lot about them. And hair like Max's, long and luxurious with a bounce in the relaxed waves, indicated she was hiding behind the curtain of strands. Afraid of change— taking chances; quiet with an aura of mystery. The thing was . . . Max pretended to be unafraid of everything, most of all me, but that was a lie. The girl was hiding, and I was going to break through and watch her crack.

I was pissed I couldn't read her thoughts. It made my job harder, protecting a woman I had no idea what was channeling through her brain. Information was my advantage and I was good at finding it and using it to get what I wanted. Maybe it was better I didn't read her thoughts; it was too intimate and my obsession with her was already fucking with me.

"Like what you see?" she said, eyes flashing open.

The corners of my lips twitched up—smartass. What I'd discovered with Max was she was feisty. The way she'd handled Jules made me want to grab her and kiss her until she moaned my name. I knew

Jules wanted Max to think we were fucking, but the truth was there was nothing between us anymore. We'd fucked a few times a couple years back, but that was it. And normally, I wouldn't give a shit what another girl thought, but Max . . . it bothered me overhearing her talking to Julianna. I didn't like her thinking I'd fucked her.

"Yeah, I do." No point denying it. Shit, I wanted to taste her, caress her, sink inside her so badly it was like my cock hung by a noose, strangling with need.

The thing was . . . I had a feeling once wasn't going to be enough and that bothered the fuck out of me. Still didn't stop me from wanting her. Hadn't stopped me from watching her for months either. Besides, I took what I wanted and dealt with the consequences later.

My cock swelled as her sweet glassy eyes looked at me. I didn't like when she had no expression, face stiff and controlled. She had a magnetic smile she rarely used and when I had seen it, it was like she'd handed over a piece of her soul. Fuckin' brilliant.

I'd yet to hear her laugh and damn it, I wanted to. I bet she'd tilt her head back slightly, revealing her slender, pale throat and her eyes would sparkle like blue sapphires. The sound . . . fuck, it would have the sweetness of syrup with the heat of a hot sauce.

She uncurled her legs and put her feet on the floor, searching for her shoes. The jagged white scar and discolored skin on the bridge of her foot overtop what was her tattoo caught my eye. I'd seen it a number of times and it was obvious someone had purposely destroyed her Ink by burning it. From what was left of it, the Ink had been some sort of spider.

A roar rose in my chest threatening to escape my throat as the image of Max being burned, tortured . . . fuckin' hurt. My entire body stiffened and I wanted to punch something, destroy. Jesus, what was wrong with me?

I never gave a shit what scars, physical or emotional, people had. We all had them. Made us who we were . . . good and bad.

But I wanted to know exactly what happened to her. I wanted to kill the bastard. He was mine to destroy.

"What happened?" I nodded to her foot.

She immediately shoved her foot back in her shoe. "None of your business."

I was expecting that answer. Max was as closed off about her past as I was. "It is my business. You're my business and until I say otherwise, you're going to tell me anything I need to know about you." I didn't really need to know shit about her. All I had to do was keep her ass safe and if I couldn't do that, then I had to kill her. Should've been a simple job. But it was complicated as hell and fucking with my emotions. I tried to play it off as lust, but my obsession was more than that. I didn't just want her, I wanted to own her. And the crazy-as-fuck part was that I wanted her to want to be owned by me.

Max's lips pursed together and I knew I was getting to her. When I'd met the girl, she had a shield around her emotions the size of Asia. But I was chipping away at it and she was crumbling.

"And I don't feel like telling you."

This time, I did chuckle. She frowned and her spine stiffen which jutted out her sweet breasts that I'd got a taste of pressed up against me for hours on the bike. I flicked the switch for autopilot then reached for her foot.

"What are you—" she squealed as I yanked off her shoe.

Her fist hit the underside of my jaw—hard.

"Let me go!"

She twisted in her seat, attempting to get away, but she had little room to move. It was cute as hell. Fuck, I'd like seeing her fight lying beneath me naked. "Babe, what happened to your Ink?"

"Nothing."

"Sunshine, tell me."

She stopped fighting and blurted, "He burned it okay. He held me in his arms and stroked my hair all sweet-like while his vampire minion took a burning rod and scorched my Ink." Fuck. Fuck. Fuck. I froze, staring at her. "That was day one."

She bent her knee and I should've seen it coming, but my hands were wrapped around her delicate ankle, and I was busy reeling, the image suffocating me. She kicked out and hit me in the side of the head, throwing me off balance. My hands slipped from her ankle and I grunted as my vision blurred for a second.

"Jesus, you have one hell of a kick."

She was on her feet and standing behind her seat, hands curled around the back of it. "Touch me again and my blade will be the last thing you see. Got it?"

Her blades were in my bag under my seat.

"Got it?" she shouted.

She was trembling, her face pale and the blazing anger was mixed with fear . . . fuck. I was a bastard. I shouldn't have pushed her on the Ink thing. What was my deal? My deal was I normally didn't give a fuck what anyone thought of me, but that was changing. I realized I did care. I cared what Max thought. And instead of making a cold remark back at her, I had the urge to apologize.

I swore to never care again. It was dangerous, and in my line of work, it could get anyone I cared about dead really fast.

"Yeah, babe. I got it." I picked up the headset and put it on.

ten

Max

I WAS STILL SHAKING WHEN the plane descended and my ears popped. Then a thump and the tires skidded down the runway. It had been an hour since Jasper had tried to see my Ink and every inch of me was screaming at the memories of Drake's voice as he calmly held me, whispering soothing words in my ear. But nothing was soothing. His words were a knife stabbing me with every syllable.

I couldn't walk for weeks after he killed my Ink.

"Max." Jasper stood beside my seat, his hand rose as if he was about to touch my shoulder, but he lowered it to his side.

I counted to ten, bringing the shield down over my mind. I couldn't let him get to me. I wasn't that vulnerable girl anymore. I knew how to fight. I knew how to protect myself.

I titled my chin up. "Touch my Ink again and I'll kill you."

He met my stare head on, and for a second, I thought he was going to shoot back a smartass remark, but this time he surprised me and gave an abrupt nod. "Yeah." He walked to the side door, opened it and strode down the steps.

When I came down the stairs, he was leaning up against the plane, arms crossed with the confidence of a proud lion defending his mountain and the mountain was Fiona. I walked over and reached for my blades he had in his hand. He put them behind his back and with his other arm, snagged me around the waist and pulled me tight to him. My hands automatically went to his chest, one palm flat against his heart.

His voice was low and graveled with that panty-dampening hint of an accent. "I'm sorry, Max. I shouldn't have . . . fuck, I'm sorry."

My breath caught in my throat. There was no cocky grin, no playful gleam in his eyes; instead, I saw concern with furrowed brows and lips pulled downward.

I was so taken aback by the simple yet powerful words that I remained quiet and still in his arms. I knew something had changed between us in that moment. His ability to apologize and mine to . . . yes, I accepted it because I knew getting those words from Jasper was monumental.

"What happened to you, Jasper?"

His expression immediately hardened. He put his finger under my chin and his thumb slowly caressed the dimple. The softness in it completely contradicted the harsh, cold look in his eyes. "I'm good at three things: killing, fucking and not caring whether I've done either one." His fingers trickled over my chin, down my neck then between my breasts and lower. Then he was under my shirt, his skin touching mine as he lightly graced the pads of his fingers over my naked skin. Suddenly, his hand left me and he moved away. "Max, I want you to . . . I need you to never forget that."

I couldn't understand him. He was playful and flirted, yet was cruel and unkind as if he wanted to hurt me. But I felt something when we touched and it was more than desire. It was stronger, and if either of us gave in to it, I had a feeling it would be the destruction of who we'd become.

"Max?"

I gasped at the familiar voice and turned. Xamien shut the door of a black Audi and walked toward me with a broad smile on his face. The tension in my shoulders instantly disappeared as I met the bright warmth in his eyes. If there was one person in this world I cared about, Xamien was it. Every time I saw him, the memory of him lifting me up in his arms and carrying me out of Drake's hell brought a wealth of relief.

It was like being saved all over again.

I knew he wouldn't hug me. I'd kept my distance from everyone, including him, but something had shifted in me and I wanted to feel the familiarity of Xamien around me.

I stepped toward him and wrapped my arms around his waist. It took him a second before he embraced me and then kissed the top of my head. I pressed my cheek to his solid chest and he squeezed me. The Taldeburu exuded an intense sexuality with the way he held himself. Tall and muscular with aristocratic features and an air of confidence. He had never pushed me to tell him anything about myself and now I knew why . . . he'd known I was a Healer and probably suspected I was hiding it because of what I'd been through. It didn't matter though. Xamien had given me a home and most of all, he'd trusted me when I'd given him nothing to trust.

"You okay?"

I nodded and pulled back. "Yes, sir." I heard Jasper grunt.

My gaze shot to him and I noticed his eyes flicker down to Xamien's hand still settled on my waist. The glare . . . it was filled with irritation. I was a Healer and couldn't feel emotion like a Scar Reflector, but no one needed an enhanced ability to feel the tension radiating off him.

Xamien was obviously pretty immune to Jasper's assholishness or knew that it was a cover because I was learning fast that everything out of Jasper's mouth wasn't the truth.

Jasper's eyes trailed back up to my face and his scowl deepened. All those little things he noticed about me . . . how he watched me . . . how he looked after me when I had the nightmare . . . those things couldn't be actions of a man who didn't care.

And that realization made my heart skip a beat as we stared at one another until Xamien's voice drew us apart. "I can sense the attraction between the two of you."

Xamien was a Reflector and could read emotions; however, a Reflector didn't have to break through your shields to feel them. When I looked up at his face, it was murderous as he glared at Jasper. What made it worse was Jasper shrugged.

"It's not like that," I quickly said.

Xamien ignored me, his focus on Jasper. "You told me you wouldn't. I warned you to keep your hands off." The words were ground out one by one, like a fist pounding on a drum. "I should've known better. I did know better."

The tension between them caused the air to shift and I quickly put my hand on Xamien's arm to draw his attention back to me. "Xamien, I'm fine. We're okay."

"I don't give a fuck about him."

Whoa. I hadn't expected something like that coming from Xamien. He was always laid back and casual, but this was the side others feared. Xamien reached forward and pushed my hair back from my neck. I heard Jasper cough and mutter something under his breath. Xamien must have distinguished his words because he started to go for him, but I latched onto his arm.

"What's going on, Xamien?"

Xamien raised his head and looked toward the car. The air grew colder and then a grey cloud of mist appeared.

I stiffened as a figure emerged from the fog and I met the ice-blue eyes of Waleron. He looked at me and for one second, I wondered if he knew who I was.

He was an ancient, upheld the laws above all others and protected the Scars with his life. He was exceptionally private and no one even knew where he lived. But two things everyone did know was that he endured sixty-one years of torture by a CWO, a Lilac, and he would do anything to protect the Scars—anything.

He strode toward us and I shifted a little closer to Xamien, who responded by squeezing my waist reassuringly.

"Xamien. Jasper," Waleron said then turned to me. "Max." I shivered as he said my name. It was as if he knew it wasn't my real name. Was it possible? Did he know I was Breanna and lied about my name all these years?

Xamien nodded with respect. Jasper didn't say anything; actually, I noticed he avoided looking at Waleron all together, which was odd because Jasper met everyone head on.

"You tell her who is after her?" And Waleron's voice matched his ice-cold glare—abrupt and harsh.

My heart jumped and then started running a sprint. Heat flooded my body as my nerves began to shoot off like fireworks. *No, don't say it. Please don't say it.*

"Not yet," Xamien said.

"What the fuck are you guys talking about?" Jasper's hands curled into fists at his sides. "Waleron, damn it. You bastard. You told me you didn't know who the fuck was after her."

Waleron didn't even flinch as he stood calmly and kept his eyes on me. I knew. No one had to say anything. I knew what they were going to tell me.

"The Scar looking for you," Xamien said. "He's been seen all over the world for the past six months looking for a girl. A girl about twenty years old with scars on her and a burn on the top of her foot over a tattoo." Bile rose in my throat and I had to swallow several times. "His name is Drake and he's an ancient Scar, Max." Oh, God. It was Drake. "This Scar . . . the Goddess killed his Ink because he was too powerful. He wanted to destroy the Scars and be the only one to rule. When his Ink died, it weakened his lungs and took most of his powers away including his ability to Trace."

I didn't hear his words anymore and I didn't need to. I knew the story. What they didn't yet know was that Drake had kept me prisoner for six years as his private Healer.

And now he was looking for me and didn't care who knew it.

Black spotted my vision as the overwhelming fear catapulted me into a soaring reel of emotions that suddenly crashed to the ground and left me gasping for air.

"Max," Xamien gently pulled me around to face him. "The house I found you in . . . there were vampires but . . . were they followers of Drake? Was he who we rescued you from? Is that why you hid that you're a Healer? Because you've been scared he'd find you?"

My breath locked in my throat as I thought of Drake. He could Trace again. He was looking for me. He had hordes of vampire followers to help him. He had humans helping him. Who else? CWOs?

"Max, we need answers in order to protect you." Xamien rubbed my arms up and down, trying to comfort me, but all I could think about was Drake.

"Yes. I healed him for six years." I closed my eyes as the fear grabbed hold of me and brought me under. I trembled and heard voices echoing, arguing, but I couldn't focus on anything except that Drake was the one coming for me.

Drake would kill Xamien. He'd kill anyone who got in his way, just like he had my Talde and my mother. He was resilient, unwavering, determined.

I felt as if I was standing naked in the freezing cold and frost bite was slowly eating away at my skin.

"Max!" It was Jasper's curt tone that cut into me and I slowly opened my eyes. Jasper had his hands on my hips and I was clutching his shirt as I stood in front of him, not even knowing how I got there. "He won't find you."

But no words could calm the rising storm of emotions. The numbness Jasper had chipped away at was crumbling—fast. "Yes, he will." I forgot about Xamien and Waleron as I looked up into Jasper's eyes, tears filling them as everything I'd fought to avoid came crashing down on me. "Did you know he walked the streets of different cities every day? All around the world just so he'd be able to Trace to any place he wanted. I healed him every week so he'd be strong enough to Trace." Jasper's entire body pulsated with tension as he looked over at Waleron who stood beside us. "I was taken when I was ten. He killed my mother and Talde. He burned everything and then he . . ."

Then he tortured me for six years; watched me suffer. Forced me to heal him. He had left reminders on my body, so every time I looked at myself in the mirror I saw him.

"Jesus, the Talde in England. The little girl, Breanna," Xamien said beneath his breath. "Everything was burned to the ground."

I nodded and stepped back from Jasper's grip on my hips. I was instantly cold and wanted the comfort of his hands again. It was possessive and protective and yet, Jasper was neither. Not really. He was both at that moment merely because he was paid to be.

Xamien put his hand on my shoulder as if knowing I needed some sort of support. "But there are no Healers missing. How is it that the bastard can Trace now? You said you had to heal his lungs every week so he'd be able to Trace."

Everyone was quiet.

Waleron had yet to react to anything I was saying, but he rarely reacted—stone cold.

"You should've fuckin' told me it was that bastard who did that to her. That it was Drake after her." Jasper's voice erupted in the silence. I jerked but his abrupt words weren't directed at me; they were at Waleron. "Jesus." He turned and strode away and I watched him, the muscles in his back tight and his hand running through his hair as he stalked to the car then slammed his fist down on the roof. The sound echoed and I knew there had to be one hell of a dent.

When he turned around and started walking back, his eyes never left mine as the fear slid over my skin in a suffocating black tar. My fear was not of Jasper; it was what I knew had to have happened. This was worse. Way worse. There was only one possibility as to how Drake was strong enough to Trace without a Healer.

Jasper reached me and without hesitating, he wrapped his arm around my waist and tugged me into him while his other hand cupped my chin. "I can protect you." I tried to shake my head, but his hand prevented me. "I'm good at what I do."

"You're a killer. That is what you do." I said it gently and I hadn't meant it to be mean, just that it was the truth. Jasper was a killer. He was good at that. He was the hunter, not the hunted and at the moment, we were the hunted by an ancient Scar that could Trace and now . . . now he was stronger than ever. Because Drake was now vampire.

Jasper's jaw clenched and his lips pursed together. Then his gaze drifted to Waleron as he said, "Yeah, well someone has to do what needs to be done." I thought I saw Waleron give a microscopic nod, but I couldn't be sure and his expression never changed.

"He's vampire," Waleron said as if reading my thoughts. "It's the only way he could be strong again without a Healer."

Xamien swore under his breath. There was no other possibility, except that Drake had gone hybrid. "Balen has a strong ability to Track vampires. We can call him."

Balen was a Scar Tracker who was with a Talde in Toronto. He had once drunk vampire blood in exchange for saving a woman's life. He'd nearly Transitioned into a vampire, but fought the hunger of the blood thirst and defeated it.

But it wouldn't matter if they found Drake. If he'd Transitioned, then he was more than likely stronger than ever and would stop at nothing to find me. But why would he want me now if he didn't need me to heal his lungs?

My legs gave out when I realized why. Jasper held me tight against him, his breath up against my neck.

Drake knew. He knew I could heal his Ink. That was why he was searching for me. It was the only possibility. The timing was right. Six months ago, I'd communicated with Waleron's Ink. Six months ago, Drake supposedly started asking questions about a girl with scars.

"What is it?" Jasper whispered in my mind.

I couldn't tell him. I couldn't tell anyone. If they knew I was capable of healing Drake's Ink, Waleron would kill me and then Xamien would retaliate. But healing Drake's Ink would make him almost undefeatable. A hybrid with an Ink so deadly the Goddess had to kill it . . .

Then it hit me. Drake wanted to change me into a vampire. I'd be a slave to him—he'd be my master. I'd have no choice but to do what he wanted and I'd be forced to heal his Ink. But I had one small advantage. If Drake got to me, I had to *willingly* drink his blood in order to Transition.

But no matter what, if Waleron knew, he'd never allow me to live and risk the lives of the Scars.

I looked over at Xamien who was scowling at Jasper. I loved Xamien; he was the closest I had to family and just like my mother and Talde had tried to protect me, so would Xamien. He'd even go against Waleron.

"I'll stay with her," Xamien said. "If he's a vampire, then I'm better protecting her than Jasper."

Jasper's arms tensed around me and for a minute, I thought he was going to argue, but he didn't and I hated that I felt disappointed. Then I was mad that I did.

"Xamien," Waleron said in a calm, steady voice. "I need you with me. We have a better chance finding him being able to Trace. You and I are the only Scars left with the ability besides Drake." He nodded to Jasper. "Two weeks. Take her."

Jasper hesitated and then nodded and grabbed my hand, pulling me toward the car. "Jasper wait." He kept tugging me behind him and I looked back at Xamien who was now head to head with Waleron and the tension was palpable.

"No way am I letting Xamien have you." Jasper's voice was abrupt and I was startled at his choice of words. What he didn't realize was that I hadn't been about to say that. I'd wanted to say goodbye to Xamien. "I want my payment and I won't get it if you land in that asshole's hands." He ground out the words as though he was angry at them.

I stopped as fury boiled over in my chest. "I'm already in an ass-hole's hands," I shot back.

"Very funny, princess."

"So, now I'm a princess?"

"Yeah, you're a fuckin' princess. And right now, you're my prin-cess." He pushed down on my head. "Get in the car."

I did and he slammed the door.

"Max . . . or do you want me to call you Breanna now?" Xamien's comforting voice entered my head.

"Max, sir," I replied. That was who I was now. For six years, I was no one, something used, an object, and when I became Max, I was a person again. Xamien didn't use me or hurt me. He just loved me for the broken girl I'd become.

I was stronger than Breanna. I fought to bury the fear Drake had instilled in me and even though it lived there still, it didn't own me like it used to. And now Jasper . . . I looked over at him as he folded into the car. Jasper unearthed the fear and made me want to fight for the girl I was now.

"We'll find him," Xamien said. *"You know I won't let anything happen to you."*

I did know and that was what terrified me. *"Xamien?"*

"Yeah?"

"I . . . love you. Not like . . . well . . ."

"Love you, too, Max." He paused. *"Promise you'll be careful with Jasper. You know what I mean, right?"*

The time to be careful had already passed. *"Yeah, I'll be careful."*

Jasper skidded out of the small airport gates and horns honked as he went through the red light. He didn't say anything and neither did I for ten minutes.

Finally, I broke. "What's with two weeks?"

He glanced at me and his grip on the steering wheel tightened, the leather crackling beneath the pressure. "My job's over."

"And then?" My voice quaked and I hated that I was letting the fear back in, but it wasn't just Drake who now blanketed me with uncertainty. It was Xamien's safety and the feelings I had for Jasper. It was what I might have to do in order to protect them all. What my Talde should've done years ago. What I should've tried to do during those six years with Drake, but I was too scared and weak.

"Jesus, Max. He won't get to you. Do you hear me?" When I didn't answer, he repeated, "He. Won't. Get. To. You. Say it."

I didn't because eventually Drake would get to me. "And if he's not caught before your job is over?"

"You'll be fine. I have a place you'll be safe."

"So, you just leave me there and that's it?"

Jasper slammed his hand into the dash and the vibration shook the car. "Max, damn it. I can't give more than that. I'm already too clos—" The car jerked forward even faster. "I can't."

I was uncertain what he meant by I can't. But it sounded as if he was talking aloud to himself rather than to me.

I looked out the window.

He pulled up to a hotel a few hours later and this time it was a nice one with a beautiful garden out front and a yellow arch over the driveway. It was small, maybe fifty rooms, and was only four stories. The mountains were behind it and I imagined there was skiing here in the winter.

I got out and followed him into the lobby where we were greeted by stunning marble floors and a cascading staircase. Jasper ignored it all and guided me to the front desk where a young, impeccably dressed woman greeted us.

I noticed her eyes roam appreciatively over Jasper and expected him to procure a half-cocked grin. Except this time, he was all business to the girl's obvious disappointment. He insisted on a room on the ground floor and then paid for it in cash. Without looking at me, he grabbed my hand and we walked down the row of rooms until we reached the last one. He unlocked the door, flicked on the light and then yanked the curtains closed, blocking the view of the mountain.

"Get some rest."

I stood at the door while he checked the room over. "I was thinking," he went into the bathroom and washed his hands. When he came out I continued, "what if we use me to lure Drake?" I knew it was risky, but they didn't know Drake like I did. He'd never give up. He was relentless in his pursuit to be the most powerful Scar. That was all he talked about.

Jasper bent over and shuffled through his bag, ignoring me.

"I can talk to this Adrian guy and make certain you get your money." Fear could break you, but it could also drive you to conquer it and I'd been trying for four years by practicing with my blades. Needing to feel strong again. I was a weak puppet used by a man for my ability. "I know him. I know his weaknesses." And I was stronger now. I could destroy his Ink so it never had the chance of being reborn again. I didn't know for certain if I could do it or if it was possible, but at the moment it was the best I had.

"No!" Jasper stood up straight and kicked his bag to the side. "Fuck. No."

"It makes sense. He won't kill me. I'm a possession to him. I belong to him. He wouldn't—"

"Jesus, Max. You hear what you said? You don't fuckin' belong to him. And that isn't happening. Period."

"I want it to end, damn it!" I shouted. "I'm sick of living in a bubble. I want out, Jasper. We can use . . ."

Jasper started toward me, his hands curled into fists, tension in every part of his body. I raised my chin, but my heart was slamming into my ribcage and it wasn't in fear. I wasn't scared of Jasper, his words may be harsh, but there was something in him I trusted. That speck in his eyes that refused to let me in, but revealed his vulnerability, his softness.

He grabbed my arms, fingers bruising. "He is never getting near you again. Two weeks, two fuckin' years, two hundred years. He isn't touching you again."

"I know him better than anyone. I can get him to trust me and—"

"You think he'll trust you for one second? He'll chain you up and make certain you never escape him again. Then if you're lucky, he'll only torture you. Unlucky, he'll find someone you care about and torture them right in front of you. And then . . . then you'll willingly drink his blood and become his slave."

"But if we can—"

"What would you do if he had Xamien hanging from his fingernails being tortured day after day? Tell me, Max. Will you break then?

Or will you watch him suffer for weeks? Hear his screams, hoping someone will come in time to save you both." His jaw pulsated and his voice was laced with anger. I realized, this wasn't about me—this was about him.

"Jasper—"

"But they'll come too late and she'll be dead."

My breath hitched. He said she. What had happened to him? Who was she?

"Fuck!" Suddenly, he pushed me away from him and strode into the bathroom and slammed the door. "You don't belong to him," he shouted. "And he won't get to you."

I heard the tap turn on and then a loud bang. There was no doubt something in Jasper's past was exactly as he said. Coldness seeped into me as I imagined what could have happened. Had he made a choice like that? Was that why he was alone? Why he kept his distance from everyone? What made him this way?

He opened the door again half an hour later. Water dripped off his chin and the strands of his hair. And his face—darkness. Ravaged pain had crept into the depths of his eyes and sat there unhidden beneath the cocky confidence he exuded. A beast lingered and it looked ready to attack.

While curled up in the chair, he went to walk by me. I don't know why I did it except it was instinctive. I reached out and placed my hand on his forearm. There was a stark contrast to my white skin against the black vivid ink of his tattoos. We contrasted in a lot of ways . . . except for what we both hid from others and ourselves.

"I'm sorry. For whatever happened to you . . . and her."

He jerked, but not away from me, just muscles flexing beneath my palm.

Our eyes met and I saw the moment his raw pain shifted and became hidden beneath a veil of cocky confidence. I slid my hand down his arm until my fingers linked with his.

He glanced down at our interlocked hands. "Unless you want to fuck right now, let me go."

I knew he was acting out, just like I did by being cold and silent. It was my safety net to stay closed off. Jasper was doing the same thing.

But I was tired of my safety net and I wanted it to break.

I slipped my hand from his, stood, then grabbed the bottom of my shirt and yanked it up over my head.

eleven

Jasper

"WHAT THE HELL ARE YOU doing?"

She pulled off her shirt and tossed it on the floor. All the blood rushed from my head right down to my cock. Her pearl white skin against the black lace bra covering her breasts left me speechless. *Fuck.* Everything about her threw my usual steady composure into unchartered territory.

I wanted to fuck her. Hear her scream and beg, and I wanted it over and over again.

The sound of the zipper on her jeans had my heart slamming like a freight train into my ribs. I swallowed. Why was I just standing here? Why couldn't I react? I should grab her and fuck her to get it out of my system. I'd never expected it would be her doing the instigating and me the hesitating.

I grabbed her arms. "No." What the hell was I doing? I hadn't been laid in months. I'd stalked her; watched her for months and now . . . now I was pushing her away.

But I was selfish and harsh and she'd said it herself . . . I was an asshole and suddenly I didn't want her to see me that way.

"Why not? You want me and I want you. It's sex. I'm not stupid enough to think it's anything more, Jasper."

I jerked at her words. For some reason, Max's words bothered me—big time. That should be even more of a reason I should fuck her and prove to myself this was just that—sex. "How long since you fucked a guy?"

"What?" Her arms moved as if she was about to cross them over her breasts and then decided against it and put them back at her sides. "What does that have to do with anything?"

"Because when I fuck you, it will be hard. I need to know if you can take it." I'd expected her to grab her shirt and put it back on. That was what I had intended. To scare her. Instead, she stared at me as she undid her bra and let it fall to the floor.

Fuck.

I was a guy. A guy that didn't give a shit if a woman hated me in the morning, but they never did. I may be a selfish bastard but I never left a woman unsatisfied. And it was more a self-serving reason as I could always get seconds when I wanted. But this was different. Everything about it was different. Max was different.

And that should've scared me enough to walk away.

But Max . . . staring at her milky white, naked skin . . . her handful of breasts with nipples erect and waiting for my mouth to suck on them. I should've walked back into the bathroom, shut the door and jerked myself off in the shower.

I didn't.

She wiggled her hips, slid off her jeans and stepped out of them.

Jesus. It was that word for two reasons. She was fuckin' gorgeous even with scars all over her legs and a few on her stomach. Some of them were faint lines like what would come from a knife, but others looked raw and raised, maybe burns from something.

And that fucked me right up imagining her being held down and burned and cut, her screaming with pain, thrashing against the very bastard I was protecting her from. I could picture it, hear it and it was fucking with my head because I'd lived it. Watched as a child had been thrown carelessly into a grave after hearing the screams.

Shit, Max deserved more than me. I couldn't do it. I wanted to prove to myself that I could and still walk away from her, but I knew I was already feeling more for her than I should. For months I tried to convince myself it was nothing, but it was something. It was a fuck of a lot of something. "Put your clothes on." I turned away from her, walked around the other side of the bed and lay down. I put my hands beneath my head and closed my eyes. Unfortunately, all I saw was Max standing naked and willing in front of me.

"Is it because of my scars?"

Now, that pissed me the fuck off. "Jesus, Max. No. That's not fuckin' it." And it wasn't. Her scars made her more beautiful because they made her real. Not some fake piece of ass I didn't give a shit about.

Fuck.

Fuck.

I didn't give a shit about Max. This was a job. She was a fuckin' job. But she wasn't. She had never been a job. She was Max. The girl I watched for months because I couldn't stay away.

The mattress sagged and creaked and then—

My eyes flashed open when her hand brushed across my thigh. She had one knee on the bed and the other leg lifted and went over top to straddle me. My hands flattened against her naked thighs and I groaned. I didn't have to ask what she was doing. I knew damn well what the hell she was doing. And I'd given her an out . . . that out expired the moment she straddled me.

I couldn't resist. Not anymore. "Fuck, sunshine."

My palms slid up her thighs, curved around to her hips and then over the bare flesh of her ass. A finger slipped into the string of her thong and I pulled upward—hard.

Her breath hitched and her body tensed with her head slightly titled back. I fisted the strap in my hand and pulled up again so the thong was tight in her ass and panties putting pressure on her pussy. I tugged upward again. She pushed back against the pressure. There was defiance in her eyes mixed with the smoldering desire I had craved since the day I met her. It was for me. She wanted me just as much as I wanted her.

"I'm not nice, Max."

She raised her chin a bit. "I know."

I looked away for a second, nodding and said quietly, "Don't hate me in the morning." I'd never said that to a woman before because I never cared whether she did or not. But Max . . .

"Oh, I already hate you, so sex won't make a difference." I saw the slight twitch at the corners of her mouth and that did it. All resistance and doubts crumbled.

I grabbed her around the waist and in one motion, tore off her panties and had her flat on her back. I locked her wrists above her head with one hand, my legs straddled her, weight pinning her beneath me, helpless and unable to do anything but submit to me.

That was what I wanted—submission. I wouldn't get it completely, for that I needed her to trust me and that wasn't in the cards. But I'd take what I could like I always did.

And at the moment—that was her.

I reached over the side of the bed and searched inside my bag for a condom. Quickly, I ripped it open with my teeth.

I didn't take off my jeans, but unzipped them, pulled out my cock and rolled the condom on. This was sex—raw, uncomplicated and without the intimacy of kissing. From the hard look in her eyes, she knew exactly what I was going to do and I didn't need to check if she was wet. I knew she was. Her body quivered with anticipation beneath me. Her skin flushed. Her pulse thumped frantically in her throat.

I held my cock as I slid it up and down between her legs, her wetness clinging to the condom. Her legs bent on either side of me and I let her wrists go to put one leg up on my shoulder. "You're soaking."

"Must be your glowing personality," she replied.

I cocked a smile, ran my hand down her leg, over the raised scars to her thigh, across her abdomen, then lower. The second I touched her clit and put pressure on it, her body tensed and I thrust my hips forward and drove my cock inside her.

It was a harsh move, knowing she was already tense and clenched, but I never said I was sweet and gentle, just the opposite and I saw her expression, heard her sharp intake of breath. Shocked at the sudden intrusion. Pain. And then acceptance as desire blazed from the depths of her eyes.

She was fuckin' tight as hell, clinging to my cock as I moved. I put more of my weight on her, jeans rubbing up against her, my pelvis rocking so it hit her clit with every thrust.

I pulled all the way out then hesitated and pounded back into her over and over again. She was panting, eyes closed, hands curled into the pillow on either side of her head.

I watched her tense with every shove of my cock deep inside. The pain, the relief and then the ultimate pleasure as I did it over and over again until her body quaked and knew she was close.

I pulled out. Her eyes opened and met mine. It was in that second I knew I couldn't do what I was hired to no matter the consequences. Maybe I'd known all along, but tried to convince myself otherwise. Prove to myself I could if I had to.

But this wasn't just raw fucking. This was her—Max. And no matter what went down with Drake, I knew killing her wasn't an option.

"You going to finish me off?"

I flipped her over so she was on her stomach. "On your knees." She did as I ordered and I ran my hands over her ass. Jesus, it was perfect. A little plump so I had something to hold, to grab, to slap if I wanted to.

I groaned and my finger slid down her ass crack and then between her legs where she was soaking wet. Fuck, that was the best turn on. A woman who was wet as hell. I shoved my finger inside her and she moaned, her front end lowering like she was a cat stretching.

"Hurry."

I grinned and then pulled my finger out of her and looped my arm in front so I could slap her clit.

"Fuck," she cried and tried to move away.

I tugged her back hard against me and hit her clit again with two fingers. She tried to sit up and I shoved my hand down onto her neck. "Stay there."

"That hurts."

"Yeah. But you like it. You want it. Right?" I didn't have to ask because I knew she was like me—hiding a part of herself.

But sex was where I'd found release and whether she knew it or not, so would she. It was where I could let go and finally just feel. I wanted Max to experience that. To drop the shield and let the pain in, and with it, the pleasure.

She didn't say anything and I did it again. This time her body trembled after the pain. I knew she could take it. "Scream, sunshine." I rubbed her clit back and forth and she moaned. Then I flicked it and her back arched. She was giving in to it, pleading for it, wanting the pain.

"Let go, baby." I grabbed my cock and slid it down her ass crack.

Then with a hard shove, I pushed inside her and at the same time tapped hard on her clit.

She screamed.

"That's it." She gave herself to me as her cheek pressed into the pillow and all the tension in her body released, becoming mine to do with as I wanted. The denim of my jeans rustled as I thrust faster and faster into her, my fingers playing with her at the same time.

"Jasper. God."

Was that her begging? No, not yet. Not fuckin' yet. I wanted more from her. I stilled my hand, but kept my hips rocking back and forth harder and harder, her body moving forward so hard she placed her palms on the headboard to keep from banging her head into it.

I saw the second her hand left the pillow and moved down between her legs. "Not a chance." I was sunk deep when I stopped thrusting and latched onto her wrist. "Only I do that."

"I need to come."

"You'll come when I say you do." I knew she wouldn't like that, but I didn't give a shit. I was holding onto my control by a fuckin' thread. I was betting my cock was shouting profanities at me for holding off this long.

"Get off me. I'll finish this myself."

I kept my voice steady. "Put your hands back where they were." She tried to elbow me in the ribs, but with my arm snug around her waist, my cock inside her and my weight pushing her into the mattress, she didn't have a chance. "Put them back."

The moment she gave in, her body relaxed and she slowly slid her arms back over her head. She hadn't fought that hard, and I knew it was because she was feeling exactly what I was—teetering on loss of control. This was the only place both of us could let go and she had yet to learn that. I had to push her until she broke, not to hurt her, but to set her free.

"Are you going to use that cock or let it go soft inside me?"

I snorted and did what I had been dreaming about doing since the day I'd met her. I pulled out of her, pressed my hand into her lower back and then with the other hand smacked her hard on the ass.

She screamed and tried to wiggle away, but I was stronger and determined as hell. I smacked her again.

"Jasper. Stop."

Smack.

She managed to get hold of the top edge of the headboard and with one yank pulled herself out from under me and to her feet. Before she could jump off the bed, I was on her and slammed my body up against her, pushing her into the headboard.

"Let me go, asshole." She tried to kick back, but the mattress was soft and she lost her balance. I seized both her wrists and locked them on either side of her head against the wall.

"I feel you quivering. Do you like this? The fight?"

"Fuck you."

"No. I'm fucking you." She pushed back into me and I chuckled because she didn't have any leverage—just the way I liked it. "Open your legs like a good girl and let me fuck you, Max."

What I got in response was a heel to the knee cap which had me grunting and growling. I grabbed her around the waist and threw her down on the bed then fell on top of her. She tried to clock me in the face with her elbow and I managed to jerk back before she made contact.

"You're not fucking me anymore. I don't fuck guys who spank me."

"You've never been spanked. How would you know? And right now, I'm betting you're so fuckin' hot for me that your pussy is throbbing and wetter than it's ever been."

Max was a fighter. She may have remained quiet and reclusive for years, but she was a rebel, and that was dying to get out. And I was going to be the one to release that part of her.

"Don't ever lie to me, sunshine. Not when we're fucking. Not when we both can win here." I ran my finger up and down her through the moisture and then brought my finger to her mouth. She was breathing hard and her eyes were wide.

Uncertain.

Passion blazing.

Need and want.

All of it.

"Taste how wet you are." I caressed my finger over her lower lip and then her tongue darted out as she licked my finger.

I just about came right then. "Fuck. That's hot." And then I did what I hadn't planned on . . . I replaced my finger with my mouth.

It wasn't just a kiss. It was the assault of our mouths—bruising, craving, tasting, what we'd been starved for. The vibration of her moan beneath my lips erupted a fierce need inside me. I kept her locked down with my body and my mouth as I grabbed my cock and pushed it back inside her—where it fuckin' belonged.

Her legs wrapped around me and then I was kissing and fucking her and everything was exploding. Hand clenched in her hair, I thrust faster and faster, the taste of her mouth giving in to my fierce possession and then . . .

She stopped kissing me. She stopped breathing. Every muscle in her body tensed, shivered and trembled.

"Fuck," I groaned as my final thrust inside her drove deep. I came harder than I ever had and it was almost painful.

I fell forward, my head in the crook of her neck, breathing in her scent, filling me up until I was on the brink of giving her more of myself.

It was then I noticed I still had my clothes on. What the fuck was I thinking fucking her with my clothes on? It was what I normally did with one-nighters. I wanted to be naked and have her curled around me.

"Please, get off me." Her hands pressed on my chest.

I frowned, and for a moment, I thought of shutting her up by kissing her red, bruised lips. Instead, I sat up, tugged off the condom and tied the end in a knot, then shoved my cock back in my jeans and did them up. She tried to escape by sliding out from beneath me, but I saw her movement and clamped down on her arms.

What the hell? "We had sex. We both wanted it. And it was great fuckin' sex. Why are you running?" Fuck. I should've just got off her and let her go, but I couldn't. I couldn't let her go.

She stared at me, and for a second, I thought she was going to tell me as her mouth opened and then she clamped it shut. I saw the change in her, how she stiffened and then the turmoil in her expression. "Let me go, Jasper."

For some reason, there was a hell of a lot more meaning to those words than me just crawling off her, but I slipped away, and the second I did, she was off the bed.

"Max?"

She ignored me, snatched her clothes off the floor and went into the bathroom.

I heard the lock turn.

twelve

Max

I GRIPPED THE EDGE OF the sink, head down, breathing hard and my body still throbbing. What had I done? What was I doing? He took everything I hid away and blew it apart. He'd broken through.

Jesus, he'd found me.

I closed my eyes and breathed through my nose. In and out. In and out.

He spanked me.

And I wanted it. It turned me on. God, what was wrong with me?

I was scrambling to find the peace again. The steady control I lived with. Jasper just fucked it right out of me and I had no idea how to get it back. I needed it back.

If Drake found me . . . I needed the numbness.

God, his hands roamed over me like . . . it was like he didn't even notice my scars. No pity. No questions. Just the raw need for one another.

Then he spanked me.

A tweak of desire hit me as I thought of his hand coming down on me, then the instant pain then . . . then pleasure. A wild release of beauty. I shouldn't like it. But I did. Because I knew exactly what he'd done

110

. . . he was getting me to feel. To scream. To free me from the shell.

I rubbed my hand over my butt, closing my eyes as the tenderness raised the desire in me again. I pictured him behind me, his hard thighs against mine, hands on my hips and then running down me.

"No!" I shouted and pounded the edge of the sink and turned away from the mirror so I didn't look at myself. See the blush in my cheeks, the satisfied look in my eyes.

He'd find me. Drake would find me and break me this time. I couldn't let that happen.

"Max?" Jasper knocked on the door.

I slid to the floor, leaning against the bathtub and pulled my legs up, resting my cheek on my knees. I didn't like what was happening to me. It was as if Jasper was spinning the lock to my emotions and each number he got right set free another emotion in me.

"Open the fuckin' door." It sounded like his palm slapped the flimsy wood of the door.

"There are washrooms in the lobby."

I heard a rough snort and then—

The door frame gave as his foot kicked it open, but it did more than that; he left a huge hole in the middle of the door. I refused to be provoked by him and kept my spot as he stood in the doorway, staring down at me.

He stepped closer and then crouched in front of me. I kept my eyes averted because . . . because I was still trying to put my pieces together and they were getting further and further away with Jasper so close.

He didn't say anything as he stared at me, and it was the way he did it, as if he held the fragile pieces of me in his grasp. At his mercy to be crushed or gently cradled.

He dropped down beside me, knees bent, arms casually hanging over them.

It was what he did. Just like when I had a nightmare.

Every muscle in my body was strained as I waited for his smartass remark, but he sat beside me and said nothing. After a while, I relaxed and closed my eyes as I listened to his rhythmic breathing beside me.

I don't know when it happened, but I ended up with my head on his shoulder, his arm around me, fingers slowly stroking my shoulder. At some point, I fell asleep with Jasper cradling me in his arms.

I woke in the morning, in bed, legs tangled with his and his tatted arm over top of me, my lips nestled next to a smooth, hard naked chest. And no matter how good it felt, it was wrong for more reasons than just Drake. I didn't regret having sex. I wanted him, but Jasper was wrong. I had to remember why we were here, why he was here.

I tried to push him off me, but he merely groaned and tightened his arm around me, locking me down. "Jasper, get off me."

"Relax, baby." His tone was playful and casual as if we were . . . more.

"I want to get up." Because I was already feeling moisture between my legs and what happened last night couldn't happen again.

"Are you trying to get another spanking, because all you have to do is ask."

I smacked him with my palm in the shoulder and he laughed, one eye opening as he looked at me. "Can you not be an ass for one second?"

"You see, you're even thinking about asses."

I raised my knee as hard as I could. He saw it coming and dodged out of the way still laughing. "Damage the goods and I'm not getting you off again." He came down on top of me and his hard cock pressed into my thigh. An invasion of heat hit me and I couldn't stop my heart from racing or the clench between my legs.

The best I could do was glower at him as he hovered above. "I can look after myself."

"Oh, I know you can, but you won't. Not when you have me to look after you."

"Oh, my God," I muttered. "That won't happen again."

"Yes, it will. I've decided I want all of you."

"You don't get to decide that."

He lowered until his lips were inches away from mine and my gaze shot to his mouth and then back to his eyes. "You want to kiss me right now, don't you?"

Fuck, yes. "No." Last night, Jasper did way more than fuck me; he broke through me.

A slight quirk upward at the corner of his lips and then he lowered a little more, his warm breath drifting across my skin. "Don't lie to me." I clenched my jaw and pursed my lips together. "Fuck, baby, you're beautiful."

My breath hitched. He said it not in a playful flirty way, but as if he really meant it. Except I wasn't beautiful; I was the beast with the scars all over. He was the beautiful one, but still it made me feel for that one second truly beautiful and that the scars didn't matter.

His cell rang and he groaned, lifted off me and grabbed it from the nightstand. "Your timing sucks." He listened for a second and then hung up. "So much for the idea of slow, lazy morning sex. We need to move. A horde of vampires were seen at the airport asking questions. They must have caught on to the ruse with Damien and tracked the plane." He snagged his jeans off the end of the bed and strode into the bathroom. He said over his shoulder, "There is going to be a lot more than a second time, Max." I heard the water turn on in the sink. "Babe, grab the toothpaste in my bag and come brush your teeth."

I rolled my eyes and got out of bed, quickly throwing on clothes before reaching for his satchel. I found in it a little black leather case which had his shaver and . . . I sifted through it . . . cologne, a wad of bills, deodorant and condoms.

"Max." His face was wet, water dripping off his chin to trail down his naked chest. I walked over and passed him the leather case. "Find anything interesting?"

"No."

He took it from me. "I have nothing to hide. You'll never find any-thing important."

"Except for condoms," I said offhandedly and it was more to me than to him.

He chuckled. "Ah, baby. You're fuckin' cute jealous." He reached out and hooked his arm around my neck. It was unexpected and I stum-bled into him. "No reason to be. I haven't fucked anyone since the day I met you."

Before I could even contemplate his words, he bent forward, shift-ed his hand to the back of my neck then kissed me. It was hard and possessive, just like him, taking what he wanted, when he wanted it. It made my heart pump madly and my stomach flip-flop as if I was jump-ing on a trampoline.

Just as quickly as he brought me into him, he let me go. I stood flustered and heated, the ache between my legs demanding attention.

And his words were still whirling around in my head like confetti.

Jasper casually picked up his toothbrush and put toothpaste on it then stuck it in his mouth. He put a glob on my toothbrush and passed it to me.

Our eyes met in the mirror as I shoved the toothbrush in my mouth and we brushed our teeth, watching one another's reflections. A moustache of white clung to his lips and I wanted to lick off the minty freshness and then have him kiss me again.

I didn't know if my shield around my thoughts was wavering, but Jasper grinned and winked at me. It wasn't with cocky arrogance, but with tenderness.

I looked away and quickly swished, finished brushing and walked out.

He came out of the bathroom a few seconds later and took a t-shirt out of his bag, pulling it over his head. I caught myself staring as his muscles flexed just before the shirt fell into place. He crouched, packed the bag and then zipped it up.

"You slept through the night."

I jerked and looked into his charcoal eyes not realizing I was still staring at his tatted arms that had been wrapped around me last night. "Huh?"

"No nightmare."

I threw the pillow that was on the floor back on the bed and shrugged.

"Just saying, Max. Thought . . ." He stood, picked up his bag and threw it over his shoulder. "Never mind. Let's go."

He held out his hand and I walked over to him and took it. I had no energy to argue with Jasper and if he wanted to hold my hand, then I'd allow it. He tossed a wad of bills on the dresser and I looked at him questioning.

"Bathroom door."

Shit, right.

We walked through the hotel, stopping to grab water and croissants and then went out the front door where he passed the valet his car keys.

His cell rang again. "Yeah? . . . Fuck. We'll leave it here." His hand tightened on mine and his entire body went on alert. "She can make it." He started walking, pulling me along behind him. "I said, she can make it."

We were leaving the car? I glanced back over my shoulder and saw the valet searching around for us.

Jasper moved at a slow jog and I kept pace as he said short, curt answers in the phone. "No." He glanced over at me. "Things have changed." He was quiet and I could hear someone yelling on the other end. "I don't give a fuck," Jasper replied calmly. "If it comes to that, then I'll deal with it . . . No. Too fuckin' bad . . . Then come kill me." He pressed end, and then threw his phone on the ground and crushed it with his boot.

"I gather you don't like him?"

Jasper didn't say anything, but his lips were pursed together and his jaw was clenched. After a few seconds, he ground out, "Something like that." He nodded to the all-encompassing mountainside. "We're headed up there and we need to make it by nightfall. You up for it?"

He could have been referring to anywhere on the mountain. "Do I have a choice?"

Jasper sighed and ran his hand through his hair. Something was off, agitating him and I didn't think Jasper was capable of being agitated. At least not by the looming threat of vampires and some guy who may have pissed him off on the phone. "No."

"Then why are you asking?"

He shrugged as if uneasy with the question and then he said, "Civility, sunshine."

"Really?" That surprised me.

"Yeah." He averted his eyes from mine then took his satchel off his shoulder, unzipped it and reached in pulling out a brown paper bag with the freshly baked croissants. My mouth watered as he passed one to me and I quickly took it and bit into it.

"What's up there?"

He hesitated and stared up at the mountain. "A place to stay for a while. Normally, we could drive part way up, but with the vampires finding out we flew into that airport, there's a chance they'll eventually track the car to the hotel."

"You think they will?"

"I've lived this long because I bet on every possibility."

I didn't know who had been on the phone, or what was waiting for me up in the mountain, but despite Jasper's attitude, I did trust him to keep me safe, which for now, was my best option.

My legs were quivering after several hours walking through the rough terrain uphill. We'd crossed two streams and my shoes were soaked, and just when they felt dry, we came across another one. Jasper merely trudged through as if it was dry land.

I refused to complain, but as the hours dropped away with the sun and temperature, coldness sank into my bones. I shook uncontrollably by nightfall, my thigh muscles burning and the arches in my feet aching.

I didn't think I could take another step when Jasper turned to look at me for the first time in an hour. His gaze trailed down my shivering body to my soaking wet feet then back up again.

"Jesus," he muttered then strode toward me. He grabbed my arm and backed me into a tree. "Lean against the tree, baby." His body pressed into mine and the heat emanating from him was like he'd wrapped me in a wool blanket.

He scowled as he rubbed my arms up and down several times. "You should've told me you were fuckin' cold." He lowered his bag to the ground and took out one of my blades. He placed it in my hand, curling my trembling cold fingers around the handle. "Stay here. I'll be right back." He kicked his bag closer to me so the trunk of the tree hid it, and then he pulled out his knife from the leather holster across his chest.

"Jasper—"

"Don't move. I need to make sure the place is safe first." He didn't wait for a reply as he crept off into the darkness.

I stood leaning against the tree, my muscles screaming from exertion and cold, and my blade held in both hands in front of me. I was uncertain what damage I could do if I was attacked. My hands were numb and I suspected I'd collapse if I took one more step.

It was only a couple minutes before I heard his voice and then he was there in front of me again. "Max." There was a large bruise on his cheek and he had dried blood on his lip. He caught me looking at it and shrugged. "Run in with a bear. I punched him. Fucker punched back." There was a slight twitch at the corner of his mouth. God, I liked when he was playful like that; it made me forget the type of man he was. But maybe that wasn't a good thing. He held out his hand. "Come on. Let's get you warm."

I gratefully took his hand and he bent, picking up his bag. We walked another couple minutes before I saw an orange glow through the trees. A few seconds later, a large wooden log cabin appeared with firelight blazing in the window. It was pretty massive and I had pictured something small and rustic, but this was beautiful with a wide deck in the front that had one of those double-seater wood swings.

Jasper tugged on me.

I hadn't realized I had stopped walking and was staring at the house. I think partially it was my body finally shutting down with relief. And then it hit me . . . a woman. This place belonged to a woman of his and that was where the punch came from.

"A bear or woman?"

At first, he looked confused and then he grinned, which had me hating him more because despite my reservations on what I was walking into, when Jasper grinned so casually and without the hardness . . . it lit up my insides like a Christmas tree laden with colorful blinking lights.

"Holden—my brother."

I jerked. "Oh." Now, that shocked me. I hadn't considered Jasper having a brother or family. It just seemed . . . foreign.

"I sent him on an errand. He didn't like it. Now, can we go inside before you freeze to death?"

I nodded.

The moment we stepped inside and the heat from the fire blanketed me with warmth, I closed my eyes and sighed. Jasper led me over to the fireplace, set me down on the floor and I immediately put my hands out to warm them. He hesitated, before gently lowering his hand and stroking my hair. I glanced up at him, his fingers curled into the back of my neck and his hard features flickered in the firelight.

I swallowed, my eyes trailing down to his mouth, wanting to taste him again.

Jasper nodded. I wasn't sure at what, then he turned away, tossed his bag on a black leather couch and walked into the kitchen and began opening cupboards.

"You like tomato soup?" He held up a can.

"Sure."

I watched him move around the kitchen easily, as if he was familiar with what he was doing. I wondered if he had a house of his own and what it was like. Did he cook? For the type of person he was, I didn't think he would, but I was beginning to see him differently.

I imagined him having a small house, nothing special—simple. It would be on the edge of a cliff, the ocean crashing against the jagged rocks below. He'd stand out on his porch when he couldn't sleep and listen to the rhythmic sound of the waves.

I was staring and as if sensing me, he glanced up from stirring the soup and looked at me. The stirring stopped and my breath hitched as his grey, penetrating eyes let me in. They were naked and open and without shields. I saw him—Jasper. Casual and easygoing, but still with a wealth of self-confidence. I knew it was a glimpse of who he'd once been and who he hid from everyone.

It was beautiful.

The wood suddenly crackled and snapped, making me jump. Turning away and distracting myself, I grabbed the iron poker hanging on the hook beside the fire.

The second I did, I froze and the poker slipped from my grasp, making a loud clang as it hit the floor. The shivers were no longer from the cold but from the memories as they plowed into me. The red hot tip of the iron, the agony as it pressed into the top of my foot while Drake held me in his arms.

The smell. God, the smell of my burning flesh had been worse than the pain. I screamed and cried and begged Drake not to do it, but he rocked me back and forth while the vampire burned the bridge of my foot, killing my Ink.

"Max. Max." Jasper crouched in front of me. "Max." He reached forward and I jerked away. "Jesus, you're crying."

I hadn't realized I'd been crying and quickly used of my arm to wipe away the tears.

He put his hand around the back of my neck, fingers weaving into my hair. It wasn't harsh and insisting like I expected from Jasper; instead, it was gentle and comforting. With his other hand, he pushed back the few tendrils that clung to my damp cheek. "You're safe here. You're safe with me."

Jasper may think so, and he was cocky enough to believe that, but I knew differently. If Drake was after me, then I wasn't safe no matter where we were or who was trying to shield me from him. "I'm fine."

"You can lie, but I'll always know the truth." I was about to argue when he leaned closer, his mouth so close to mine I could taste him on the tip of my tongue without even touching. "I won't let him near you."

I stiffened. "For two weeks, you mean."

His fingers flinched on my neck. "I won't let him have you."

"Yeah," I whispered.

"Max . . ." He brushed his lips against mine and instantly my stomach whirled and it was an invasion of butterflies. "Fuck, baby. I don't know how to do this," he said beneath his breath and then let me go. Standing, he strode toward the kitchen. "Sit at the table."

Whatever haunted him, lived and breathed inside him, he smothered it with his attitude, his flirting, his indifference, but he was opening up and it scared me because it made me want him more.

I walked over to the long wooden table that looked like it belonged in an old medieval castle and sat. Jasper placed a steaming hot bowl down in front of me and then sat at the end of the table two seats away. "Thank you."

"You're welcome." He took a spoonful of the tomato soup, and without looking at me, he ate.

I was stunned. Such simple words and yet coming from Jasper . . . it was different. We were different. And they weren't just words; they had meaning.

Jasper was my mirror and we shared a similar darkness. He tried to hide it by being an asshole, by doing what he did so he didn't have to give a shit.

I did the same thing. I rarely spoke, kept to myself, and didn't get close to anyone except I was civil about it. I didn't hurt anyone by how I'd chosen to live. Jasper did.

I didn't want to care. I shouldn't. I knew better. Jasper was clear about who he was and yet . . . he'd slid through the cracks. He was an assassin. He'd been a jerk and yet I'd seen a side to him that was genuine. I just didn't know if I trusted him. Was he suddenly nice to me because he needed something from me? He used people. He'd told me that.

Was Jasper using me like he did everyone else?

His spoon clattered in his bowl as he dropped it, and then he pushed away from the table and looked at me. There was no cocky grin, no flashing brilliance of playfulness in his eyes; instead, what I was looking at was the man who had no compassion for anyone. And I hated it. I didn't want to see this side of him.

"Yeah, I use people." Oh, God, he'd read my thoughts. Horror crushed me like a hammer and I saw the hurt in his grey eyes. "You want the real? I get paid to kill people. Those I don't kill, I use for my own benefit. And you know what, princess, I don't give a shit if you trust me, actually it's better you don't. " His lips curled into a cruel smile and a shiver tap danced across my skin, and it wasn't from desire this time. "What? You don't like knowing you fucked an asshole? Well, too late for that, sunshine. You did."

"Why do you do this? It's like a light switch you turn on and off. I never know which side of you I'm going to get." I pushed the bowl away and it sloshed over the sides and splattered onto the table. "I don't understand you." I had to get away from him. From me. From everything I was feeling.

I knew what he was doing. He wanted me to hate him. It was how he protected himself, to drive people away. Well, it was working because tears welled and I needed to escape before he saw them.

Jumping to my feet, I headed for the door. I was suffocating under everything that was happening. I was a job to him; an object to Drake; a liability to everyone.

"Where the fuck are you going?" he asked.

I managed to get the door halfway open before he came up behind me and his palm slammed it shut. He grabbed my arm and yanked me around to face him then pressed into me so his chest was up against mine. "Where the fuck do you think you're going?"

"Away from you." I tried to shrug his hand off my arm, but he tightened his hold.

"You're not going anywhere."

"What are you going to do . . . force me to stay? You don't have that power, Jasper. I'm not a prisoner."

"You sure about that, sunshine?" he shot back.

I eyed his bag on the couch a few feet away where my blades were.

He followed my gaze and then grabbed my chin. "Are we going to have an issue here?"

"We've had an issue since the day we met."

"Yeah, I've wanted you. And I'm not letting you go."

I had no idea if he meant as in not letting me walk out the door or more than that, but at that moment, I didn't care. I just wanted to escape all of it. For years, I'd been dead to emotions and it was like everything inside me was exploding.

I raised my hand to push him away, but he moved to the right and then used the movement to push into my side and lift me up so I hung over his shoulder. "Jasper!"

He ignored me and strode through the house and down a hall. He stopped for a second, opened a cupboard and shuffled around. I pounded on his back with my fists and tried to kick him, but he was holding my legs with one arm.

"Jasper, let me go."

He started walking again, then opened a door and kicked it shut with the heel of his foot. He threw me down on the bed and I scrambled to get up, but he latched onto my ankle and dragged me back. Pulling me up to the headboard, lying on top of me, I squirmed underneath him.

"What are you doing? Jasper."

"Making sure you don't leave."

Then I saw it.

The sight of the rope had me screaming and yelling and punching at him. I wasn't getting anywhere as his weight kept my movement to a minimum. Within seconds, he had my wrists tied together and strung to the post on the right side of the bed.

"I wasn't leaving. I have nowhere to go, damn it. I just want to get away from you."

"Well, you're getting your wish."

"Let me go, Jasper."

His jaw clenched and he ran his hand through his hair. His gaze trailed up my arms stretched above my head then back to my face.

"Max . . ." He pursed his lips together and I saw the conflict in his expression, the turbulence in his grey eyes like a thunderstorm. "And for the record, I don't trust you either."

"You don't trust anyone," I replied.

He nodded. "True." He turned and walked to the door. "You need to realize when I say something, I mean it."

My fingers curled around the rope. "Xamien hears of this, he'll kill you."

He had his hand on the doorknob. "Good. He's the only one who's earned it."

Shit. I couldn't let him leave. He couldn't leave me here like this. "I'll go after him." I shouted the only thing that might get his attention. "And you can't stop me."

He slowly turned. "What?"

"You heard me."

"Yeah, but it was so stupid I thought I'd misheard."

I pulled on the ropes, trying to slip my hands through. "It's not stupid. It makes sense. Instead of us—"

"You aren't going near him."

"Instead of waiting for him to hunt me, it would be more productive to—"

"More productive?"

"Jasper, just untie me."

"No." He crossed his arms and leaned back against the door. "But please, continue. I'd like to hear your plan to go after a Scar-slash-vampire who is an ancient and can Trace. But no matter what you say, it won't make me untie you."

Our gazes clashed and heat rose inside me. I didn't have a plan; all I had was frustration and . . . desire. He'd tied me up and was going to leave me here, yet instead of being royally pissed off, a sweet ache throbbed between my legs.

Screw it.

"Kiss me," I said. His arrogant expression faltered with a subtle flicker of uncertainty and then it was steady again. "Kiss me."

He scowled and I thought he was going to walk out the door, but suddenly, it was as if all the caged emotions broke free and he came at me.

My fingers curled around the rough rope as he hovered over me for a second, and then he was on top of me. His hand came around my neck, fingers bruising as he squeezed. "You want my cock inside you,

Max? Because a kiss isn't going to do it."

I tried to nod, but he was preventing me from doing anything. "Yes," I managed.

Jasper's grip tightened and air trapped in my lungs, but I didn't fight him, which was a test. His own test to see if I'd trust him to let me go.

Just when I thought I'd pass out, he let me go. As I sucked in air, he stole it with his mouth slamming into mine. I moaned beneath his harsh assault. It was like he wanted to punish me, yet it was filled with need and unrestrained passion.

"Sunshine." His voice vibrated across my lips. It was a soft whisper, and yet there was nothing soft or gentle about him at the moment. It was angry and fierce as his mouth tore into mine, tongue violating, hands tearing at my clothes at the same time. He pulled my shirt up over my arms and left it there then undid my jeans and dragged them down my legs.

He swore when they got caught on my shoes and had to yank them off first.

He took off his shirt and my breath caught as I stared up at his perfectly muscled chest and carved abdomen.

He kicked off his boots and they went flying across the room, hitting the dresser. Something crashed to floor, but Jasper didn't seem to notice, or if he did, he didn't care. He was a wild animal trying to get at his prey, frantic that if he didn't soon, it would disappear on him.

"Jasper. Untie me."

"Fuck, no." He growled and then disappeared into the bathroom where I heard drawers being opened and shut. When he emerged, I saw the condom package in his hand. He ripped it open with his teeth and then finally looked at me, shirt torn open, chest heaving, hands tied above my head.

He froze. Time stood still as we let our desire simmer over us. For those few seconds, we connected on a level neither of us expected.

I knew what he was feeling. I could see it in his smoldering grey eyes; it mirrored my own. It had been trickling from me since the day we met—there was no hiding or running from this.

The cockiness was gone and the anger had dissipated. And I saw the fear of what was between us. It also looked like he was about to run when he glanced at the door.

His brows lowered and there was a twitch in his jaw. I was losing him and despite knowing this was a bad idea, I wanted him. "I'm not going anywhere." I gave him a playful smile as I tugged on the rope. "Kiss me, Jasper. I want you to kiss me and then I want your cock inside me."

His eyes roamed the length of my body and there was anger and tension in him again. I knew what he was seeing—my scars. I closed my eyes, not wanting to see his disgust; afraid he'd walk away and leave me.

The bed sagged and then I gasped as his lips caressed one of the scars on my stomach near my belly button. Then another kiss on the one just under my right breast. His tongue slid over the raised surface and goose bumps scattered as I arched my back into him.

His hands settled on my hips to keep me still as the velvet heat of his tongue kissed every scar across my chest and abdomen and then . . . then he unsnapped my bra and drew my nipple into his mouth and suckled.

"Jasper," I breathed.

His teeth grazed the sensitive peak as if in warning and then he bit down just enough to make me tense and moan. His mouth eased the throbbing pain with the tantalizing sweetness of his tongue before he repeated it on my other nipple.

Desperate to touch him, I pulled hard on the ropes, but his one hand came up and held my wrists down on the pillow. "Don't fight, baby. Not this time." His mouth claimed mine again and it was slow and hinted a teasing playfulness before it became forceful and claiming again.

It was then that I let him have everything—all of me. My need to escape, to have some control over this was washed away by his kiss, his touch and I let him devour me. And it was devouring as he took his time exploring my body, never once hesitating at my damaged skin.

"I'm not good for you." His voice was ragged as he kissed my neck. "But I can't stop."

"I'm sure you say that to all the girls." I tried to make light of it, but Jasper pulled back and his brows knit together.

"No, because I don't care what they think. Just you, Max. Only you." He sat up, his cock pressing against me, so I pushed up, needing him inside me.

"Did you really watch me for months?"

"Yeah." Then he made a strangled groan. "Fuck, angel, I want to hand you the world, yet I can't promise you anything."

What he didn't realize was he had already let me in by telling me that. "I don't want promises." I wanted truth and that was what he gave me by admitting he couldn't promise me anything. "I want you. I've wanted you from the beginning."

Silence. I waited, heart pumping madly, blood raging through my veins and desire throbbing between my legs.

"Jasper?" I was overflowing with anticipation of having him inside me again. And all this talk, listening to his low graveled voice, feeling his hands holding me . . . Jesus, I was sizzling.

The heat in his eyes blazed an inferno ready to assault, to wreak havoc with my body and set each piece of me on fire.

"Max," he murmured, kissing me again.

The denial was over.

But there were no promises.

Just here and now.

His hand reached under my naked thigh and hoisted it up to his shoulder. My muscles stretched and ached, but the pain felt good as he used the bed for leverage and pressed hard into me with his weight.

It didn't matter. I knew pain. I grew up with it and it was part of me. And for a second, I thought of Jasper spanking me and how it turned me on. Was it just him or was it the fight? Both. The shocking pain released a new kind of pleasure and suddenly I wanted that again. That harsh pain and pleasure that awakened me. Made me feel alive.

"Fuck, Max," Jasper moaned against my mouth. "I need inside you. Now."

"Yes," I breathed. He bit my lip hard and I tasted the sweet iron of my blood. I licked my lip just as he slid his hand between my legs and cupped me. I swiftly inhaled as the clench intensified.

"Jesus, baby. You're fuckin' wet." His fingers began to play with me and the urgency to feel his harsh thrusts, his cock filling me had me pressing my hips up, my wrists pulling on the rope that kept me locked in place.

"Do it. Now."

I thought for a second he was going to deny me as his smoldering gaze ran over my swollen lips and then up to my half-lidded eyes. "I don't like being told what to do."

I kept my smile to myself, because I damn well knew that. Jasper hated anyone controlling him. He lived free from everyone, everything including his emotions. "Neither do I."

"Then we're going to have a problem here."

"Yeah," I whispered. "But you won this time."

And that was when he grinned and a piece of me fell—hard. I knew it was wrong. I knew there was nothing good about what I felt for him. Yet he'd chipped away at my resistance and made me want to live again. Made me want to fight for something. For those I cared about. For myself.

He shifted upward and then came back down on me. I screamed at the sudden intrusion of his cock filling me. It was tight and painful. It was like he was tearing me apart and then the pleasure of being pieced back together. "Jesus."

His lips came close to my ear as he said, "My sunshine." And then he thrust and it was him showing me who had the control as he took me.

I didn't care. Nothing mattered except this moment of pure, unrestrained pleasure.

Our bodies met again and again with a harsh, raw passion as he slid in and out of me. His back arched, hips driving forward with a hard rhythm that pushed against my clit.

I opened my eyes just when the orgasm hit me. There was no warning as I screamed out, my hands gripping the coarse rope as my entire body tensed. He pounded harder. Faster. Then he groaned long and deep.

He throbbed inside me as I lay completely still. Trailing small kisses down my neck, I slowly moved my aching legs off Jasper's shoulders, and his cock slid out of me.

He lifted his head and the second our eyes met, it was something more. There was no mistaking this was a primal need, but it was a primal need undeniable by either of us. There was swirling confusion in the depths of his eyes, I had no doubt, matched my own. And maybe this wasn't something we could deny. We'd both fought enough in our lives; maybe it was time to stop fighting.

"You good?" He tucked a strand of hair on my cheek behind my ear.

"Yeah," I replied.

He nodded and then I saw his mouth open as if to say something else, but then he closed it and his brows lowered. He slid off me and headed to the bathroom. I watched as he rolled off the condom and threw it in the garbage.

He came back and leaned over me and his fingers slid up my arms to my wrists and then he undid the rope. The gentle caress of his hands massaging where the ropes had rubbed my skin had me moaning.

He cupped my chin, his thumb stroking back and forth. "He doesn't get you." He leaned closer and kissed me long and slow before he slipped in bed behind me, arms coming around my waist, tugging me in close to his naked, heated body. His breath whispered across my neck as he trickled kisses across my skin. "Just so you know, sunshine, my cock is in you. No other cock, tongue or fingers go anywhere near you."

I stiffened. He knew. He knew Drake had sex with me.

"I hate to think about him touching you." He tightened his hold on me. "I need you to know I'll do whatever it takes to keep you from him. Can you trust that, Max?"

I didn't know if I was wrong for trusting him, but without the risk, there was nothing, and I didn't want *nothing* anymore.

His hand slid up my abdomen to my ribs and I stopped breathing when his finger lightly flicked my nipple; instantly becoming erect. I held my breath as my body reacted to him. He caressed back and forth over my throbbing nipple, his knuckles barely touching.

I half-moaned as I arched closer, desperate for more.

His hand stopped, knuckles resting on the cusp of my nipple. He put his leg over mine and his hard cock pressed against my ass.

"Jasper?"

"Yeah, baby."

"We need another condom."

It ended up being two more. When we finally fell asleep, Jasper cradled me in his arms; our hands linked, resting on my abdomen.

thirteen

Jasper

I WOKE ON MY BACK with her cheek on my chest and her palm resting on my abdomen. The sheet was down at my waist and just covered her breasts. Her hair was tucked behind her ear except for a few strands that escaped and curtained across her nose and mouth.

I'd fucked her hard, soft and lazy, and then . . . then she fucked me. I never wanted it that way. I liked control, but her straddling me, the slow grind of her hips and the ecstasy on her face . . . it was worth giving her that control.

I was royally fucked. Should've known that from the beginning. Christ, I *had* known but I played it off as lust, tried to act as if it was nothing. Convince myself she was just another chick.

But she never was.

How the fuck did I get here? To wanting her more than I should. To craving every inch of her, needing to hear her voice or watch her move. I couldn't fuckin' breathe without her.

It was suffocating and was fucking everything up because not only would we have Drake to worry about, but Waleron and Adrian. I didn't even want to consider Xamien's reaction to everything. He was going to kill all of us.

It was too late now. The dice had been thrown and I had to deal with the consequences.

I slipped from the bed, careful not to wake her, pulled on my jeans and walked out into the living room. My brother was sipping his coffee, leaning against the mantel. I'd heard him arrive back last night when I was getting up to snag a third condom from the washroom.

Grabbing a mug, I reached for the carafe of coffee and poured the steaming liquid into it. I heard him approach, but didn't bother looking as I set my mug down at the kitchen table and pulled out a chair.

"You plan on sticking around or fucking off before she wakes up?"

I sat, curling my hands around the mug. "Fuck you, Holden. I'm not that much of an ass." Yeah, I was. I fucked plenty of women and did just that. She deserved better than that. She deserved a hell of a lot better than me. Didn't mean I was letting her go.

Holden pulled out the chair beside me, sat, and then stretched out his long legs, crossing them at the ankle. "You weren't at one time. You are now."

Yeah. And I never gave a fuck. Until now. Until her.

Now, I'd told off Adrian which rolled over into Waleron and neither were Scars to fuck with. I didn't know what the fuck I was doing. I always had a plan . . . now I didn't. All I knew was that the job was never a job. It was a way to get close to her. To make sure she was protected and no one else got near her. That was more crucial than ever.

I put my hand on the hilt of my knife when Holden reached into his side pocket. Max was right; I didn't trust anyone, not even family. Holden and I were inseparable as kids until the night I fucked up and Beth paid the price. Holden hated me ever since and I didn't blame him. Last time we saw one another, he called me a self-destructing fucked-up, cold bastard. I'd agree with the cold bastard part, but I called it self-survival.

"Easy, Wasp," he said, pulling out a cigarette which he didn't light; instead, he just rolled it back and forth between his thumb and finger.

My brother started calling me Wasp when I was a kid and tried to take a nest down by hitting it with a stick. Nest fallen, the swarm of pissed-off wasps came right for me. I ran right into the pigs' pen and dove head first into their swill. Escaped without a single sting, which, as a ten-year-old, was something to be proud of. "Fuck, man, you're worse than the last time I saw you."

I snorted. No, I was just feeling emotions I shouldn't and had to get my shit together. My edges were peeling away and she was under my skin so tight I couldn't breathe without her.

I'd thought after fucking her the first time, the obsession would ease, but it fuckin' heightened. I couldn't even look at her walking up the mountain or I would've thrown her against a tree and fucked her over and over again like some teenage boy instead of an immortal assassin. Not a place I should've even been thinking about fucking a woman when this mountain had all kinds of memories attached to it.

Then when I saw her cold and shivering . . . all I wanted to do was hold her in my arms and make it better, make everything fuckin' better. And that type of thinking was what made her dangerous to me. It scared the fuck out of me because I was acting irrationally and irrational got you killed and worse; it would land her right back where she started—in Drake's hands.

But that was never supposed to happen. I was chosen because I'd make certain that wouldn't happen. I'd said I'd do whatever it took to keep Drake from ever using her to get his Ink back.

An Ink that would stop at nothing to destroy every living being. I knew the penalties if I didn't do my job. It was catastrophic and yet . . . there was no fuckin' way in hell I'd do it.

"So, is this the girl Drake's after?"

I stiffened and my head snapped up to look at him. "You heard?"

"Xamien and Waleron have every Scar out hunting him. Yeah, I heard, but what I can't figure out is why you brought her here. You hate this place. You hate me. You hate our Talde. Fuck, you hate everyone."

I didn't. I tried to hate Holden, but the truth was I stayed away from him because I did care about him. My tainted shit would never touch him and yet here I was.

"You want us to leave?"

"Fuck, bro. I have no right to tell you to leave. But I haven't heard from you in ten years, then all of a sudden you show up here with the pretense that you need a place to hang for a bit. That's bullshit. If you don't want to be found, you won't be. So, what's the deal? Why are you here?"

From the moment I took the job, I knew I'd bring Max here. It was the only place I could think of that hadn't been touched by my job.

"Needed a place few have Traced before." That was true. I doubted Drake had ever been here and it would give us time to escape if I heard him coming.

Holden was taller than me, but only by an inch and broader in the shoulders, more like a muscled, fit linebacker while I was a quarterback. His dark walnut hair hung over his ears, in light curls he was forever pushing back from his face. He was a Scar Tracker and could track scents like a bloodhound. He'd used it to find me when I fucked off in the night to go to the pubs. Then when I was sixteen, he used it to track me when I was left hanging to rot. But it had been too late for our sister.

"Adrian's pissed."

My back stiffened. Fuck, Adrian must have called Holden when he couldn't get a hold of me since I destroyed my phone. "When isn't he?" Holden often spoke to Adrian to get info on human-trafficking rings. Holden's Talde focused mostly on children being kidnapped and taken for reasons I didn't want to know about. The Talde went in and got them out.

Holden's brow furrowed. "You screw up a job?"

"About to." My job had been simple. Now it was complicated.

"What's going on, Wasp?"

A whole lot of fucked up.

Holden sighed. "Whatever you're thinking, don't do it."

I shoved my mug away, the taste now bitter in my mouth. "Don't do what? You have no idea what's going through my head."

Holden abruptly got up, shaking his head. "I do. I know exactly what you're thinking. You're my brother. I was there, remember? Do you think I don't know what you've done all these years? Trying to erase what happened by not giving a shit about anyone." I looked down at my feet. "Jesus, that's it. You care about her, don't you? You like this girl."

I got up so fast, my chair toppled over backward. "They should've fuckin' hunted him down the day they found her. Xamien and his Talde should've known the place wasn't just a hideout for vampires." I knew what I was saying was illogical, but after being with her, holding her, kissing each scar, I wanted to crucify the bastard. "Jesus, Holden. She has scars . . ." Scars I'd licked and kissed and touched, trying in some crazy fucked-up way to make them better. Make her better. "He fuckin' hurt her," I whispered in a ragged tone.

Holden stepped forward to put his hand on my shoulder, but I jerked away from it. From him. "And you're not responsible for what Drake did. Just like you're not responsible for what happened to Beth. No matter what you did or didn't do, Wasp, they were going to kill Beth. I know what you're thinking. You want to go after this sick bastard. Fuck, you hunted those vampires for twenty years until each and every one of them was dead. Pissed off a lot of vampires, too." And it was worth it. Worth the sacrifice of all the lives I killed in order to get to them. I had no regrets about what I'd done. "You care about her, then stay here and do your job. Protect her and let the others find him."

"Protect her?" I huffed, shaking my head as I met his eyes, coldness seeping into me as I spoke the words I knew would change everything. "No, Holden you have it wrong. I was hired to kill her."

Holden tensed. "What?"

I clenched my jaw and curled my hands into fists. "Anyone can protect her, hide her away someplace. Think about it. Why me?" I sneered. "Because I'm the only fuckin' one who would kill her if there was a chance Drake could take her."

"Fuck." Holden staggered back, his hand in his hair as he sat back down on the chair. "And Xamien knows?"

"Fuck no. Xamien would never consent to anything like this and that's why he's been kept in the dark."

"But Waleron knows?"

I snorted. "Who the fuck do you think set it up? He'd never risk a multitude of lives for the sake of one." Waleron had suspected Max's ability six months ago when Max had touched his Ink and calmed it. According to Adrian, Waleron didn't think much of it until word spread that Drake was looking for a young girl with scars on her who was a Healer. "Drake is after her ability and it's damn vital he doesn't get her to use it on him—ever."

I picked up quiet movement in Max's room. The mattress creaked as she got up then walked across the hardwood floors. I looked up as she came out of the bedroom and walked down the hall. My heart pounded hard against my ribcage as if it was attempting to break free so it could race over to her, beat next to hers.

Jesus Christ. I was fucked. Cemented. That was what it felt like. All this time, I thought I was chipping away at her shield when she'd been chipping away at mine.

I cared. I fuckin' cared. Holden was right. She was in me and it wouldn't matter how many times I had her; I'd want her again.

"Word is she's a Healer and that's why Drake wants her back. But that isn't a reason for Waleron to want to kill her, Jasper."

"It isn't."

"So what the fuck?"

She was in the doorway and our eyes locked. She didn't smile like I'd hoped. Fuck, the girl never laughed. I hated that. I wanted to hear her laugh while she lay in my arms and I teased her.

Her steady gaze slid from mine to Holden's. "Because I can heal his Ink."

Holden looked at me, brows drawn together. "Whose Ink, yours? Or Drake's?"

I closed my eyes, lowering my head.

Fuck.

fourteen

Max

"YOURS?" MY STOMACH CHURNED AS my eyes shot to
Jasper. He slowly raised his head and I knew. I knew in that
second he was aware of my ability to heal Inks. He'd known
all along. I felt as if I was rolling down the mountain out of control, my
limbs flailing to latch onto something.

Jasper's Ink was dead. His tatted arms had no scars, no cuts. I'd
have seen them when we were together. But Inks could die from other
reasons.

"Max." Jasper rose and started toward me.

I held up my hand to stop him and he did, although he scowled and
clenched his jaw and I knew he didn't want to. "Tell me I'm wrong." I
ignored, who I suspected was his brother, watching us. "Tell me what
I'm thinking isn't true."

He remained unmoving, mouth pulled tight, eyes drained of playfulness and the speck of darkness spreading across the glistening surface. His silence made me angrier because I wanted an excuse. I wanted him to tell me it wasn't true. God, I wanted him to lie if he had to.
And that made me angrier that I'd be so pathetic to want him to lie to
me. But after last night . . . I didn't want to lose what we shared and I

was. All of it was crumbling and falling down the mountain with me.

"What? You're afraid of telling me? Man the fuck up, Jasper."

His brother quietly got up and walked out the front door. Jasper stayed where he was, watching me as I pieced it together. With his silence came the truth. He didn't need to say anything; it fit perfectly.

Why he was chosen to protect me when he was an assassin not a babysitter.

Why he cared that I stayed alive.

Why he had asked about my Ink.

He knew.

He knew what I was capable of and wanted to use me to heal his Ink.

Just like Drake.

I swallowed, raising my chin, unblinking as I met his unyielding stare. I wouldn't be the one to falter and I wouldn't be used. I'd been used for six years by Drake and then locked myself away from living.

"Max." His accent was more pronounced as his voice sliced through me.

I wanted to run. To do what I was good at and conceal my emotions behind a shield of ice, but he'd torn through that and given me a taste of living, of feeling and despite the hurt that came with it, I wanted my life back and yeah, I wanted the truth—needed it. "Don't you dare lie to me."

His eyes never left mine as he strode across the room, the usual cocky swagger gone, but still self-assured. This time I didn't stop him, and from his fierce expression I didn't think he'd listen anyway.

He stopped inches away and my breath locked in my chest as I felt him. I felt him, damn it. He was in me. It was too late to stop any hurt as the web of betrayal spread through me.

Was that why he had sex with me? Why he'd kissed me? Why he'd held me in his arms when I broke?

"No. I see it in your eyes, Max. Don't even go there." He grabbed my forearms, fingers curling into me and I wanted to fall into his arms and . . . cry. I wanted to cry and that made me hate him more. "Stop." He shook me once, fingers bruising. "I slept with you because I wanted you. Fuck, I still do. It has nothing to do with . . ." He swore beneath his breath then let me go and ran his hand through his hair as his expression tightened as if in pain. "The payment."

It was like he punched me in the stomach and I was winded as he said the words. His payment wasn't money; it was my ability.

I reached out and placed my hand on the wall for support. I bit the insides of my cheeks as the tears welled. I was being used in some deal. I didn't even know anyone else knew about my ability and they used it to convince Jasper to protect me from Drake. How many more lies? What else was he keeping from me?

"Damn it, Max. It's what I do. I've never pretended otherwise. I just . . . I didn't know that . . ."

His voice trailed off and I closed my eyes, unable to look at the man I thought was . . . different. My expectations had been too high and I'd thought . . . I'd seen something else in him. Felt the melting of his outer core to reveal someone hurting. Hiding. But it wasn't an outer core. It was his whole core.

I wanted him gone. "Then let's do it."

"What?"

"Why wait until your two weeks are up. That's when I'll have to give you—the payment—for saving my life for two weeks, right? That's the deal?" I took my hand away from the wall. "Why wait. Let's get it done and then you can go on your merry fucking way." I glared, meeting his startled eyes. "What? You suddenly growing a conscience? We both know that's impossible."

He stood frozen, muscles flexed, hands at his side curled into fists. But it wasn't anger; it was shock and I wanted to silently cheer, but nothing could make me happy at the moment. I knew he was bad news. I knew what he was like. I fucking knew he was tainted, yet I had seen more in him. At least I thought I had.

"What? You want more? Did the deal include sex with me afterward? Well, you got it before. You don't get to touch me again. You don't get to protect me. And you sure as hell don't get to use me again." I shoved my palms into his chest and he staggered back a step, but he didn't make a move to touch me. "I'll heal your Ink and then you walk away. That's my fucking deal."

I heard the front door open, but kept my focus on Jasper. I saw the cavalcade of emotions whirlpooling in his eyes as my words hit him. The rage mixed with disbelief and . . . pain. I didn't think Jasper could feel that emotion any longer, but I was glad. I wanted Jasper to hurt.

My past had messed me up, too, but I didn't hurt those around me. I didn't use people.

His tone was harsh as he said, "I'm not walking away."

I shoved him again, this time with both hands, but he'd been ready for it and didn't move. "Then I will." I pushed by him, but he grabbed my arm, pulling me around. I put out my hands to stop from crashing into him and they rested over his heart. It wasn't the usual steady beat. It was frantic.

"You're jumping to conclusions. And you're not leaving." His eyes flashed black and his jaw clenched. He always had this power in him, this overwhelming control over the room and I hated that I wanted to bend to him. "Things changed. It's not like that now. Fuck, it was never like that."

I didn't want to hear excuses. I wanted to get this over with. "Where's your Ink?" He refused to answer and I raised my voice. "Where the fuck is your Ink?"

"It's on his left shoulder," his brother said from the doorway. "On his back."

"Fuck you, Holden." Jasper swung around taking me with him as he glared at his brother. "Stay out of this."

His brother leaned against the front door and crossed his arms over his broad chest. From my quick glance, he was making certain of two things, that I didn't leave and neither did Jasper.

I wasn't stupid and had no intention to leave until I had a plan. "Take off your shirt," I said. At any other time, I knew Jasper's usual response would've been a cocky smirk, but all I got was a scowl with lowered brows and the crease between them.

"We are not doing this." Jasper shot a glare at his brother then put his hands on my waist and slid them down to grasp my hips. "Max, I told you, shit changed. It was a job. Now, it's not. Shit, it wasn't from the beginning. I took it to protect you."

I lowered my head. "Yeah." They were words with no meaning. I didn't trust anything he said.

"Sunshine." A sharp pain hit my chest at his soft drawl. "Fuck. I took the deal and . . ." He grabbed either side of my face and forced my head up so I'd look at him. "Max, I didn't know I'd fuckin' care.

I haven't cared about anything for a goddamn century." I averted my eyes and he tightened his grip, fingers curling into my hair. "Jesus. Don't pull away from me." His tone quivered and softened as he said, "Please, Max."

I wanted to believe him, and maybe there was a sliver of truth in his words because I'd felt it. But it didn't change the fact Jasper had been using me for my ability.

"Tell her the rest." Holden's voice abruptly cut through the air. "Tell her or I will."

Jasper's hands fell away and my heart skipped a beat with my breath catching in my throat. "What?"

Jasper stepped away, the color draining from his face. Oh, God, it was bad. Worse. I clutched at the denim of my jeans on either side of me as I waited for the wrecking ball to do its final destruction.

Jasper looked at the floor for a second and then he took a deep breath and met my eyes again. "If Drake got too close, I was supposed to kill you."

My breath hitched as I shook my head. No. It couldn't be true. Xamien . . . Xamien wouldn't let that happen. But suddenly I was uncertain of anything and I was drifting away into the abyss of deceit. I was drowning in the depths as I was yanked under by the force of the waves, pulled into the darkness where I was safe.

"Baby, it's not—"

Anger flashed and I went for him. He must have seen it coming, but he didn't do anything to stop me as I slapped him across the face, his head jerked to the side from the force. The sound echoed in the silence of the room and then I was punching his chest as emotions I'd kept locked away for years suddenly released.

It was like gravity pulling me down further and further as I hit him repeatedly. I'd slept with a guy who'd been hired to kill me. I'd lain in his arms. I developed feelings for him. And all this time, he'd known that he'd kill me if he had to.

"You're a cold son-of-a-bitch," I yelled as I completely lost it. "Do you get off sleeping with women you're hired to kill? I bet you do. I bet you—"

An arm looped around my waist and dragged me backward away from Jasper. "Go, damn it," Holden ordered. I struggled against the hard body holding me, my mind spinning and every emotion I'd locked away suddenly set free as I cracked wide open.

Bleeding.

Draining.

Drowning.

The words kept repeating in my head. Jasper was hired to kill me if things went bad. Xamien never said anything. They all knew about my ability and they wanted me dead rather than end up in Drake's hands.

Deceit.

Lies.

Betrayal.

"Xamien didn't know. He still doesn't," Jasper said, and then turned and walked out the front door.

I pushed Holden away from me, staggering back until I crashed into the wall. Sobs racked my body as the anger turned to pain and I collapsed onto the floor. I thought I was strong. I thought I was stronger, but I felt like I did living with Drake. An object. Used and beaten. Maybe this time it wasn't physical wounds, but this was worse. Jasper had reeled me in, made me feel safe and strong, and alive before he cast me out into an ocean of starving sharks.

I lay on the floor for a long time. The crying stopped and the cold numbness slowly seeped back in. I didn't open my eyes as arms lifted me up and carried me to the bedroom, and then lay me in the bed. I knew it was Jasper. I'd always know when he was near. I had right from the beginning. And I knew he never left the bedroom, but stayed sitting on the window ledge. It was then I finally slept.

"Baby, wake up."

So cold. Why was it so cold? I couldn't stop shaking. I tried to pry my eyes open but they wouldn't open. Drake hovered over me sneering with his hand outstretched.

"No. No, don't touch me." I didn't want this.

Don't make me.

His arms came around me and I screamed, pushing at him, struggling to get away. I had to fight. I needed to fight him. I hadn't fought him last time. But I was stronger now. I wouldn't let him win.

"Max. Wake the fuck up!"

I jolted at the sound of his voice and my eyes flew open. "Jasper?" He had his arms around me and we were on the floor, me between his legs as he cradled me to him. "Jasper." I tried to escape his arms as everything came flooding back, one nightmare replaced with another.

"*Shh*, relax. You're not going anywhere." His tone hardened as he whispered in my ear, "And neither am I." He held me tightly to him and his warmth seeped into my trembling body. I didn't want to feel comfort from him, but I did and that made it worse. I was being comforted by the man hired to kill me.

"*I'd never kill you.*" Jasper's words intimately caressed my mind and it was as though he was inside me. "*Fuck, I could never hurt you, baby.*"

But he had.

I closed my eyes as he locked me to him, refusing to let me go. My fingers clutched at his shirt, and his heart beat solid and steady beneath my hand.

"I got you." His gentle words pulled me into him, despite trying to fight it. A finger stroked back my damp hair from my face and tucked it behind my ear. "I can't take back what I did, Max. It was a job and I didn't know . . ." He sighed and tugged me a little closer. "I didn't know I'd care this much."

I searched his words for the truth, but I didn't trust myself. I didn't trust him. "It doesn't matter now." Because it was too late. Anything that had begun to build had been ripped apart and stomped on.

"No," Jasper said abruptly. I jerked at the fierceness in his tone. "It's not too late."

He'd read my thoughts. Oh, God, he'd found a way through the cracks. I pulled against him, shoving at his chest. "Don't you dare. You don't have the right to read my thoughts. You don't have the—"

He kissed me.

At first I was shocked as his aggressive mouth met mine, one hand holding the back of my head to prevent my escape. My lips were soft against his, the twinge between my legs pulsating, my stomach whirling with flutters of winged angels.

Then sanity stabbed me in the chest and I tried to yank back, but his grip was relentless and he titled my head and forced me to accept him. To let him back in.

His lips vibrated beneath mine as he spoke. "Please." It was a haggard pleading that tore another piece off me because whatever had been happening between us was lost to the murky lies.

I went limp against him, mouth unmoving as he kissed me. He stopped and rested his forehead against mine as he breathed heavily. My lips tingled and felt swollen. I ran my tongue over them, immediately tasting him and regretting it.

"She followed me one night to the river where I'd go swimming sometimes. We weren't allowed to leave our Talde at night because of the threat of vampires and we . . . well, we weren't strong enough yet." His voice was quiet and unsteady. "Holden used to get so pissed at me when I went out at night. He was always the practical one and I hated rules."

His hand slid down my back and settled on my hip. "I didn't think there was any harm in her coming with me. There'd been no sign of vampires in months. I was pretty . . . confident in my Sounding ability and I thought . . . I thought I was strong enough at sixteen. I wasn't." He stumbled over the last words and cleared his throat, his hand tensing on me for a second before he started talking again. "I didn't even make it to the river before I heard her muffled scream from behind me. My world collapsed hearing that sound. It shredded me, but it was nothing compared to what happened over the next few days." He glanced at me and tears filled his eyes, but they didn't fall, just pooled in his bottom lids. "They wanted to know where Lillian, a really powerful Healer, was. I wouldn't tell them. I'd never give in. But then her screams . . . my sister's cries . . ." He dropped his head forward and his voice lowered. "Three days. I told them where Lillian's Talde was after three days. They promised to let Beth go, but I knew they wouldn't. Fuck, I knew they wouldn't and I told them anyway because I hoped maybe . . . fuck, maybe they would just kill me and let her go."

I should've got up and walked way, but I didn't. I sat in his lap as he told me the devastating story of what happened to his ten-year-old sister. The torture he endured, the suffering as he hung from the tree for days, listening to her cries and begging. Then his sister being tossed like garbage into a shallow grave right in front of him. The laughter as they kicked dirt over her lifeless body. "My parents . . . their grief . . . it ruined them. I had to leave. I couldn't watch what I'd done to them anymore. I never saw them again and I spent the next years hunting the vampires who killed Beth. And every day I did, I cared less and less about . . . everything. It was easier that way. To never care about anything . . . anyone again." His hand found mine and he linked our fingers. "I've lived that way every single day since—until you."

I had no words and I didn't think I could speak them as his story settled into me. I knew what Beth had suffered. Maybe my story was different, but I knew the fear she must have felt before she died. We'd been the same age, taken from those we loved, our home.

But his story didn't change anything.

I crawled out of his lap and he let me. I stood on shaky legs and looked down at him sitting on the floor looking completely . . . vulnerable with sadness misted in his eyes and his mouth drawn downward. But it didn't matter anymore.

"You're Xamien's friend. He trusts you." I tilted my chin up as I thought of the day I met Jasper. "I wasn't a stranger, Jasper. You met me six months ago and yet still you took a deal to use me for my ability. A job with the possibility that you'd have to kill me."

Jasper's face blanched and I heard his sharp inhale. "Max, fuck. I wouldn't have done it—"

I snorted and I raised my brows. "That's not good enough. I'm sorry for what happened to your sister. But sharing why you're the bastard you are . . . doesn't change the fact." I spun on my heel and walked out of the bedroom.

fifteen

Jasper

I BENT MY KNEES, RESTED my arms on them and hung my head, closing my eyes. I fucked up. I put off telling her the truth about the job and what I was feeling for her until it was too late to fix what I'd done.

She was right. It wasn't just her I'd fucked over; it was Xamien. Despite what I tried to ignore, he was my friend. Was being the optimal word because Xamien would kill me when he heard about this.

"Jesus." I put my hands in my hair as the overwhelming need to go after her hit me. I knew she hadn't left; I could hear her on the porch swing as it creaked back and forth. Shit, I couldn't stop my ability from honing in on her wherever the hell she was.

How the fuck did this get so out of my control. When I met her six months ago, I'd known then something was different. I stalked her for fuck's sake. When I was away from her, it was as if I'd left my heart behind so it could stay with her.

But I fought it. I pretended it wasn't more than lust when I knew it was.

"Would you have killed her?"

I jerked my head up, seeing Holden standing in the doorway. I was so focused on Max I blocked all other sounds out. He had his hands in his pockets, and for once, no judgment in his expression. I even thought I saw a flicker of sympathy.

"No." I may have tried to convince myself otherwise, but she . . . Max made me feel as if I was breathing pure, untainted air. She fed me the life I'd submerged into the earth with Beth. I took the job to be closer to her, to protect her, and at the same time, my self-destructive side took it to try and convince myself I didn't care about her. That I could do the job and walk away with my scattered fragmented pieces.

What I hadn't realized was Max had been slowly repairing me without me even knowing it. I didn't give a fuck about my Ink being healed and I took the job so no other bastard would kill her.

I took it to make her mine.

None of it mattered now.

"Stop thinking of what you've done and fix it." I snorted and Holden's lips pulled downward with that disappointed glower he would always give me when I fucked up as a kid. "It's salvageable, bro, and she's worth it, isn't she? Worth trying. Worth whatever it takes?"

She's worth everything. "Fuck yeah."

"Give her some time then talk to her. Not your bullshit, Wasp, really talk to her."

My head snapped up as my ability picked up someone approaching the house. I jumped to my feet and was shoving past my brother when he called, "It's just Guise. He's staying a few days."

I made it into the living room just as the front door open. Guise stopped and we stared at one another for a minute. I hadn't spoken to him or seen him since that day he and Holden found me; watched me dig for Beth.

He chin-lifted to me. "Wasp." He strode into the kitchen and pulled a mug from the cupboard then poured steaming coffee into it.

And typical Guise, he didn't make a big deal of the reunion.

Guise was a Visionary, meaning he had the ability to see real damn far. The odd thing was he wore glasses, light rimmed, subtle and sitting casually on the bridge of his nose. They made him look intelligent and warm when Guise was anything but.

The Scar was clean cut, dressed immaculately and there wasn't a tattoo visible, although he had to have his Ink somewhere on his body.

Guise lived with one purpose in mind—kill. He may do it quietly and with finesse, but when he slit a man's throat or decapitated a body, it was as if he was cutting up a watermelon. Smooth, easy and without concern. Unlike me though, Guise didn't take money for his kills.

Guise was also my brother's best friend. Was mine at one time too when we were kids, although he'd been much older than me. Adrian gave me updates on him and Holden, whether I wanted them or not. Over the years, I just accepted the info and there was a slight wave of relief when I heard something; it meant they were alive.

The swing stopped rocking and Max's weight shifted. I heard every step she made as she walked across the porch to the door. She walked in the house and Guise's eyes roamed the length of her. I watched as the corners of his mouth tilted upward, then the barely noticeable straightening of his back.

No fuckin' way. A low growl simmered inside me and I curled my hands into fists. I had no misconceptions of what Guise looked like to a woman—muscled, tall, dark hair like mine, and stark defined features that softened with the glasses—a costume of disguise. Exactly, how he got his nickname. Nothing was as it appeared.

The air shifted when Max saw me and froze. Her red rimmed eyes glared and every second she looked at me was like she was squeezing her hand around my heart and attempting to rip it apart.

I deserved it. Shit, I deserved a hell of a lot worse for all the shit I'd done in my life.

And Max . . . Max was made up of all goodness. But she was also made up of contradictions. Quiet and subtle on the outer edges while attempting to keep herself locked behind her shielded mind, but beneath that—fire. And I'd felt the burn of that fire blazing with her unrestrained anger. But I'd rather have her anger than the closed-off girl I'd met six months ago.

I watched Max, every muscle stiff, pulsing and eager to respond to what I was fighting—myself. Guise walked toward her holding out his hand to pass her a coffee, the perfect fuckin' gentleman and yet . . . Guise was the perfect deception. He'd slip his knife between her breast bones without a backward glance or regret if she was a criminal who hurt the innocent.

Just like I would. Usually. Normally. Fuck, I wasn't so sure if I could do it anymore and in a way it made me want to do it just to prove that I could. But the thought of never having the chance with her . . . I'd already lost her.

"Thank you." She nodded to Guise and her voice drifted across the twelve-foot space between us like a sparrow on the wings of a gentle breeze. The way she said thank you hit me and it had my legs already running toward her. And it was totally fucked up because I wanted to drag her back into the bedroom and fuck her until she forgave me.

"You're welcome . . . Max," Guise emphasized her name in a slow drawl.

I cleared my throat as it tightened. I wanted to shove my fist down his throat then beat the shit out of him. It would be a crapshoot as to who would win, but if he touched her—

"Leave it, bro. He knows you're watching and is trying to get you riled. Payback for throwing away his friendship for the last century." Holden's voice held a deep, resonated tone as he came up beside me. It was a warning that calmed the roar fucking with my control.

I sighed and dropped my gaze from Max. "I can't fuckin' breathe, Holden."

"Yeah, it's called giving a shit. Welcome to the living." He patted me on the back. "She needs time, Jasper." Max sat at the table and curled her legs up beneath her and then lifted the mug. I held my breath, waiting for it. She pursed her lips and then lightly blew on the steaming coffee. I saw the subtle tremble in her hands and knew it was me who caused that. Not Drake. I made her tremble and it wasn't in a good way.

When she lowered the coffee, Max looked at me and our eyes met. Then my cock jerked and I shifted my position to ease the discomfort. Jesus, I wanted all of her and I didn't like Guise sitting near her at the table. I didn't like that he was quietly talking to her. I went to take a step toward them when Holden grabbed my arm.

"She's already broken . . . don't finish the job."

I hesitated, unable to look away, captivated and bound by her. I knew words weren't enough for Max. And there was only one way I had a chance at bringing her back to me.

"Keep her safe." I turned to go back down the hall to grab my bag and then leave out the back door.

146

"Whoa. Jasper. You're fucked up right now. Don't be stupid. I know what you're thinking, but it's not the only way."

"Words mean nothing to her. I'm doing what I should've done the second Adrian offered me the job." Because I'd known then that I loved her or at least was falling in love with her. I started to walk down the hall, but Holden followed me.

"What? Get yourself killed. Fuck, Wasp. You're not indestructible. You can't go after an ancient Scar alone. How are you going to find him?"

I snorted. "Not an ancient Scar, he's a hybrid ancient Scar, but one thing I've excelled at over the years . . . is maintain a reputation for being an asshole."

"What are you thinking?"

"Drake will have heard of me. He knows what I do for a living and he knows I'll turn for enough money."

Holden shook his head. "I don't believe you'd ever do that, Wasp."

I shrugged. "Maybe not now. But he doesn't know that."

Holden grabbed my arm and yanked me to a stop. He pulled his cell phone from his pocket and passed it to me. "I think this is a mistake."

"You can think whatever you want."

"At least . . . Jasper your Ink. You can get her to—"

"No!" I threw his arm off me. "Never. I'll never have her touch my Ink." I stopped myself from looking over at her one last time, knowing I might not leave if I did and then I walked away.

sixteen

Max

I GOT UP FROM THE table when Jasper disappeared down the hall with Holden. The Scar, Guise, had been saying something about his Talde and what they do, but I'd been focused on Jasper and hadn't heard a word he said.

"He's leaving," Guise said.

That got my attention. I abruptly looked at him, casually sitting back, his long legs stretched out, ankles crossed. "Leaving? Where?"

He shrugged, glanced past me and gave a subtle nod. I turned and Holden stood looking at me, his expression solemn with the edges of his mouth pulled down and half-lidded tired eyes. I felt the slow spread of unease.

"Jasper?" It was all I could manage at the moment with my throat tight and fear skidding into me. I didn't want to care, but I did. I didn't want to go after him, but my legs were already running in my head.

Guise got up.

Holden approached.

"Tell me." I directed my words at Holden.

"He's gone after Drake."

My heart crashed through its protective barrier and dropped to the pit of my stomach. "No." I shook my head. "No. He can't." Drake would kill him without a second thought. He was an ancient, his abilities ten times stronger than a regular Scar. And now he was a vampire with the unquenchable thirst for blood. His cruelty knew no bounds and I had the scars to prove it. A slow precision to his method of destruction in order to break you to his will. He wouldn't just kill Jasper—he'd rip through his mind and take every morsel he could use against him and then torture him until he got what he wanted.

And in this case it was me.

I'd done everything I could by remaining quiet and alone at Xamien's. I'd made myself invisible, kept to myself. Hid my abilities from the Scars so there was never a chance Drake would hear about me. Discover where I was.

Never kill anyone I cared about again.

But it wasn't enough.

I did what my mom wanted. I did what I was supposed to do and never healed his Ink. They didn't die for nothing. For six years I survived Drake. Finally free of him, I had to stay hidden so he'd never find me again and kill more people.

But Jasper found me. He'd dug and dug until he unearthed the trapped emotions and I finally felt—alive. And I liked it. I liked fighting with him; I liked feeling the heat between us. I liked the teasing and the lightness in my chest whenever he was with me.

Jasper did that.

I felt something.

Holden's large hand slid into mine and gave a reassuring squeeze, before letting go. "What are his chances?"

My breath locked in my throat and I couldn't swallow as my throat tightened with the words. "There isn't a chance." Tears welled up in my eyes and my throat tightened. "And Adrian is right," I said. "I'm too dangerous alive."

Holden abruptly grabbed my shoulders. "No. Not an option. We'll find another way."

I stiffened my spine and raised my chin as I let the cold rush over me. "There's me."

seventeen

Jasper

I FOUND HOLDEN'S CAR HIDDEN in the side of the hill with a shitload of brush all over it. I yanked each branch off with frustration. Ever since I left the cabin, I had the urge to go running back.

To beg. Beg her to forgive me.

Jesus, it was pathetic. I was pathetic.

The paint chipped off the roof as I dragged a heavy branch across it and whipped it aside. I watched it fly through the air, land hard and roll down the mountain out of control.

Like me. I felt like that branch, unable to stop the caring. Bombarded with emotions I hadn't let myself feel in a century. Maybe it was partially because of where we were. Here in the mountains where I swore I'd never come again.

My heart sat in the pit of my stomach, no longer steady and rhythmic but all fucked up and stealing my calmness. I didn't like leaving her. But I had no choice. The risk was too great that Adrian would find someone else to do what I had been hired for. Drake had to be taken out before that happened. And Holden and Guise were the best to keep her safe.

I was betting I had two days. Two fuckin' days to hunt down the bastard who hurt her. I wanted nothing more than to cause destruction, but there was way more to this than I cared to admit.

I loved her. I fuckin' cared and I loved her and I had to fix this. I couldn't lose her.

I wanted to hold her in my arms while I slept. I wanted to watch her walk across a room toward me knowing she was mine. I wanted to be the one to make her laugh. See the flash of brilliance in her eyes as she tilted her head back and released the sound trapped inside her.

I loved her fight; the way she tried to hide it behind her soft words in the beginning and then . . . and then her smartass remarks back at me. I thought of when she purchased two rooms that first night, her tiny smirk and lift of her chin as she strode away from me. Defiant and cute.

She hadn't been scared of my reaction. She wasn't scared of me, but she sure as hell was terrified of Drake.

"Jesus." I smashed both fists onto the roof of the car. I knew what I had to do. I had more connections in the underworld than anyone and it would be easy to get word to Drake that I wanted to meet him to make a deal. My reputation would make it possible. Anyone who'd heard of me knew I'd do anything for money. And I was betting on Drake knowing that. What might give me away was Drake being a Scar Reflector and able to read and feel emotions. If he discovered my feelings for Max, he'd see right through my plan.

My plan. Fuck. It was a risk . . . no, it was a high-risk that had been tapping at my mind since the moment I found out he was a vampire. I didn't know I'd go after him until now, but I was alive because I never stopped thinking every scenario in my head. And fuck, I wanted to kill the bastard who took Max . . . no, Breanna . . . the little ten-year-old girl who saw her mother die, her entire Talde and then broke her for six years. Six fuckin' years.

He crushed her soul until she buried every part of who she was, and that girl . . . that girl with the defiance, the fight, the strength and the gentleness that soothed all of it with her beauty. Fuck, she'd trusted me. Gave herself to me and there were no words to repair the damage I'd seen in her eyes.

Words wouldn't repair it and I didn't deserve another chance with her, but I'd take away the fear she tried to hide from everyone by killing Drake. I knew he was stronger than me. Fuck, he was a hybrid, an ancient who could Trace. He was alive because he was intelligent as hell and despite the Goddess killing his Ink to make him weak, he'd become strong again. Drake would never stop until he got what he wanted.

But I knew how his mind worked because I'd encountered the cruelest unsavory fuckers in this world, and there was one way he'd trust me. I'd have to become like him—a hybrid. A vampire.

I folded into the car and drove down the treacherous dirt path, and the further I went the more anxious I became. It was as if my cells were running frantically through my body searching for her . . . for Max.

I took out Holden's cell and scrolled the contacts until I found Xamien. It did a half ring before he answered. "Holden?"

"Jasper."

"Max okay?"

"She's safe. For now."

Xamien was quiet, but I could hear the tension in his breathing.

"Waleron with you?"

"Yeah and Balen. We've picked up the trail not far from you. The vampires who came to the airport are headed in your direction. You sure she's safe there? We should catch up to them before they get close but—"

"Can you get away from him?" I didn't need Waleron overhearing the conversation and Xamien was going to erupt the moment I told him.

Xamien paused, obviously already suspicious that something was going down. "Who?"

"Waleron. And you need to keep your shit together."

"What the fuck, Jasper?" I heard the denim of his jeans as he walked. He must have put his hand over the phone as his voice became muffled as he said, "Waleron, give me five . . ." then it was clear again, "tell me."

"I was hired to protect Max, but if things went bad and there was a chance he'd take her . . . I was hired to kill her. I didn't know it was Drake at the time—"

"You're dead." Xamien's low tone was menacing and I could tell he was barely holding on. Any second he'd hang up on me and then . . . then he'd hunt me.

"She can heal Ink, Xamien. Waleron knows. That's why he had Adrian hire me." I heard his sharp intake of breath and then the phone crackle, and I knew he was walking again and suspected he was going for Waleron. Shit, I would, but I wasn't Xamien who was generally controlled and not impulsive. "Don't do it, Xamien. Waleron did it to protect the Scars. That's what he does. That's who he is. If Max healed Drake's Ink, the repercussions are too great and now . . ." Now that he was a vampire it was even worse. "Drake will try and destroy the Scars. I think we all know he wants control of the underworld. The Goddess can't kill him because she's his creator so we have to before he has the chance to get near Max and bring his Ink back."

Xamien was quiet but I didn't hear him walking anymore, and I knew he was contemplating whether to try and kill Waleron or come after me. But Xamien was also sensible and one of the most intelligent men I knew. He never acted impulsively and that was what made him an honorable Taldeburu.

"You touch her . . . your death won't be swift." Xamien's voice was steady and in control, but laced with ominous truth in each word.

"I know." And I deserved it, but I didn't care about me. I cared about Max and I had to make certain Xamien stayed close to Waleron. "Drake and I have a few things in common. Both our Inks are dead and we are both assholes. I can convince him I want to join him in his quest for power."

Xamien scoffed. "You want to die now? Because that's what is going to happen. Drake will never trust you."

I put the phone on speaker and set it down on the passenger seat when the road became tricky to navigate. "Maybe not, but I'm not waiting until Drake or someone else comes after her and . . ." Everything in me went silent. It was as if my heartbeat, my blood, my cells stopped for that one moment before she spoke. The calm before the raging storm.

"Jasper."

The silence broke and my heart thumped and the blood rushed through my veins. *"Max. What is it?"*

"I don't know. The air . . . it's colder and . . . my hands are burning."

I slammed on the brakes, put the gear into reverse and pressed my foot on the gas heading up the mountain. There wasn't a road all the way, but I could make it part way back before I'd have to run. I ignored Xamien's shouting in the phone as I spoke to Max. *"Baby, get Holden and Guise."* I waited a second, nearly tangling the car around a tree. I swerved to the right, my neck cranked back to try and see where the fuck I was going. *"Are they with you?"*

"Yes."

"You need to tell them. Get your blades, baby. I'm coming back."

"He's close," she whispered. *"My hands, they get warm when he's near."*

Jesus. It was like a sledgehammer slammed into my chest and my breath was gone. Drake was near. How the fuck? How close was he? Could he get to her before me? *"Get out of the house. Tell Guise and Holden and get out."*

I tried to spin the car around but the hood smashed into a tree and crinkled like an accordion, steam and hiss started escaping from the engine. "Fuck." I reached over, grabbed my phone and put it to my ear. "Drake is near Holden's. He can't Trace, but I don't know how many vampires he'll have with him." I was already out of the car and running toward the cabin as I said the last words and shoved my phone in my pocket. *"Max, he can't Trace where he hasn't been."* But if her hands were reacting to his closeness, Jesus, he could be closer than I was.

I ran harder as I reached out to my brother. My lungs screamed for air and I pushed harder, muscles quivering, heart pumping and fear crawling through me like a slow web, suffocating me. *"Get her out. Jesus, get her out of there."*

"Wasp, calm down. I'm trying to Track him and I can't find him anywhere close."

"Her ability won't lie. It's trained to heal him. Fuck, he might not be able to Trace there, but he sure as hell can use his fuckin' legs. And if he puts one hand on her, she's gone."

"We'll meet you at the river."

I stumbled then fell to my knees and split my palm open on a jagged rock. *No. This wasn't meant to go down like this.* I screamed in my head. Fuck. I got up and ran harder up the hill. I had a mile to go to reach the river.

I slid into Max's mind and tried to control my breathing as I spoke to her. *"Sunshine, you need to cover your hands. He's a Reflector and feels your emotions. He'll sense the healing and be able to track you easier."*

"Jasper?"

Just her saying my name with that slight quiver to her voice raised the haunting fear I'd tried to run away from since Beth. *"I need you to do it right now."*

"I'm not . . . I'm not scared to die, Jasper. It's the right thing, but . . . not you. Don't let it be you who does it."

Jesus Christ. Those words ripped a hole through my heart and it was as if I was bleeding out. *"Fuck, baby, you're not dying. You're not fuckin' dying and he isn't getting you."*

I swallowed the bile in my throat as I thought of running through the bush toward Beth, her screaming and knowing I was already too late.

Don't be too late.

Fuck, don't let me be too late again.

"Okay,"

She was out of breath and I knew they were running. Holden and Guise would keep her safe. They had to.

I ran until my lungs bled, until finally, I sucked in a gasp of air and it was sprinkled with her.

"We're at the river."

"That's my girl. I'm nearly there." Because no matter what she was thinking right now, I knew she was mine. And no one would take her from me. All these years I'd easily killed, became the best at what I did . . . it was all for this. It had a purpose. I had a purpose.

To save her—Max.

I heard the swoosh of wind from a few hundred feet away to the left of me and then the distinct smell of black licorice. Shit. Vampires. They'd be on me in ten seconds.

I skidded to a stop, my breathing harsh as I looked in the direction of the river. That was when I caught a glimpse of her, blades in her hands, Holden and Guise flanking. She took a step toward me and my brother grabbed her arm, pulling her back. He knew. Of course he knew. He'd know why I'd stopped running and he'd do what needed to be done.

"Do it, Holden," I said calmly.

"Jesus, bro."

I was fifty yards away when the air shifted and then swooshing like a fire crackling in a tornado. *"Holden. Now. I'll hold them off as long as I can."*

Within seconds, I was surrounded.

"Jasper. No, Jasper. We can—" Max's panicked scream echoed in my head, but I ignored it, cutting her off from my mind.

I didn't glance back at her because I knew by now Holden and Guise would already be running with Max, whether it was willingly or not.

I counted nine vampires. I would've fought. And there was always a chance I'd make it out alive, but not this time. This time I had to talk my way out of it and give Max enough time to get away. Drake was on foot, so his advantage of Tracing was gone, and Holden knew this mountain like his own backyard. We both did.

"Ahhh, the famous Scar Assassin, Jasper," a deep, raspy voice emerged out of the trees and following it could only be Drake. "And I can smell her all over you. Interesting and . . . not too good for you. She won't like it much when I cut you into little pieces. Or maybe I'll let her watch your body burn like I did her mother."

The opportunity to get Drake to trust me slipped through my fingers. I sensed the possession in him, the heated rage of need swirling in the depths of his red, gleaming eyes. He didn't like it one bit that I'd been with Max and *that* was what was going to kill me.

eighteen

Max

"NO. NO," I MUMBLED BENEATH Holden's hand smothering my cries.

Holden picked me up and started running. I flailed and kicked and elbowed him so hard in the ribs, he staggered, but didn't let me go. "He'll kill him."

Memories of Drake carrying me away as my mother lay dying. Knowing I could heal her and being forced to leave. *"Jasper. Jasper."* But my voice hit a brick wall and slingshot back at me. He'd closed himself off.

Jasper. I couldn't lose him too.

But hadn't I already? He left because of me. I drove him away because he felt he had to prove to me he meant what he said. He took the job to protect me from any others from killing me.

Did I believe him? Did I trust him? Was he using me for my ability?

But I knew. I felt it when we were together. It couldn't have all been lies. It didn't feel like lies. There had been devastation in his grey eyes when I learned the truth. That wasn't a man who didn't care.

The way he kissed my scars last night . . . how he held me in his arms . . . how he sat with me after my nightmare. How he admitted to watching me for months. How he knew the little things about me.

He cared. Jasper cared. I knew it was huge because I understood what it was like to lose someone you loved and never want to go through the agony again.

I knew what it was like to lock yourself away. I did it so Drake wouldn't find me and to protect everyone. And Jasper . . . Jasper did it to alienate everyone so he never had to care about them. Never have anyone used against him.

I hung limply over Holden's shoulder as he ran down to the river, then across it and up the steep embankment, and into the cover of the woods. Guise was a few feet ahead, but kept looking over his shoulder, his eyes glowing a brilliant gold as he used his Visionary ability.

I expected fear to blanket me again knowing Drake had finally found me, but it wasn't Drake I feared. It was my fear for Jasper. Because I knew Drake would show no mercy. He didn't have it in him and yet we were running away. Leaving him. His own brother was going to let him die.

Holden stopped and slid me off his shoulder. Before I could do anything stupid like run back for Jasper, Guise grabbed my hand.

They nodded at one another and then like a well-oiled machine, each knowing what to do without hesitation, we started running again— without Holden.

"Guise. No. We can't leave them." I stumbled behind him and he didn't hesitate as he swooped me up and threw me over his shoulder and kept running through the brush.

After what felt like an hour but was more than likely ten minutes, he stopped and set me on my feet. I took one step to head back where I'd last seen Jasper, which had to be miles away now, when Guise snagged my arm and yanked me forward so hard I fell to my knees. He glared down at me, his face a harsh, unyielding statue of rage. "You're going to run, damn it. You don't run, you're responsible for killing Holden because he is making certain we get clear."

I blanched, stomach churning as I fought to keep from throwing up.

"We can't let Drake have you." He grabbed my other arm and shook me. "No matter what. And I don't kill innocent women. So, you'll fuckin' run until I tell you to stop." He cupped my chin and locked his threatening eyes on me. "Jasper sacrificed his life for you. Don't throw it away."

It was like he kicked me in the chest and tossed me down the mountain as the choking sob wrenched from my throat and pain filled me.

I shook uncontrollably and with each breath, it hurt . . . but I ran. I took Guise's hand and I ran.

It was a while before Guise stopped and held up his cell phone searching for reception. I collapsed against a tree, bent over, gagging and spitting as my lungs screamed from exertion. I put my hands on my thighs, my hair a curtain across my tear-stained cheeks.

"Xamien." Guise's voice seemed far away, but he was right in front of me, his booted feet pacing back and forth. "At the base. Jasper . . . yeah . . . not sure about him. Look for Holden. He stayed back . . . Okay . . . the hotel at the base of the ski mountain."

He said something else but I'd blanked out as I sank to the ground and wrapped my arms around my knees. I could've stopped him. I could have stopped Drake from killing him. Made an exchange. Done something.

"No, you couldn't," Guise abruptly said. There was a strong push at my mind as he read my thoughts. I was weak and unable to block him. Did it matter? Did I care if Guise or anyone else read my thoughts anymore? What did I have to hide?

He crouched in front of me. "Jasper fought all his life trying to redeem himself for something he had no control over." Guise reached out and rubbed his thumb over a spot on my forehead where I undoubtedly had dirt. "He cared for you. Anyone could see it within seconds of seeing him look at you. Well, he got the chance to prove to you and to himself that he was worth something."

I broke. I wanted to be strong and fight against the anguish that was eating me alive. I knew how. I'd done it for years, but it was gone. The shell had cracked and I was vulnerable to the pain.

I opened up all my shields, hoping if Jasper had any life left in him, he'd hear me. *"Jasper,"* I whispered his name in my mind, praying I'd hear the hint of his Scottish brogue sweep across my mind.

"Breanna. There you are, my sweet."

I jerked my head up and Guise tensed, leaping to his feet and taking me with him. My heart thudded at the deep, raspy voice I hadn't heard in four years. *"How did you find me?"* He could've tracked us to the hotel, but not to Holden's in the mountains.

"It was a simple deduction once I discovered who was protecting you." Jasper? *"I have many vampire followers, my love. Vampires who really don't like that pathetic, worthless Scar. Seems he pissed off a few too many a long time ago hunting down those who killed his sister."* His chuckle vibrated in my head. *"Once we tracked the car to the hotel, all fell into place. The house in the mountain . . . did you know that the river close by is where Jasper and his sister had been going to swim that evening?"* Oh, God. No. *"According to the vampires whose friends he killed, Jasper had a house built nearby but would never live there."* He clicked his tongue like he was scolding a child. *"Such a shame, he will bleed to death in the same spot his sister had. I give him an hour, if he doesn't move too much. A lot longer than I gave your mother."* I couldn't stop my stomach from lurching and I fell to my knees as I threw up. It was a collision of relief Jasper still lived and terror that Drake had him.

I recoiled. Guise was saying something, but I couldn't hear him as I blocked out everything except Drake's voice.

"Did you fuck him, Breanna?"

"Don't kill him." Jasper was alive. He still had a chance.

He chuckled again. I remembered the sound so clearly and a thread of fear sliced into me. Because I knew what came next. And I'd do anything to save Jasper's life; that was why Drake hadn't killed him yet. *"You know what I want. Don't make me chase you . . ."* he paused and I could hear him breathing in my mind. *"There will be consequences for leaving me and for lying to me, you know that. But I will make it easier on you if you stop running."*

"And Jasper?"

"Max!" Guise's hands gripped my arms and shook me, trying to get my attention.

"Jasper?" I repeated.

"He'll live if you come to me. I'll even be generous and let you heal him. But he leaves and you come back with me. To where you belong, Breanna."

I had one chance and if I failed . . . I wouldn't fail. I was stronger now, and if my plan worked, I'd have help. I knew Drake better than anyone. He'd kill Jasper. He'd never let him walk away no matter what he said. His acid-laced lies spilled so easily from his mouth. *"I'll meet you. But if Jasper isn't alive, I will never heal your Ink."* I had no intention of ever healing his Ink even if my idea didn't work.

"As my slave you will."

"Know this, Drake. If he dies, I will never drink your blood. And I will spend each and every day fighting you. I know how you hate it when I fight." My chest swelled at some of the power I had over Drake. It was no longer fear but determination. It was no longer submission but rebellion. He could torture me and hurt me and mentally destroy me, but what he couldn't do was take my will away. In order to become a vampire and his slave, I had to willingly drink his blood and I wasn't the little ten-year-old girl anymore who had no one.

I had something to fight for—Jasper.

"And I will torture him until you do," Drake said confidently.

"No, because I will heal him and then you will let him go. He walks away first. So, you better make fucking certain he stays alive, Drake." He hissed, knowing I had the upper hand. *"And the blades I hold to my throat. I'm not afraid to die. You made sure of that. Don't fuck with me, Drake."*

He was quiet, and for a second, I thought he'd left my mind, but the cold, cruel blackness still lingered and I knew he was deciding how far he could push me.

"There is a white house by the road across from the hotel where you stayed . . . with him. Find a way to get there. You have less than two hours. Remember your house burning with your mother inside? That is what will happen to him in two hours if you don't show—alone Breanna."

And then he was gone.

nineteen

Jasper

I WAS PICKED UP UNDER my armpits and forced to stand. I hung
limply between two vampires and I could barely lift my head; I was
so fuckin' weak. Blood soaked the wound in my chest and it was
only a matter of time before it flooded my lungs and I took my last
breath.

But she got away. I knew she did otherwise the bastard wouldn't
be standing here with me.

I ground my teeth as Drake grabbed my chin and forced me to
raise my head. "She wants you alive. Enough to sacrifice herself for
your wretched, pathetic life."

Fuck, no. No. Jesus. My heart and lungs seized and my stomach
revolted. I had to swallow continuously to keep the bile from rising. I
tried to hide my reaction, but inside, it was a roaring agony of horror.
What'd she do? Why would she ever risk her life for mine? She knew
there was no chance in hell Drake would let me walk away. She knew
the consequences of healing Drake's Ink, of its re-birth.

She wouldn't do it. She was smart. Even as a child, Max hid her
ability from Drake. Six years of torture and pain and whatever the fuck
else he did to her that I couldn't even think about. But what scared me

most was knowing Max wouldn't do it. She's tried to protect everyone by hiding herself and her ability, so there wasn't a chance in hell she'd heal Drake's Ink. No, she'd kill herself or have someone else do it before she did that.

Jesus, Max.

"I'd have killed you already just for touching what's mine if you weren't needed—for now. Bring him."

My head dropped forward as he let go of my chin and I used what little strength I had left and raised my head again. Drake had already turned and was walking to a black SUV. "She's not the same girl you broke." I forced out each word. "And no matter what you do—she'll never belong to you. She never did." Because Max was stronger now and I knew no matter what Drake did to her, she'd fight and that terrified me.

In death or life, the connection we had was undeniable and unbreakable.

I'd been hers for months, watching her, falling for her every day a little more and yet denying it. Fighting it. And Max . . . maybe she didn't love me yet, but I'd felt inside her, been in her thoughts and she gave me all of her. She gave me the pieces of her that she hid from everyone.

Drake spun on his heel and came striding toward me. I kept my eyes on him, his fury raging in his eyes as they blazed red. But he wouldn't kill me. It would risk too much and despite Drake being a fucker of a Scar, he was intelligent.

I tensed as his fist flew toward me and pummeled into my chest. My breath sucked from my lungs and I keeled over, but the two vampires hauled me upright, making the pain worse. Blood rushed violently through my veins and my knife wound pulsed and throbbed brutally. I finally caught my breath then started coughing and gagging as the pain ripped through every part of my body.

"We'll see about that when I have you begging to end the pain while she watches."

I clenched my jaw, my stomach rolling in a battlefield of determination to fight, and surrender so I could take another breath just to love her for one more moment.

But surrender wasn't in me. And it wasn't in Max. Both of us had once surrendered in different ways and it led us each down a different path of destruction.

My legs dragged out behind me as I was taken to the SUV and then tossed into the back. It was only minutes before the agony of the vehicle bouncing down the mountain road finally blurred my vision and my mind became a haze just before I passed out.

I had no idea how long I was unconscious but I woke up with my arms tied behind my back around a wooden beam in what looked like a basement. No windows. Like a large wine cellar but most of the wooden slots for the bottles were empty.

I shook my head to clear my vision as everything swayed back and forth as if I was drunk. But I knew it was from the blood loss. I tested the chains around my wrists and winced as they pulled the muscles around my wound.

Fluid slowly filled my lungs and each breath became raspier. I was surprised I'd lived this long, however long it had been.

Fuck. I couldn't stop the trembling as my body could no longer maintain warmth and was barely functioning. I'd been like this before. Weak and unable to do anything but slowly die.

I heard her before I saw her. The subtle beat of her heart that matched her light steps—a fawn; a fawn entering a slaughter house.

I waited for it, the moment I'd see her. It was crushing knowing she'd come and at the same time—fuck, I wanted to see her. But not here. God, not fuckin' here like this.

Jesus. I closed my eyes as her steps drew closer and with them—his.

The doorknob turned and then the door clicked open.

I couldn't stop myself from looking and it was a mere heartbeat before her eyes found mine.

twenty

Max

"OH, GOD." THE WORDS SCORCHED my throat as the strangled cry emerged the second I saw him. I tried to wrench free of Drake, but he jerked me back. "Rebirth to my Ink first, then I will allow you to heal him."

I held back the tears that threatened to fall and make me into the weak little girl who broke under the man who now held me in his grasp. But I wasn't that little girl anymore. I'd fought to keep my secret hidden. I'd fought to stay alive and now I was fighting for Jasper's life. That was more powerful than the nightmares of six years with Drake.

I raised my chin and met his red flashing eyes. "No, Drake. I heal him first."

He hissed revealing his fangs and looking scary as hell, but I refused to waver, knowing our one chance was if I could get to Jasper first.

I thought I'd be more terrified of him, but I wasn't. He was a pitiful disgrace to the Scars and what they stood for. There was no honor in him and he was weak. He used vampires and a little girl to get him here. He was a monster who destroyed others in order to make himself feel better.

I didn't dare look over at Jasper again. I needed Drake to believe he had no choice here. If he thought for one second I would break, he'd kill Jasper and take me away and wait until I gave in and drank his blood. But I knew Drake. He wouldn't want to wait. He wanted his Ink alive now and that was what I was banking on.

Finally, Drake nodded and his hand slowly slid from my arm. I took a step toward Jasper when Drake grabbed me by the back of the neck, his fingers squeezing as he pulled me into him so hard I slammed into his chest. "Remember who you belong to, Breanna. Don't do anything foolish."

I knew exactly what he was saying. I was not to touch Jasper except to heal his wound. "I *belong* to no one, Drake. I'm your prisoner." I shoved at his arm, gritting my teeth as the pressure on my neck increased before he let me go.

It took everything I had to walk slowly and steadily toward Jasper when all I wanted to do was run and throw my arms around him. My heart thumped erratically, and my blood rushed through my body like a torrential rainstorm.

I knew the Scars had to be looking for me by now and I planned on it. I hadn't known at the time how I'd get away from Guise, but when we went into the hotel bar to wait for Xamien and Waleron and hopefully Holden, I knew it had to be then or I'd never have a chance. I waited ten minutes and even that was a struggle as I kept glancing at the clock up above the bar. I had an hour before Drake blew up the house Jasper was in. And there was no question in my mind he'd do it. He had nothing to lose if I didn't show up.

Luckily, Guise was a Visionary and not a Reflector because I was betting no shield I put around my emotions could stop what I was feeling from being read. This meant I had to leave before Xamien arrived. He'd see right through me and know what I was up to.

My opportunity came when the waitress asked if we needed anything in French. She switched to English when neither of us answered her. She looked me up and down, frowned then glared at Guise who glowered back. I was a mess and suspected I had more than a few cuts and scrapes from our mad run through the bush.

She offered her hand. "Come on. Let's get you cleaned up. Men." She shook her head, her lips pursed together as she sneered at Guise.

"It's always the hot ones who are such assholes."

Guise snorted and stood when I did. "Where are you going?"

"I'm calling the police if you don't behave yourself," the waitress, I glanced at her name tag, Vee, said. "Your girl here has dirt and cuts all over her. You want to explain to the police what happened to her?"

Guise's scowl grew fierce, but he sat back down. "Don't go far. We're leaving the second they get here."

The waitress flicked her hair over her shoulder and then tugged me to the washroom in the far corner of the bar. It wasn't that difficult to get rid of the waitress saying I needed some time alone and then she smiled as if in understanding. I waited a few seconds and then peeked out the door and saw her serving a couple at the bar. Guise was on his phone. I snuck out in the shadows of the hall and went out the back fire exit door.

Then I ran. I suspected Guise and the others would track me pretty damn quickly to the house, but I just needed enough time to do what I had to.

And now . . . seeing Jasper again, I knew I did the right thing. I could do this. I had to. I wanted to.

The beam Jasper was chained to stood from floor to ceiling and was thick and solid. I'd need to find a way to undo the chains. Not now, Drake would be watching everything I did but when the time was right . . . after I killed him.

There was a good chance that I couldn't. That my plan would fail, but this was the only way to try and save Jasper. Drake would've killed him if he had a hint of any Scars with me.

I stopped in front of Jasper, our eyes having never left one another since I began to make the ten agonizing steps toward him. *"Sunshine."*

I pursed my lips and frowned, hoping he understood what I was saying. Drake was an ancient Scar and I'd learned to barricade him from my thoughts, but now he was also vampire and he might be able to intercept our telepathy. I couldn't take the chance that he'd hear us. I just hoped Jasper would understand what I was doing.

My instinct was to scream and cry and hold him in my arms, but if I did, it would destroy all I had to do in order to save us both.

I couldn't tell him I believed him. That I trusted him.

I put one hand on his left shoulder as if to steady myself and slid it back slightly, so my fingers were touching his shoulder blade. His brows drew together and his body stiffened, but he didn't say anything. I called to my healing ability and put my other hand on his chest just below his heart.

I shifted all my healing to his shoulder, instead of his chest. Jasper must have felt it because his breath quickened and his eyes widened with surprise.

I closed my eyes when the images hit me and I saw it all. Jasper hung by his wrists from a tree, the tips of his toes just able to touch the ground. He had chains wrapped around his shoulder to keep him from calling to his Ink and there were bruises all over his body, yet he wasn't bleeding or wounded. The stars shone down on his naked skin as he trembled so violently the chains rattled.

There was a ravaged expression on his face, rage pulsating through him as he hung helpless to the elements. I moved a little closer to him as I heard the screams of the girl echoing in his mind. The little girl's screams that were tearing him apart as he dangled, unable to do anything but listen to her.

His sister. Beth.

The images came quicker like a movie played in fast forward and I weakened, just as Jasper had with each day they left him there. His body began shutting down and then . . . his Ink. Its strangled cries begged to be released from the chains the vampires had thrown over the tattoo to keep it trapped.

But it was locked in his body as he grew weaker.

I heard Drake's footsteps walk toward us and knew if he came close enough, he'd notice the wound on Jasper's chest hadn't been healed and my hand on his shoulder was the only one burning with heat.

I had to take the chance Drake couldn't hear us. I needed Jasper's help. I moved both my hands to his shoulder blade and used everything I had to bring his Ink back to life. I had seconds. *"Rise. He needs you. Breathe."* An Ink couldn't be called upon if the Scar was wounded. But I could. At least I think I could. I communicated with my mother's Ink many times. If I brought Jasper's back to life, then I could call to it without him.

The burning in my hands was so intense it was as if I was holding them in the flames of a fire. But I'd couldn't stop. I'd never stop. *"Jasper, what's your Ink's name? I need to call to it."*

"Baby, what are you doing? My Ink . . . he can't . . . he can't come to form when I'm wounded."

"By you he can't. But I can call him. Jasper, there's no time, tell me. Now."

I knew Drake was behind me and then . . . he hauled me backward so hard I fell on my ass. I heard Jasper's roar and the chains as he struggled to break free.

"Groar. It's Groar." He stopped moving and I saw him close his eyes and knew he was trying to help me call Groar to life.

I had no choice. I needed to say the words aloud as they were more effective than telepathically. "Rise Groar. Jasper needs you. Live and fight for him. Protect him."

"What did you do?" Drake grabbed me by the hair and I winced as he pulled me to my feet. "You bitch." He raised his fist and I braced for the pain, knowing if he knocked me out, our chance was lost. Jasper's Ink would be sluggish and even worse was that it would weaken Jasper further.

But his fist never connected as something crashed into the both of us. I landed hard on my side and I was dazed for a second before I looked for Drake. He was on his back with a snarling wild boar-like monster, with silver skin covered in tattoos, on top of him. There was blood splattered all over Drake. I scrambled toward them and saw the damage the Ink had done with its first leap. Its razor-blade horns were covered in Drake's blood that had penetrated his chest.

But he'd heal. He was a half-vampire and within minutes, he'd heal again. Drake grabbed the Ink by the horns and as soon as he did, his palms bled as they cut into him. Ignoring the damage, Drake tossed Groar across the room. There was loud squeal as he hit the wall and fell on his side and then he was on his hooves again and tearing for him.

I scrambled to my feet and ran for Drake at the same time

"Max. No." Jasper's words were lost to me as Groar leapt on Drake again but this time Drake was ready and dove to the right and then whirled around and grabbed Groar's leg and yanked so hard I heard the crack as the bones broke.

But Ink's never gave up and that was what I depended on. Groar would fight until death or until his master called him back.

Saliva foamed at the corners of Groar's mouth as he panted several times. Then he made a deep screeching growl, spun on his hooves and tackled Drake to the floor, his fangs going for his throat. Drake held him off, with his hands pushing on the thick neck.

I dove for them and pressed my hands onto Drake's chest as Groar pinned him to the floor. I didn't have long. There was no question Drake would win against the Ink; physically he was stronger and faster. My advantage had been surprise, but all I needed were a few minutes.

I called to my ability and my hands heated. I was dislodged for a second as they flipped to the side and Groar used his horn to carve a five-inch long gouge in Drake's cheek.

"I'll kill him," Drake shouted. "You'll wish you were dead, Breanna. You'll beg me for it and I'll never kill you."

I glanced back at Jasper and he was watching me. God, he was pale and could barely keep his head up. He had to call his Ink back before it drained all his strength. My hands burned as I pressed them as hard as I could into Drake's chest, but instead of healing, I did the opposite. I drained him of everything living.

"What are you doing?" His voice was a whisper as I took all that he had. His heart slowed as I bore down on him. Drake's hands slipped away from Groar's neck and then his eyes rolled in the back of his head.

I stopped blood flowing through his veins. His organs from functioning and then . . . lastly . . . I stole the air from his lungs. Lungs I'd healed for six years.

Drake's sudden harsh, cruel laugh with his last breath sent cold shivers through me. His eyes flashed open and they met mine for a brief second as he said, "He will die with me anyway. Remember your house, Breanna. He will burn just like your mother."

Jasper's Ink jammed his horn into Drake's neck at the same time as his heart hesitated and then . . .

Nothing.

I collapsed to the side, my body trembling and cold, even my hands were freezing. I couldn't stop; I had to get to Jasper. I crawled to my feet, staggered and fell to my knees. *"Go to him,"* I said to Groar. The boar with its broad shoulders and heavy weight walked past me, blood dripping from its horns to leave droplets on the floor along its path. He then leapt into the air toward Jasper, following the bright string of light that bound them. The beam of light dwindled as it merged with Jasper again and I saw his body jerk at the impact.

"Jasper." I scrambled to my feet again and ran to him, collapsing against his chest, arms wrapping around his neck. "Jasper."

His eyes were closed and he was freezing cold. His heart was so faint I had to press my ear to his chest in order to hear the slow, irregular beats. "Hold on, baby."

I put my hands on his wound but they remained cold. They weren't warming. They weren't heating up. "Oh, God," I cried as I pressed them harder into the wound. "Please. Please."

I choked back the sobs as I focused and tried to re-awaken my healing, but I'd used all I had in me to take Drake's life and I was too weak.

"No," I sobbed as I desperately tried to bring heat into him. There was a spark, like a match being stroked and his heart began to beat stronger as a flicker of heat began in my palms. "Come on, Jasper. Fight with me."

He groaned and I pushed further, forcing my body to transfer my heat into him. "Baby." His haggard whisper strengthened my resolve and I pushed more and more until he raised his head and his eyes flickered open.

"Stop," he said. "Fuck, stop." He strained against the chains. "You'll die. Max, it's too much. Stop."

My heart slowed and staggered as the coldness I took from him leaked into me, but I'd never stop. Not until we left here together.

Suddenly, a loud boom from upstairs vibrated through the room and I fell backward. Dust and debris crumbled from the ceiling as the house groaned under the pressure. I looked at Jasper and his face was contorted in agony at the sound. Being weak, he was unable to tone down his ability.

I climbed to my feet then ran for the door. "Max," he called.

Another loud bang as if furniture was falling. I threw open the door and the instant I did, I smelled the pungent smell of smoke and heard the distinct crackling of fire.

"Max, get the fuck out of here. The ceiling is going to cave in."

I ran to Drake's body and searched through his pockets and found his phone. It flashed the clock screen.

"Oh, God." He killed his vampire followers upstairs just to make certain Jasper didn't escape. That he'd burn here, just like my mother and Talde. And he would if we didn't get out soon. The house would either collapse on top of us or the smoke would suffocate us.

I ran back to Jasper and tried to undo the chains. "Jasper. I . . . I can't undo them." Panic gripped me and my breathing quickened, making me lightheaded. I had to calm down. We'd get out together. We'd make it. The Scars had to know I was gone and then they'd see the fire and come for us.

"A gun. Something," I said and ran to Drake's body, quickly searching for any kind of weapon to break through the lock. "There has to be . . ."

"No," Jasper said. "He was never planning on letting me go, Max."

"No. No." I shook my head as I yanked off Drake's boots looking for a knife—anything. "He wouldn't do that."

But I knew that was exactly what he'd planned. That was why I knew I had to try and kill him. What I hadn't anticipated was being unable to get Jasper out of the chains.

"Max, come here." It was his calm, steady voice that drew me from my frantic searching. "Come here."

I pushed up and then ran to him, my arms wrapping around his neck as I pressed my lips to his. "There has to be a way."

He pulled back and I stroked his cheek. "You killed him. You stopped him, angel."

"We did," I corrected. "We have to find a way to get you out of here."

"I want you to listen to me, Max." He tilted his head down and looked at me while I cupped his face in my hands. The grey in his eyes wrapped me in its intensity as he waited until I calmed my breathing and my eyes were steady on his.

"Good girl." He quirked a half-smile and then it was gone and I knew. I knew what was coming. "My heart is yours, sunshine." My own heart crashed through its protective cage and dropped into my stomach. "Never knew I had one until you. It lost its beat a long time ago when I lost myself. I never thought it would beat again—until you."

"Jasper. No." I knew why he was saying this and I shook my head. "No. I don't want it. I don't want it without you." I clutched at his shirt, tears staining my cheeks as I pleaded with him.

He grunted and his muscles flexed. I frantically reached around again to try and undo the chains on his wrists. I choked on the sob catching in my throat. "Help me. Help me. Your Ink. Groar can—"

"Baby," Jasper whispered.

I ignored him, yanking on the chains, desperation blurring the reality of what I was doing. I had to get him free.

"Baby, stop."

"No. Fuck you, Jasper. Fuck you. You don't get to give up."

"I need you to look at me, Max." I clawed at his trapped wrists until he added, "Please."

My trembling hands slid down his stretched arms and away from the chains that were going to break us; tear us apart before we were even brought together. I shifted so I was standing in front of him again, ignoring the escalating sounds of the crackling and banging upstairs.

"I can't," I said. Because the second my eyes hit his chin, I had to close them. I couldn't look at what I knew I'd see.

"Yeah, you can. Because it's all I have left."

Oh, God, the pain crushing my chest was so debilitating I had to grab hold of him to stay upright.

"Look at me so I can see the stars in your eyes. Going to take them with me, angel."

I collapsed at his feet, my hands on the floor, my curtain of hair hiding the anguish in my face as reality hit me. There was no escape for him and I was helpless to save him.

"You going to give me your eyes, sunshine? Because fuck, I don't want to die without seeing them again."

I crawled back up him, my legs vibrating so badly I needed to use him to keep myself standing. I raised my chin and then my blurred, tear-filled eyes slid up his body, past his chin, his nose and then . . .

We locked. And it stole my breath and stilled my heart.

This was what it was about. This was why anyone would go through suffering because on the other side was this . . . the encompassing brilliance of what Jasper and I shared. It was us merging, with that one look and becoming one.

"That's it, baby. Fuck, you're beautiful. I'm so proud of you." He cocked a half-smile and from the wince after, I knew it was painful for him to give me that. I traced his lips with my fingers as the tears continued to stream down my cheeks. "Max. I need you to get out of here. Take Drake's shirt and put it over your head, stay low and run. Use your telepathy to try and reach the others. You have to go before it's too late."

But I was too weak to use my telepathy and I wouldn't leave Jasper. Never. I wasn't scared to die; I was scared to walk away.

"No. I won't leave you." I stood on my tiptoes and curled my hands around his neck and then kissed him. His groan vibrated beneath my mouth and I deepened the kiss, my tongue tasting, my need so intense it was like I was unable to breathe without him.

"Max. Go," Jasper mumbled when I refused to let him go. "Fuck," he grunted and tore his head to the side to break us apart. "Get out of here. Give me that. Let me die knowing you're safe."

"I'm not safe. I'll never be safe without you. You're my safe, Jasper. Don't you see that?" I flinched as his eyes hardened. No. No. I gagged on the tears, the sobs, the clenching pain that had my heart in its hand and squeezed until I felt as if it burst and I was drowning inside from my own blood.

"Do this for me. Jesus. I can't watch you die. Don't make me. You're free, Max. You're finally free of him."

But I couldn't give him that. I wouldn't. I'd lived my whole life locked away doing what I had to in order to protect everyone. Now, I was doing what I wanted and I'd never leave him. Never.

I pulled away from him and this time when I met his eyes, I raised my chin and refused to falter under his determined harsh expression that he was using to try to get me to do what he wanted.

"I'm not leaving you."

We stared at one another for a few seconds, both unwavering. It was Jasper that broke first and it was him sighing. Then every muscle relaxed as he hung, accepting what he couldn't fight. "Come here, baby," he whispered.

I buckled into him and it was at that moment I felt as if I took his heart and he took mine. Because every day I suffered in Drake's hands, every day I hid away, it was all worth it for this moment, knowing that

Jasper was mine. That he was giving the pieces of him that had scattered into the wind so many years ago.

I'd caught each one and brought them back and now they were mine. He was mine and I was his.

"Fuck, you're stubborn." His voice was a ragged whisper and I heard the tinge of fear. "But I love you, Max. I fuckin' love you."

I pressed my forehead against his chest, his heart still thumping strong and steady despite the walls that crumbled around us. It was getting closer. The heat burning my back and the smoke leaking beneath the door to make a light fog in the room.

"I love you. I love you. I love you," I said as there was a sudden crash of what sounded like parts of the roof.

"Jesus, Max." I knew he must have heard the fear in my voice. But it wasn't fear of dying; I'd always accepted that. What I was scared of was us not dying at the same time. Of holding him dead in my arms or him seeing me being burned alive.

Jasper kissed my forehead. "Don't look, okay. Kiss me, baby. Just kiss me and we'll go together."

I jerked as the door burst open and the inferno of smoke and heat filled the room. I slammed my mouth down on his and kissed him with all I had left. Because this was all either of us had.

I kept my eyes closed, ignoring the agony of the heat burning my back, the smoke filling my lungs with each breath that was Jasper's and mine together.

But my kiss ended too fast as I struggled to breathe and my hands slipped from his neck as I coughed violently. No. No.

Suddenly I was yanked away and a cry escaped my lungs, not knowing what happened until a wet cloth came over my nose and mouth and I saw the cold ice-blue eyes of Waleron.

Then Xamien came up beside us and something else. An Ink. A brilliant light linked the black shadow of a massive beast to Xamien. It was transparent except for the mouth, eyes and claws that glowed bright turquoise. It had to be over seven-feet tall with faded grey markings all over the black shadowed form. Xamien took me from Waleron then spoke to his Ink.

"The chains, Grief." The Ink moved like the wind and shifted past us. It snarled and razor sharp fangs emerged. It lowered its head and clamped down on the chains around Jasper. Within seconds, they fell to the ground.

Waleron grabbed the now unconscious Jasper around the waist as he collapsed and threw him over his shoulder. I reached out to Xamien's Ink, no longer hiding what I'd been forced to for ten years. *"Thank you, Grief,"* I whispered to the Ink in my mind.

His glowing eyes darted in my direction and then he tilted his head to the side as if he was trying to ascertain whether he heard me or not. After a few seconds, Grief bowed his head to me then swept across the floor and merged back with Xamien.

We made it out of the basement just as the ceiling gave way.

twenty-one

Max

Twenty-four hours later

JASPER PACED.

I watched from the bed, my legs crossed beneath me as he strode back and forth like a caged animal. His hair was tussled and slightly damp from his shower and his jeans hung low on his hips, button undone as if he'd quickly yanked them on. He wasn't wearing a shirt which I took great pleasure in because I admired his muscles that at the moment were flexed. And they were flexed because Jasper was . . . agitated. No, it was more than agitated, it was pissed off.

We'd been back at Xamien's for a few hours after the long trek back.

Despite Xamien's protests that I was too weak, as soon as we escaped the burning house, I healed Jasper enough so I was certain he wouldn't die. I'd attempted to heal him completely but it was Guise who had dragged me away the moment I began shaking from exertion. Guise was scary as hell in a quiet, subtle way, but I still fought him to get back to Jasper and finish healing him. It was when Holden and Xamien came and stood in my field of vision, blocking me from Jasper with their unyielding expressions that I gave in.

Waleron left as soon as we were safe. The tension between him and Xamien was obvious from their fierce glares at one another. At some point they'd have it out and it wouldn't be pretty.

Jasper remained unconscious all the way back and I knew it was due to the blood loss. I could heal a wound and repair damage, even offer the heat from my own body, but I couldn't give blood. But his heart beat was steady even though it wasn't strong yet and he was no longer bleeding out.

Xamien flew Jasper's rust bucket, Fiona, and I was less concerned about dying a fiery death this time as I was too concerned about Jasper. Holden came with us to the manor, but Guise said he was going to the hotel. Something about the waitress, Vee, and he needed to talk to her.

It wasn't until I had him in my bed and finished healing him, with his temperature up that I finally relaxed. Holden and Xamien left me alone with him and I took off my clothes and climbed into bed with him, needing to feel him up against me.

It was hours later when I woke and he was gone. I panicked and got out of bed so fast I tripped over the sheet and fell hard to my knees. Then I heard the shower.

Now Jasper paced.

I sat on the bed in my panties and t-shirt watching the angry Scar assassin and I should've been nervous. Maybe even a little concerned about my well-being. Instead, all I could think about was how I was going to get him to remove his jeans.

"Jesus, what were you thinking?"

And this he'd said three times now as well as "you weren't thinking" and "you could've died." Freaking out. Yeah, Jasper had been on a rampage ever since he'd come out of the shower and saw me awake, sitting on the bed.

I think the reality of what went down had finally hit him and the initial relief that we were both alive had shifted to anger over how it went down.

"Seriously, Max. Why?" He stopped pacing to stand in front of me; his arms at his sides, hands curled into fists. "What if you hadn't been able to raise my Ink? Did you think of that? Christ, what if you couldn't have . . . fuck, I don't even know what the fuck you did to

Drake, but it sure as hell wasn't heal him."

"I did the opposite. I took his life from him."

He stared at me a second as if contemplating, and then he swore beneath his breath. "You can do that?"

"Well, I thought—"

"You thought," he shouted.

I shrugged. Maybe it wasn't the smartest gesture when he was reeling because that pissed him off more.

"You willingly walked right into Drake's arms—alone—with a plan to raise my Ink, which by the way, an Ink you know nothing about. You *think* you can manipulate your ability to do the opposite—to a *hybrid ancient Scar.*" He raised his voice at the hybrid ancient Scar part. "And then you refuse to leave a burning building. Fuck, Max." He bowed his head and I heard him growl low in the back of his throat. "Does any of that sound senseless to you?"

"Maybe." That was my safest answer at the moment and it had been risky, but I'd do it again. I was a Scar, a fighter and I was no longer going to hide.

I knew he wasn't done yet, so I waited quietly on the edge of the bed as he ran his hand through his hair several more times. Jasper was fighting a lot more than what we went through. He must have faced worse situations over the years in his line of work, but this was him having to face all that we were now. His past clashing with what happened. Of nearly losing someone he cares about again.

But what I wasn't prepared for was him walking straight up to me and falling to his knees, his hands gripping my hips, head dropping forward to rest in my lap. I stopped breathing. "You wouldn't leave. Jesus, you didn't fuckin' leave."

I put my hand on his damp hair. "Jasper . . ."

"Max, everything about me is ruined and sour and I don't deserve you." His fingers tightened on my hips and he lifted his head and met my eyes. "But I swear every damaged piece I have left belongs to you."

Oh, God. Tears pooled and I cupped the side of his face. "Jasper . . ."

"*Shh,* not done yet, sunshine." There was no playfulness in him and his brow furrowed as he kept his eyes glued to me. "You're the stars that burn away the darkness, Max. That's what it feels like when

I'm with you. Like I'm all lit up inside with brilliant specks of light. And when I touch you, it's like I've grabbed one out of the sky and I'm holding it in my hand. Flawless. Bright. And fuckin' beautiful." His hands slid up my sides and goose bumps dappled my skin. "I want this—us. To fall asleep with the stars in my arms. Then wake up with the sunshine. I can't ever lose you and what happened . . ." He leaned closer and pressed his lips to my neck, then trailed a slow path up to my chin until his mouth hovered over my lips. "I love you, Max."

A tear slipped down my cheek and he wiped it away with the rough pad of his thumb. "I love you, too, Jasper."

He kissed me lightly on the lips and when I leaned into him, wanting more, he abruptly pulled back. "Good because, baby . . ."—his tone hardened as did his grip on me—"you pull shit like that again . . . I will spank your ass so hard you won't walk for days."

I dragged my teeth over my lower lip as the undeniable ache heightened. He must have noticed the slight tightening in my body and my subtle change in breathing because his brows rose.

"You like that, sunshine? Does that make you wet?"

Oh, God. I swallowed. Yeah, it made me wet and I wanted him inside me.

No, it was more than that. I wanted to live. I wanted to feel every emotion there was and I wanted to do it with Jasper.

He stood and looked down at me. "Answer me, baby. Are you wet right now?"

I hesitated and I shouldn't have because Jasper took full advantage of my unwillingness to admit the idea of him spanking me turned me on. And he was quick and agile like a panther as he dove for me.

I did a little girl scream and vaulted off to the side, kicking my leg out to push him in the chest. He grunted and landed on the floor on his back. He looked up at me, mouth gaping and eyes wide, shocked that I managed to outmaneuver him. My advantage was he wasn't in top form, but that wouldn't last long.

But seeing Jasper fall to the floor with that expression . . . priceless. I started laughing. I couldn't help it. And then once I started I couldn't stop as the unfamiliar feeling took hold of me and wouldn't let go. My chest hurt and I became dizzy as I inhaled short gasps of air while laughing.

When I finally found some control and looked at him, my laughter stopped. He was up on one elbow on his side, watching me. His grey eyes soft and filled with . . . affection and wonder. His voice was husky and had that sexy Scottish lilt to it as he said, "I've wanted that since the day I met you."

"What?"

"Your laughter. To hear you laugh. And it's more fuckin' beautiful than I could ever imagine." He slowly rose and walked toward me.

"But I was laughing at you."

He half-grinned. "Baby, I'd do anything to hear you laugh like that."

"You would?"

His brows flicked up. "What do you have in mind, sunshine?"

I thought about it for a second. "You tied to the bed while I tickle you relentlessly?"

He snorted. "Not happening. Ever. Only you get tied up, baby."

I pouted, but that totally turned me on. He chuckled before he leaned down and picked me up in his arms and started back to the bed. "I want to hear it again. But first I want to hear you scream my name." My eyes widened in horror. "And we have an issue to settle." He sat on the edge of the bed and I was straddling his lap, knees on the mattress on either side of him. I saw the desire blazing in his eyes and I was pretty sure my eyes were doing the same thing because my body was already heated and aching for him.

Suddenly, I found myself lying on my stomach over his knee, butt in the air.

"Jasper!" I wiggled and writhed, trying to get away, but he held me firmly on his lap, his arm across my lower back keeping me in place. "What are you doing?"

"Next time, don't think about lying, baby. Not about this. Not about what turns you on." He yanked up my shirt then pulled down my panties with a sharp tug and then his hand was caressing my ass.

I couldn't stop the moan from escaping at the gentle touch as he stroked the surface. "I can laugh again. Let me up and I'll laugh."

"I think you want this more," Jasper said, his finger sliding down the crease into the folds that were slick with moisture. "Yeah, you do. And, sunshine . . . I will always give you what you need."

I tried again to move so I could look at him, but the hard slap on the naked surface of my butt had me screaming and arching. It hurt. Shit, it hurt. Jasper wasn't playing. Well, he was but he was making a point and I tried again to get away.

Slap.

Burning. Aching.

Slap.

Oh, God. It was like an explosion of fireworks going off inside me. It hurt like hell, but it inflamed me. It released me. It made me want to scream and shout, and fight. And I did. I struggled against him, but he easily held me in place as his hand came down on my butt several more times and it wasn't nice. It was meant to make me scream.

And I did. I screamed. "Fuckkkk, Jasper."

"That's it, baby." And that was when he stopped and stroked the burning pain, soft and gentle then slid his finger down my crack into the wetness and then . . .

I gasped as his finger drove inside me, my hands curling.

"I'm going to sink my cock into this." He pushed another finger in and then thrust in and out. "And you're going to tell me you'll never do that again. You'll never risk your life like that again."

I knew what would happen if I refused, but I wouldn't lie. Because I would do it again. "I can't do that, Jasper."

He pulled his fingers from my moisture and then his hand stoked over my butt again. I knew what was coming and my sex clenched. But the sting failed to come down on my ass. Instead, he flipped me over and tossed me backward so I landed on my back on the mattress.

He stood. I shifted up onto my elbows and watched him carefully as he slowly turned doing up his jeans. Doing up his jeans? What the hell?

"What are you doing?" I scrambled to my knees on the edge of the bed. "What's wrong?"

He strode to the bathroom, the same bathroom where we'd first met, and grabbed his black t-shirt from the counter and pulled it over his head. Only then did he look at me and his expression was tight, unbending.

"You know what I do, right, Max? You know I get paid to kill." I nodded. Yeah, of course I did. "Then I need you to agree to never

182

do anything like that again. Because my shit, the people I deal with, I won't have you coming after me if some fucker gets his hands on me."

Now, I was angry and my heart pounded as I crawled off the bed. "You can't dictate what I can and can't do. I won't hide anymore. I know how to handle myself and for once in my life, I can live."

"Did you hear what you just said? Live, Max. Fuckin' live."

I walked toward him. He was braced and ready for me, looking like a large unmovable rock. "Yes. Live." I shoved my hands into his chest. Of course it had no effect and he remained solid. "Live, Jasper. Whether one day or a thousand years, I want to live—with you. And if you're going to continue to risk your life, then you can damn well expect me to risk mine in order to keep you."

His determined expression faltered. It was a flicker of shock as his eyes widened briefly and then they narrowed again. "No," he said. But the one word was gentle and no longer held the grip of resolve.

"Protecting me isn't done by locking me away." I rested my hands on his chest, feeling his steady heartbeat beneath my palms.

He took a deep breath. "They'll use you against me."

Like his sister. "Maybe. But it won't be your fault. Just like what happened to Beth wasn't." His jaw tightened. "Jasper, love me, protect me, but let me love you and protect you, too."

He ran his hand through his hair as his eyes locked with mine. "I can't lose you."

"Then you know why I'm fighting you on this. I can't lose you either."

"Fuck it." He spun around and walked over to the dresser and tagged the phone. I had no idea what he was doing or who he'd call in the middle of our conversation, but when he put the phone to his ear, he looked at me, and it was the confident resolute man who always got his own way.

"Don't send me anymore jobs," he said into the phone then pressed end, not even waiting for a response and then he pressed a few more numbers and put the phone back to his ear. "Guise . . . yeah, I'm good. Yeah, she's good, too . . . yeah, I will . . . tell Holden I'm with the Talde . . . fuck he's here? Fine, I'll tell him myself." I heard an abrupt 'about fuckin' time' through the phone, then Jasper pressed end and tossed it on the dresser.

I crossed my arms and the corners of my lips curved up. This was how he planned to win the argument. "No more jobs?"

He shook his head. "Nope."

I saw the self-satisfied look on his face. Cocky bastard. "And you're joining your brother's Talde?"

He nodded. "Yep."

And that meant he'd have Guise, Holden and the others I had yet to meet in the Talde, who'd protect me and I was guessing stop me from going after Jasper if he ever got himself in trouble. The thing was . . . he now had a Talde to stand behind him and protect him.

"You're not always going to win when we disagree."

He cocked a grin. "Yeah, I am, baby. Get used to it." He strode back into the bathroom and came back out with a small, thin, square package which he ripped open with his teeth. Then he undid the top button of his jeans and lowered the zipper.

I pursed my lips together and watched as he slid off his jeans. He was naked underneath and already hard. I stood, throbbing, my breathing ragged as he slid the condom on. "And now I'm going to fuck you. On the bed, sunshine."

Oh, I wanted to fuck him. God, I wanted to fuck him. And I was still pulsing and aching for him, but Jasper couldn't get what he wanted all the time and despite me losing out on hot sex, I had to prove a point. I darted for the door.

I'd almost made it when his arm curled around my waist. His yanked me back hard against his chest and then my feet were off the floor as he scooped me up and carried me to the bed, my body wiggling like a fish out of water.

"Jasper, put me down."

He did. He tossed me on the bed and before I could move an inch, he was on top of me, hands grabbing my wrists and locking them together above my head. I had no leverage as his weight pressed me hard into the mattress.

His teeth snared the lobe of my ear and then his tongue licked the bitten surface. "Never try to run from me." He groaned as he moved his hips and his cock jutted into my inner thigh. "I'll always catch you." He slid one hand down the length of my stretched arms and then along my waist to my hip. His breath swept across the back of my neck as he trailed kisses and tiny nips on my skin. "And you're not always going to like it when I do." He shifted to the side and then he flipped me over and was on top of me again.

I didn't fight him. I was so hot and aching, it was torture just waiting for him to put his cock inside me. But I knew if I begged, he'd make me wait. He liked the control. No, he *needed* the control and I was turned on by it. I could finally let go and knew he'd take care of me.

"Fuck, Max, I love every piece of you. Every fuckin' piece. Even the stubborn, irrational side." He slid his hand between us while he lowered his head and his mouth took mine.

I sighed beneath his lips as our kiss inflamed the charged sparks between us. His hand holding my wrists above my head released, and my hands shifted into his hair, drawing him closer, needing him closer.

I arched as his finger circled over my sex and my legs fell open wider and then I broke from his kiss, tilted my head back, eyes closed as I moaned, "God, Jasper."

"Not yet, princess." His finger stopped and I groaned with frustration. "You will always come around my cock or my tongue. Right now, it's going to be my cock."

I thought I was ready for him. Shit, I was but he was big and he thrust hard inside me and it hurt, but damn, it felt good too. He kissed my neck, the hollow of my throat and then just above my right breast. "You good with that?" He took my nipple into his mouth and suckled as his hips moved slowly and with ease.

What? What was he talking about?

He bit down and my entire body tensed. "Oww."

His tongue flicked over the sensitive surface of my nipple and I heard the sweet suction of his heated mouth on me. He drew back. "You good with that?"

"Yes?" I still wasn't certain what he was asking, but I'd say anything to get him to fuck me harder. "Jasper . . . please."

He pulled part way out of me then slammed back in and I met his thrust with my hips so our bodies slapped together.

"Jesus." Jasper wrapped his hand around my hair at the back of my neck and kissed me, thrusting repeatedly until I was throbbing and sore.

I curled one leg around his waist and he grabbed the other and hitched it over his shoulder pushing deeper inside. Then he let me go, placed his hands on the bed on either side of me and moved faster and harder.

"Jasper," I breathed, the cusp of my orgasm latching onto me and holding me in limbo. For a few seconds, he continued to thrust and then he tensed and made a low, deep growl, sending me over the edge. I screamed his name as every part of me tightened and shook around him.

"Fuck, baby. Fuck." His hips rocked forward a few more times.

He kissed me again and this time it was filled with gentleness as his lips molded me to him.

And that was what it was, us molding into one another. Us becoming one.

We weren't fixed and neither of us pretended to be. I fell in love with the broken parts of Jasper and he did mine.

He kissed the corners of my lips and gently nipped the tip of my nose before he pulled back. I felt him lift to slide out of me, but I looped my arms around his back keeping him in place. "I want to live with you."

He grinned. "Baby, I'm not letting you go. We can live anywhere you want."

"The house in the mountains. Your house, Jasper."

He stilled. "You know?"

I knew eventually we'd have the conversation about how I knew, but for now, this was about us having a family again. "Jasper, it's time you went home. And I want you to take me with you. You're my home now, Jasper."

His head lowered into the crook of my neck and his mouth was moist against my skin. I waited quietly until he finally lifted his head again and then cupped the side of my cheek.

His eyes were glassy and his voice shook as he said, "Yeah, sunshine. I'll take you home."

The End

Hey guys,

Thank you so much for reading, *Take*. I hope you had fun with Jasper and Max and meeting the Scars. If you wouldn't mind helping me out and leaving a review on the site where you purchased *Take* it would be much appreciated. And let me know if you want more of the Scars. Thank you!

Please, come say hi on FB or send me an email, I'm always thrilled to hear from readers.

Cheers,

Nash xo

Author's Note

If you read my Senses series, which is no longer published, and what Take is based on, you probably noticed I altered a few time-frames, situations and descriptions regarding Scars and their world. I'm rewriting the three books that originally started this series, but have no release date as I have obligations for other novels at the moment. Thank you for reading Take and I hope you enjoyed!

acknowledgments

Take has been in my head for years with Jasper lurking and daring me to type out his words. It was the incredible fans of the Senses series (no longer published) who pushed me to sit down and write this story—thank you. I fell in love with Jasper and Max so long ago and now even more so.

Melissa, my plotting partner and friend, you're a precious gift. The Scars brought us together and I'm forever thankful for that. Keeping writing, chickie.

Susan, love you girl! The messages and texts over this book . . . thanks for putting up with me. You're help with Take, and all my books, is invaluable. Bring on the Alpha assholes and the toys!

My girl Paula, yep you're mine. I told you that a long time ago when I dragged you into the darkness of "Torn from You" and now there is no escape. Thank you for your insight, advice and for sticking with me on this book when I jumped genres. I'm keeping you, babe.

Stacey, my magical formatter, every book I write has the touch of your magnificent hand and I'm so blessed to have you. Thank you once again, for making my book look like a masterpiece.

Kristin, my content editor or rather my character goal finder, I love your excitement over the Scars. This book would be a scrambled mess without your clear vision. I'm telling you again . . . no leaving me!

Becky at Hot Tree Editing, I won the lottery finding you. You make my words shine and eliminate all my pesky bad habits. Thank you for caring about my words and my story.

Sarah dude . . . hooker here. What can I say except you are seriously priceless, in many ways, LOL. Yeah, I'm a little scared about your obsession over Crisis . . . you know he isn't real, right? Thank you for all your support. Our chats in the UTA Babes and PM's . . . damn I've never laughed so hard.

To the fans, the readers, who share my passion for books, I owe it all to you. Thank you for all your messages and emails. It is the greatest gift to wake up in the morning and read a message from a fan of my work. I'm truly honored and humbled.

UTA Babes . . . love you girls!

Sarit and 'the girls' . . . you know who you are. One day we are meeting up even if I have to swim across the ocean, lol. Thank you for all your support, chats and enthusiasm. Hugs xo

To the bloggers and readers who tirelessly promote and support my work, your dedication means the world to me. No matter how big or small your presence is, I wouldn't be here without you. My stories get seen because of you. They get read because of you. Hugs and kisses xoxo.

Love as always to my incredible family, animal and human.

Available Now

UNYIELDING BOOK 1

Georgie

I SMOOTHED OUT the wrinkles on my bedspread then placed my stuffed brown bunny rabbit against the white-and-pink flowered throw pillow. At sixteen, I was a little old for stuffed animals, but it had been a gift from my brother the first time he went away to Afghanistan with the military.

I straightened, then saw the sheet hanging down in the right corner and quickly tucked it back into the mattress. Perfect. I liked . . . no, I was obsessed with being organized. Everything had its place, even me. I kept to the same bland, colorless clothes, the same schedule, and the same hair style. Why mess with what worked? My brother often teased me and said I should join the Canadian forces like him. I may like neat and tidy, but I hated fighting, blood, guns, and, unquestionably, any killing.

Connor knew that. He'd helped me bury my goldfish, Goldie, in the backyard when I was seven, then the hamster, Fiddlehead, when I was ten. To this day, there is a marked stone Connor had made for him near the back fence. I could see it whenever I looked out the kitchen window.

I jerked as a car door slammed, which sounded as if it was in our driveway. The sun had just peeked over the horizon; six in the morning was too early for any visitors, plus it was Sunday and Dad had the rule he and Mom sleep in. I always rose early, wanting to get ahead of the day, another reason Connor said I'd excel in the military. Although, we both knew he'd never allow me anywhere near danger, which I was very content with. Danger to me was if my shampoo was missing and I had to use my brother's instead.

But Connor wasn't due back for another month, so that meant . . . A sudden freeze hit my body, locking my limbs in place as I realized why someone might be in our driveway at six in the morning on a Sunday. My breath trapped in my throat as if clamped hands were strangling me.

No.

No. I shook my head back and forth. Please, don't knock.

It was the newspaper boy. Early. He was an hour early today. In a second, I'd hear the clang as the newspaper bundle hit the metal screen door.

Eyes squeezed tightly shut, I waited for the familiar sound.

Nothing. I sucked in large amounts of air for my starved lungs.

Not him. Please, not him.

Connor.

Connor.

My heart thumped harder and harder in its cage and tears pooled in my eyes. I couldn't hear his footsteps, but I knew his team leader's black combat boots were walking up the stone path toward the house.

I can't lose him. Please.

Run.

Run and it won't be true.

But I couldn't move. My legs were locked in place as I waited for the nightmare to begin.

Thump.

Thump.

Thump.

It was as if each knock was a punch to the stomach. No air. I couldn't breathe. I was silently screaming and nothing could stop the fear gripping my insides.

Please. No. I need him.

I heard my parents' bedroom door open and the shuffling of feet down the hallway on the hardwood floors. The distinct click as the lock turned and then the front door opened, followed by the screech of the screen door.

Then silence.

It felt like hours as I stood in the middle of my room, afraid to look out the window and see the car I didn't want to see. Afraid to run. Afraid to move. Hoping I was still asleep and this was all a dream.

Yes, it was a dream. I'd wake up any second. I'd call Connor today. I'd tell him how much I missed him and loved him. It had been weeks since we last spoke. I should've emailed him more often. Why hadn't I?

My mother's loud wail pierced the air, and my perfect world crashed to my feet. It was like I was being coiled in the death grip of an anaconda and dragged under the water.

I fell to my knees, my arms wrapped around myself, and I rocked back and forth as my mother's cries became muffled as if she was being held against something.

There were more footsteps. Not quiet and soft like my mom's. Not slow and lumbering like my dad's. Long, confident strides.

No. Go away. Just go away. It's not real.

The steps stopped outside my door, and I heard the click as the door handle turned. It was opening my soul and ripping out my heart.

I stopped rocking.

The door swung open.

I clamped my eyes shut, not wanting to see him. Unable to face him, face what he was here to tell me.

"Georgie."

Deck's gruff tone, I'd recognize anywhere. It scared me. He scared me but what scared me more was my body's reaction to him. The strange tingling between my legs, the warmth on my skin and the whirling in my stomach as if I was falling from the sky.

I sniffled as my nose dripped, and I felt the trickle of tears slip from the corners of my eyes.

"Look at me, Georgie." If I ignored him, it would all go away. "Georgie."

It was the hint of softness in his voice when he said my name which had me opening my eyes.

My gaze hit his legs first, the long, lean length covered in black cargo pants. There was a rip in the material just above his knee. Dirt. Smudges of dirt on his pants as if he'd come straight from whatever hell they'd been in.

They. In a second, the word they wouldn't exist anymore.

My gaze moved upward, hesitant, as if my brain was fighting every step. His hands were curled into fists at his sides, his knuckles strong notches which had felt the harshness of pounding into another man. It was odd because his hands were clean, and yet I saw the dirt on his tatted arms and the . . . blood? Was it his blood or—

"Georgie."

The loud, abrupt sound of my name made me lurch and my gaze flew to his.

His jaw was tense. Eyes hard and cold—unemotional. He looked directly at me, not an ounce of compassion in his unyielding stare. But I saw other things. There beneath his stoic solidity . . . the torment, the pain, the darkness which was soon going to become my own.

I started shaking violently, and my throat tightened against the sobs that racked my body. "No." It was the only word I could get out.

Please, no.

He stood and watched me tremble and cry on my knees in the middle of my room for several minutes before he said, "I couldn't save him."

His words cut into me with the finality of the truth, and my breath hitched as more tears pooled and slipped from the confines of my eyelids. I tightened my arms around my body as if that would help the pain ease.

It didn't.

Nothing would.

Connor.

He was gone.

I'd never hear his teasing. Feel the touch of his hand ruffling my hair. Hear his voice calling me 'Georgie Girl.'

He promised to come back.

Pain.

Hurt.

Devastation.

'Chaos.'

My head screamed with anarchy as Connor's image played across my mind. It was distorted and broken with bits of light being sucked apart by the darkness.

Destruction. I had to destroy. My perfect world was no longer. Nothing would ever be the same again. I'd never be the same again.

I scrambled to my feet, grabbed my duvet and tore it off the bed, the flowered throw pillow and bunny tossed to the floor. A strange sound emerged from my throat as I dove for my dresser and swept my arm across the shiny, neat surface—books, my jewelry box, and a vase crashed to the hardwood floor. I could hear glass shattering, and silver stud earrings, pearls, and rings scattered in every direction.

I didn't stop. I couldn't.

Destruction.

I grabbed my light off my nightstand and threw it across the room. The bulb made a loud pop as it hit the wall. I needed to destroy. Everything I'd made into a neat and tidy place was no longer. It was all gone. Nothing would be perfect again. My world had just burst open, and I was bleeding. It hurt. God, it hurt.

I tripped over my duvet as I went for the closet and fell to my knees. It didn't stop me . . . the physical pain was nothing, almost welcoming to the emotional pain taking me apart piece by piece. I got up, then staggered to the closet and threw open the doors.

I wrenched my clothes off the hangers—the pretty, soft-yellow dresses, white ones, black ones. Then the plain, button-down blouses and the black pants. The empty hangers swung back and forth on the metal bar as every single piece of clothing was thrown to the floor. When the closet was empty, I picked up whatever was in reach and began tearing. Buttons popped. Silk and nylon tore, sleeves ripped from the cores—like me. This was me being shredded apart.

Carelessly, I yanked and pulled at whatever my hands could get a hold of.

Rip.

Tear.

Ruin everything. Destroy.

I was breathing hard when I finished. Nothing was left alive. Just like me. I had nothing left except to run.

Run.

Run.

Run.

I ran for the door. I couldn't breathe. I had to get out of here. Away from this ruined perfect world. He was gone. Connor was gone.

My mind was whirling and frantic.

Escape.

I didn't even see him; my vision blurred from tears and anger and pain. He blocked the doorway, his broad frame preventing my path of escape.

I ran anyway, trying to dive past him.

He snagged me around the waist with one arm and my feet left the floor. I screamed and squirmed in his hold like a rag doll. He set me down directly in front of him, his hands latched onto my upper arms in a bruising grip.

"Georgie, look at me."

I kicked and yelled, trying to leave, but nothing would set me free. I knew I'd never be free again. My brother. My best friend. He was dead.

"Let me go. Let me go. Let me go."

Run. Get away.

"Look. At. Me."

This time his voice cut through my hysterical need to escape, and I stopped struggling, staring up at his unflinching eyes. How could he just stand there? He'd just destroyed my life, my family's life. And he was standing there looking at me without a trace of sympathy.

"I hate you."

"You going to stand still?"

Chest heaving and heart pounding, I realized Deck had watched me destroy everything in my room. He never did anything to stop it. The one thing I did know about this man was that he was unbending.

Connor always said Deck was the best team leader, because no matter what shit went down, Deck would never yield to anyone. He'd stand by his word no matter what, and I guessed he wouldn't let me go until I bent to his will.

I stopped fighting.

He waited a second then released me. He reached into his back pocket and pulled out a small, leather-bound book with worn edges and a cracked spine. "He'd want you to have this."

I didn't move as I stared at what I knew was Connor's journal. Deck grabbed my wrist and shoved it in my hand, the hard surface abruptly hitting my palm.

Connor's name was written on the top in his familiar, messy handwriting.

I nearly fell, and probably would've if Deck hadn't grabbed my arm. He guided me further into my room, and I didn't object. All I did was stare down at the bound book. The last piece of my brother. It wasn't enough. It would never be enough.

I felt the softness of the mattress as Deck made me sit, and then the floor creaked as he started to walk away.

I looked up at the retreating figure. "I wish it was you, not him."

He gave no reaction to my words, and really, I hadn't expected any. It just came out. And I did hate that Deck was here instead of Connor. I hated that he could walk back to his family and laugh and hold them and my brother couldn't.

He turned his head and met my eyes. For a second, I thought I witnessed remorse, but it was so quick I could've imagined it or maybe I hoped to see it from my brother's best friend.

"Yeah." His whispered tone was barely audible as the door shut, and I listened to his steady, booted steps walk away.

The front door opened, and the screen door screeched. Both shut.

I had no idea why I did it, but I walked over to the window, parted the white sheer curtains and watched as he walked down the path. The tension in his back. The stiffness of his stride.

He stopped at the side of the car and stood still for a second. I couldn't see his face or what he was doing until he slammed both fists into the roof of the car. Then his head dropped forward and his shoulders slouched.

My fingers curled around the delicate material of the curtains, and I didn't realize how hard until they ripped from the rod and fell to the floor, leaving the window bare.

As if he'd heard it—but I knew that was impossible—Deck turned. Our eyes locked. It felt like he could see right into me with that direct gaze. I felt naked and vulnerable, unable to look away, trapped. He gave me these wounds. Wounds that would never heal. Deck was now part of the darkness inside me I'd never escape from.

His nod was barely distinguishable before he broke the connection and opened the car door.

I watched his lean form curl into the driver's seat.

The engine came to life with a loud purr.

Life. Something Connor had lost.

I turned away just as I heard the squeal of the tires on the street.

My perfect world had just been thrown into destructive chaos.

about the author

Nashoda Rose is a New York Times and USA Today bestselling author who lives in Toronto with her assortment of pets. She writes erotic romance with a splash of darkness, or maybe it's a tidal wave.

When she isn't writing, she can be found sitting in a field reading with her dogs at her side while her horses graze nearby. She loves interacting with her readers and chatting about her addiction—books.